The Way Things Are

The Stories of
Rachel Maddux

THE RACHEL MADDUX SERIES
VOLUME 2

The Way Things Are

The Stories of
Rachel Maddux

Edited, with an introduction, by

Nancy A. Walker

The University of Tennessee Press
Knoxville

The paper in this book meets the minimum requirements
of the American National Standard for Permanence of Paper
for Printed Library Materials.

The binding materials have been chosen for strength
and durability.

Library of Congress Cataloging in Publication Data

Maddux, Rachel, 1913–1983.
    The way things are : the stories of Rachel Maddux /
edited by Nancy A. Walker. — 1st ed.
    p.   cm.
    ISBN 0-87049-751-0 (cloth: alk. paper)
    I. Walker, Nancy A., 1942–   . II. Title.
PS3563.A3395W39   1992
813'.54 — dc20   91-40099   CIP

Contents

Introduction

For Rachel Maddux, as for many other writers, writing was a necessity, coming before considerations of publication, success, or fame. Early in her career, she wrote: "You do what you have to do, that's all, for as long as you are able, and if you do it well, it may live after you. But if it doesn't, why you do it anyway."

Only eight of Rachel Maddux's short stories were published during her lifetime,[1] the first in *Story* magazine in 1936 and the last in a supplement to the Toronto newspaper *The Star Weekly* in 1959. Known primarily for her novels—*The Green Kingdom* (1957), *Abel's Daughter* (1960), and *A Walk in the Spring Rain* (1966)—and her nonfiction work *The Orchard Children* (1977), Maddux was a prolific writer of short fiction, leaving behind more than two dozen unpublished stories when she died in 1983. Some of these had been submitted for publication; others had not. But all existed in typed manuscript form, indicating that Maddux, who always drafted her work in longhand, considered them to be finished.

But publication as stories was not Maddux's only ambition for her short fiction. During the 1950s in particular, she collaborated with several other writers to transform some of her stories into scripts for film or for the rapidly growing medium of television. Indeed, two of her stories, "Emmy Foster" and "A Talent with Tigers" (neither included in this collection) now exist only in script form. Although none of these scripts became television dramas,[2] at least one was performed before an audience: a one-act play based on the story "Final Clearance" was presented by the Vanney Center of Arts Theatre to the Ventura, California, USO-YWCA Club on April 14, 1957. Shelly Lowenkopf, now a professor in the graduate Professional Writing Program at the University of Southern California, worked with Maddux on the script versions of several stories, including "Final Clearance." This story, with its suggestion that the frustrating red tape of our bureaucratic society follows us into the afterlife, seems an odd choice for a largely military audience, and Lowenkopf recalls that he and Maddux "were both impressed by the fact that there could scarcely be a less appropriate group of persons to see the play unless it were a group of FBI agents."[3] Among the stories in this collection, Lowenkopf and Maddux developed scripts from at least two others—"They're Laughing" and the title story, "The Way Things Are."

Anyone familiar with Rachel Maddux's previously published work, including her autobiography, *Communication* (written in 1941; published in 1991 by the University of Tennessee Press), would recognize these stories as the products of her imagination and experience. Her fascination with childhood is central to several of the stories in this collection, as it is to *Communication* and *The Orchard Children*. Characteristic also is the use of fantasy as an element in her fiction. Two of the stories here, "Final Clearance" and "Overture and Beginners," were originally published in *Fantasy and Science Fiction*; her novel *The Green Kingdom* deals with a hidden and secret world in which a small group of people begins life all over again; and many of the characters in her stories have experiences quite removed from everyday reality.

Closely related to the elements of fantasy in Maddux's stories is one of her central themes: human isolation and loneliness. In her autobiography, Maddux writes compellingly of the difficulty people have in truly communicating with one another, so that the life that is the most real becomes that lived in one's own imagination. Nor is such isolation always viewed negatively, especially for creative children, such as the little boy in "Change" who plays basketball alone without a ball, and the little girl in "Mother of a Child" whose desire for a baby enables her to imagine a pregnancy.

Autobiographical elements are clearly recognizable in a number of these stories. Rachel Maddux was born in 1913 in Wichita, Kansas, the third and last child of a mother who had been raised on a farm and a father who had been a dandy in his youth and spent the rest of his life as a city employee in Wichita. Maddux attended the University of Wichita before transferring to the University of Kansas, where she received a degree in zoology in 1934. She planned to be a doctor and entered the University of Kansas Medical School, but the back problems and *petit mal* epilepsy that had shadowed her young adulthood forced her to withdraw from medical school in the spring of 1936. From then until her marriage to King Baker in 1941, she lived in a three-room apartment in Kansas City, working in a paint store and holding other odd jobs while beginning to write and hosting an informal salon for other aspiring writers. These were years of economic depression and impending world war, years of uncertainty and flux during which Maddux began writing *The Green Kingdom* and concluded the long relationship with an older man that she describes in her autobiography. The war years were unsettled geographically and emotionally. Maddux and her husband moved wherever the Army transferred King Baker for training: Louisiana, Virginia, and California—where Maddux settled when Baker was sent overseas, working in a date-processing plant near the Salton Sea in southern California and wrestling with decisions concerning motherhood and career. (Maddux and Baker remained childless until they adopted an infant girl in 1964.)

Following World War II, Maddux and Baker lived in the Los Angeles area until 1960 when they moved to Houston County, Tennessee, so that Baker could start an apple orchard on land that friends had bought and named "Green Kingdom Acres." In their small house overlooking acres of apple trees, Maddux wrote *A Walk in the Spring Rain* and *The Orchard Children* and continued to write and submit for publication short fiction, though she published no short stories after the move to Tennessee. Not long before her death in 1983, Maddux and her agent discussed the possibility of publishing a collection of her stories, but such a collection never materialized, and of the twenty-eight stories in the present collection, twenty-four remained unpublished at her death.

A number of these stories have origins in Rachel Maddux's own experience. The story she tells in "Mother of a Child," for example, is, in a slightly different form, part of Maddux's auto-biography, *Communication*, and the three sketches in "The Father Stories" are also childhood memories—the incident involving her sister Erma's coat is referred to in a letter she wrote to a close friend in 1981. "Guaranteed" was inspired by Maddux's trips from Kansas City to visit King Baker when he was stationed at Ft. Leonard Wood, Missouri; "The House in the Woods" is based on a period when Baker was stationed at Ft. Belvoir, Virginia. Maddux's work in a Kansas City paint store during the late 1930s forms the backdrop for "They're Laughing," as does her work in the California date plant in "My Mexican Wife." The eagerness with which a writer awaits the daily mail is re-flected in both "You Will Remember, But Strangely," and "Comfort the Small and Tender Grass."

Further, many of the manuscripts of the stories written in Kansas City and California bear the address at which Maddux lived when she completed the story. By far the majority of the stories so marked were finished at 16 West Forty-third Street in Kansas City—including "No Smoking, No Spitting," "The Little Green Velvet Park," "The Marbles," "Guaranteed," and "Change." Others are identified with various California addresses: Doman Avenue in Tarzana ("Chu Chu," "My Walks with Confidence," "You Nominate Yours; I'll Nominate Mine"); a post-office box in Mecca ("My Mexican Wife").[4] In one sense, such addresses merely reflect the caution of an author who sent her manuscripts through the mail and wished to assure that they were properly identified. But Rachel Maddux was, I believe, a writer fully conscious that her fiction depicted as accurately as possible "the way things are" at a given place and time: the barter system used by small businesses during the Depression ("They're Laughing"), the discomfort of a little girl meeting her first celebrity ("You Nominate Yours"), the human drama that goes on in an unremarkable small town in Oklahoma ("Duress"). Maddux titled her journal "The Record," and she was known to remark on her sense of obligation to write down all that she observed of human experience.[5]

Given these powers of observation, Maddux's fiction often captures the particular flavor of everyday life during definable periods in twentieth-century America. Such stories as "The House in the Woods," "Guaranteed," and "Change" evoke the period of World War II from the perspective of the wives of servicemen while "No Smoking, No Spitting," "The Little Woman," and "They're Laughing" afford glimpses of the twenty-five-cent meals and other frugalities that characterized the lives of ordinary workers during the Depression. Despite the fact that Maddux lived in or near cities until she moved to Tennessee in 1960, she was particularly adept at capturing the quality of the American small town, in the manner of Sinclair Lewis and Sherwood Anderson. Indeed, in her autobiography, Maddux recalls her joy at first being introduced to the work of Sherwood Anderson: "those stories about people JUST LIKE THE ONES I KNEW, those very simple stories, where the words coming out of people's mouths sounded just like the words coming out of people's mouths—not going through the author's head first." The town of Duress sits "in the west of Oklahoma like a piece of cold beef in the middle of a plate while the diner has been called to the telephone." In the town of Sandski, in "Chu Chu," the train stops daily for seventy-nine seconds, and the people of the town "felt a need for something more: some luxury, some unnecessary thing, for a warmth beyond comfort." Drugstores in Maddux's stories have soda fountains; children play with doll buggies and marbles; adults drink coffee and smoke cigarettes with impunity and eat Cheerioats; milk costs fourteen cents a bottle, and the bottles are made of glass.

Yet these stories are not merely period pieces, nor are they in any sense nostalgic. Maddux's need to capture the precise moment arises from her conviction that true human connectedness is both crucial and fragile—moments of the greatest importance can be missed through inattention or self-absorption. In "The Little Green Velvet Park," for example, a solitary man carries with him the memory of such a missed moment. Meeting for the first time the widow of a close friend, the unnamed character feels that "their meeting was a clean blue light in a dark place," but he moves too quickly toward intimacy, and she recoils from him. He never sees her again but always remembers her green living room as the image of potential peace and rest.

When Maddux's characters are successful in connecting with one another, it is not necessarily in the intensity of an intimate relationship; it may be a chance, though significant, encounter. In "Guaranteed," the situation is a chance encounter on a bus. The man the young female narrator calls "Russet Eyes" is far less worldly than she, but he is a good man who believes in a few basic truths, for which he takes responsibility. His simple honesty strikes a chord in the young woman on her way to visit her soldier-fiancé, and she thinks at the end of the story:

> I knew if I had asked him to he would have guaranteed *to me*, that the world is not lousy and Time is not lousy and waiting is not lousy and death is not lousy. He would have guaranteed it to me and to all the other people on the bus, . . . and he would have accepted the full responsibility for all of us, right up to the very last minute.

In "My Mexican Wife," the two central characters do not even speak the same language, but for a season they share a café and a song on the jukebox.

The title story, "The Way Things Are," also turns on a moment of human connection, and in this case one of passionate intensity that seems inevitable: "They had not called this thing any name, had not made it different from what it was, no better and no meaner, no wider and no deeper." But this story also contains several other elements and themes common in Maddux's fiction. The deep attachment of the central character to her sister, which has its origins in Rachel Maddux's relationship with her older sister, Erma, recurs in her work as the one type of human connection that is fixed and secure rather than the result of chance or effort. The rather bizarre (though not impossible) circumstances of the meeting between Penny Curtess and John Frazier suggests the isolated otherworldliness of *The Green Kingdom*, and the immediacy and necessity of their intimacy is similar to the relationship between Libby Meredith and Will Workman in *A Walk in the Spring Rain*. Each is a brief but life-changing relationship. The wit and whimsy that characterize "The Way Things Are" are also elements in other stories, including "My Walks with Confidence," "They're Laughing," and "My Mexican Wife." Perhaps most striking of all is the return to childhood represented by Penny and John playing with the 100-piece model farm[6] and the sewing kit that she has bought as gifts for her children.

One of the most remarkable features of Rachel Maddux's fiction is her depiction of children—especially her ability to assume the perspective of a child and enter into his or her imagination. In her autobiography, Maddux recreates vividly her own childhood, and her ability to place herself imaginatively in the world of a child remained central to her writing through *The Orchard Children*. In this nonfiction work about trying to adopt two children, Maddux shows her understanding of children's needs; when she writes fiction from the point of view of a child, the child's world is unmediated by an adult perspective so that the child exists in his or her own space. The nine-year-old boy in "The Marbles" has that space invaded when his father joins in the game of marbles to first win back and then lose again the marbles that the boy has been given for his birthday. The father's invasion of the boys' game represents the realities of adulthood beginning to impinge upon the boy—his father's drinking binges and his mother's attempts to hide the existence of any problem.

The beginning of mature understanding also characterizes "Mother of a Child," but this time without the intervention of adults. The little girl who so desperately wants a child of her own that she imaginatively undergoes pregnancy and childbirth understands that "there is a difference between a real thing and something you pretend" when no baby appears at the end of this process. The boy in "The Wonderful Rich Billboard of Kingston" measures social class by the quality of the billboards in various neighborhoods and has a special relationship with Mr. Hossenpeffer, whose image advertises hams across the street from his house. The creative, imaginative world of childhood is the ideal in much of Maddux's short fiction. The happiest of her adult characters are those able to retain or recapture the playfulness and spontaneity that characterize childhood—making a house in the woods during wartime, personifying confidence as an impish little man wearing yellow pigskin gloves, or making up song lyrics based on customers' comments about wallpaper.

It is not merely a fascination with children, however, that makes such childlike activities an important theme in Maddux's work. For her, writing was the result of inspiration, and she once wrote that "inspiration is the re-capturing of one's own child-hood," a period when "there is a continual teeter-totter of the real and the imaginary, the subconscious and the conscious mind." To be receptive to inspiration, Maddux believed, one must have "the ability to be again exactly as you were when you were a child, when you could as easily be Dick Tracy as to think of him, when you accepted all things first and made judgment on them afterward."[7] The strange, almost surreal elements of many of the stories in this collection come from their origin in the intersection between the childlike imagination, in which anything is possible, and the skill of the mature writer who gives the imagination shape.

Nancy A. Walker
Vanderbilt University
August 1991

Notes

1. This number does not include a condensation of her novel *A Walk in the Spring Rain*, which was published in the September 1969 issue of *McCall's* magazine. In addition to the six previously published stories in this volume, Maddux's novella *Turnip's Blood* was reprinted with her autobiography, *Communication*, in 1991. A very short story titled "Now It Is April" was published in a volume I have not been able to identify or date.

2. Others recognized the potential for dramatization in Maddux's fiction, sometimes with results frustrating to the author. In September 1945, without Maddux's prior knowledge, a dramatized version of her novella *Turnip's Blood* was broadcast on the radio; she learned of this the next day when reading the previous day's broadcast listings.

3. Letter to the editor from Shelly Lowenkopf dated September 30, 1991.

4. None of the manuscripts bears a Houston County, Tennessee, address, which suggests that most of these stories were written before 1960. "Night's Comin', Miss Alice" is the only story clearly set in Tennessee.

5. For example, when writing to her friend Savington Crampton in

1953 about an occasion when King Baker and a man he had met with on business were wearing identical ties, she reports asking Baker whether he had mentioned this when writing to Crampton, and being told that he had not. "That's the way it goes," Maddux writes in her letter. "The important things are always being lost for lack of a writer's presence. I can't be everywhere."

6. The model farm is another autobiographical element: King Baker bought such a farm for Rachel Maddux during the time that they lived in Kansas City in the late 1930s.

7. These quotations are from a talk on writing that Rachel Maddux gave about 1940.

The Way Things Are

The Stories of
Rachel Maddux

The Clay Pigeon

The minute she saw his face she knew something was wrong and automatically that section of her nervous system reserved for telegrams, long-distance calls in the night and air travel began to vibrate.

"Harry," she called. "Harry. Over here."

He was coming directly toward her through the groups of passengers now entering the air terminal, but if she had not stopped him he would have gone straight by without recognizing her.

"Why, Marcie," he said. "What . . . ? Is something wrong with Helen?"

"Why no," she said. "Silly. I just thought it would be . . . fun to surprise you."

Fun? What she had actually thought was that it would be exciting to be out driving alone at 2 o'clock in the morning going to meet Harry. She couldn't remember how long it had been (probably Helen's measles) since she had even been up at that time, let alone out. But now, remembering all the fuss and planning it had taken to get a babysitter who would stay all night and of how she had even imagined she and Harry might go to some restaurant just for the excitement of it—well, really, from the look of his face she couldn't have picked a worse time.

"Well," he said, "you certainly surprised me." And as if suddenly remembering his manners he bent and kissed her. "I suppose you've got the car?"

For a moment Marcie thought wistfully of suggesting the airport restaurant, but put the thought away. "It's over here," she said. "But where's your bag? And your briefcase?"

"Oh yes," he said. "Almost forgot."

It was not like him at all, the way he couldn't find his claim check and stood fumbling through his pockets. And even after he did have his bags, he would have gone off leaving his wallet on the counter if she hadn't noticed.

"Honestly, Harry," she said, "if something went wrong on the flight I wish you'd tell me." He had manoeuvred the car out of the terminal as one in a deep fog, but at last they were safely on the correct road home.

"Why, no," he said. "Nothing's wrong. What gave you that idea?"

"Why, you look as though you'd been hit on the head, you can't recognize your own wife in the terminal, you can't find your claim checks, you leave your wallet. . . ."

"I'm just tired, I guess," he said. "Be glad to get out of these clothes, put on pyjamas, maybe have a bite to eat in the kitchen."

At home, Marcie slipped quietly into Helen's room to reassure herself, then she changed into low heels and a housecoat and went into the kitchen. She had assumed Harry was getting into pyjamas, but when she went to ask him what he'd like to eat, he was standing in the bathroom, still fully dressed, staring into the mirror.

"What?" he said.

"Oh, never mind," she replied. It had been a foolish question anyhow. Married to the man for 12 years, she knew what he liked to eat at 3 o'clock in the morning, or any other time for that matter, and that's why the refrigerator was full of it. He came into the kitchen at last and sat down at the table.

She asked, "Is business all right?"

For a moment he came right out of the fog. "Fine," he said. "The new man we put on in Phoenix—you know the one—he's working out all right. Going to be first rate."

"That's good," she said. She poured milk into their glasses, but before she could even take a bite of her sandwich, his face had fallen into that strange sadness again.

"Harry," she said, "what's the matter? And don't tell me it's nothing."

"Really," he replied. "I don't know what you're making such a fuss about. I had a kind of shock, I guess. It's not serious. Nothing like you think. I don't know if I can even tell you about it. It . . . well, it was kind of wonderful in a way, too. And then. . . . You see, Marcie, for the first time in my life I guess. . . . Well, you know, nothing ever happens to me. I go along. I work. Well anyhow, I met this woman. . . ."

Twelve years married to the man and a thing like this happens, Marcie thought. But not Harry. Harry just wasn't. . . . And not to her. Of course, it did happen, even among their own friends. And why not to you, Marcie? a voice kept repeating. Why not?

"Harry Nolan," she said, "are you trying to tell me you've got yourself involved with some woman?"

His head jerked up, his mouth fell open. "Why, Marcie! What an idea. For Pete's sake. Where's my paper? Where's that newspaper I had with me?"

"Newspaper?"

"Yes," he said. "There's something I want to show you."

Honestly, she was so rattled. She couldn't have believed she could get so rattled. But for a second she had actually thought he was going to drop a remark that would simply cut her off at the roots, then calmly sit down and read a newspaper. A newspaper of all things.

"I have no idea," she said. How was it she could so easily have imagined cruelty from him when actually he was the kindest person alive?

"Here it is," Harry said. "I knew I wouldn't have let it get away from me. Here she is, right on the front page." He spread the paper out on the table and now, suddenly, he was himself, quick and deft and full of excitement. "Marcie," he said, "you know me. Nothing ever happens to me. I sat there on the plane reading this paper and there is this picture of a Dr. Andrews and I read how she's an . . . an astrophysicist and I'm wondering what on earth is that. Then I read how she's going to this world conference to receive a scientific award or prize or something, and I read on about some great mathematician from India who'll be there and a chemist from Sweden, and pretty soon I look up from the paper and there she is sitting in the seat beside me."

"Who?"

"Why, this Dr. Andrews."

"You don't say," Marcie said. She hated her. What in the world is the matter with me? she thought. I never even met the woman.

"Yes," Harry said, "imagine. Why I don't remember I ever met any kind of a celebrity before, then when it happens, to have it be such a . . . a. . . ."

"Such a what?"

"Well, such a real one, I mean. You know, not Miss Rheingold or somebody."

I'll take Miss Rheingold, Marcie thought. I'll bet if you'd met her on the plane you wouldn't be gray in the face.

"It oughtn't be allowed," Harry said. "It's criminal."

"What?" Marcie asked.

"Why, there she was travelling just like anybody else," he said. "God knows what might happen to her. The plane might have crashed. She might be run over in the street. Anything. Fifty bodyguards they put around a vice-president, but a great brain like that, they leave it exposed. It. . . ."

"You were on that plane," Marcie said, "and believe me, I could certainly do without Dr. Andrews a heck of a lot easier than I could do without you."

"No, Marcie," he said. "Maybe it sounds silly to you, but in the long run you couldn't. I really mean that."

"The eyes," Harry said. "You never saw anything so . . . so alive, Marcie. And yet somehow like a child's, too. A very bright child's. And then kind in a way, too. She meant to be kind, really."

"Kind? What's the matter with you, Harry? Listen to me. For two days, I've been making these big plans, getting a sitter to stay all night, getting a new dress, even. Thinking what a big thing it's going to be to be up in the middle of the night going to meet you. I go into the airport and what's there? A man who doesn't even recognize me, that's what. A ghost. Gray in the face. Mooning over a newspaper picture. Harry, what happened?"

"Gee, Marcie," he said. "I'm sorry. I guess I'm not making much sense. Well, I'll tell you from the beginning. There we sat, me thinking this was probably the only chance I'd ever have in my life to meet anyone like that, and there I was tongue-tied. I kept thinking what it must be to be like her, you know, looking out at the stars like that and being at home, so to speak, knowing what they were about and all. I got to thinking how they don't look any different to me now than they did when I was Helen's age and that got me thinking about Helen and . . . and you know what she said, Marcie?"

"What?"

"Why she said," and here Harry turned his head to the side as though he were Dr. Andrews talking to Harry, "she said, 'Isn't that curious?'"

"Curious?" Marcie said. "Why, you know I talked to Miss Randolph and she said it was perfectly natural, that all children react the same way."

"I know," Harry said. "I told her the teacher had said that and she looked puzzled. Finally she said, 'I'm sorry I can't help you about your little girl, Mr. Nolan. . . .'"

Never mind acting it out, Marcie thought, just tell me what she said. Somehow she found it infuriating Harry's trying to be this woman.

"And then you know what she said, Marcie? There was a kind of frown came in her forehead and she said, 'I've been trying to think when I had my first conception of infinity, a quite childish conception, of course, and I do remember it, Mr. Nolan. But I don't remember anything frightening at all. Just—well—excitement. I just remember being excited."

"Harry," Marcie said firmly. "At 4 o'clock in the morning I'm sitting here trying to understand how in the world a strange woman who knows nothing about children could have said two sentences to you that have you wrapped in absolute gloom."

"Oh, it wasn't that. Not the part about Helen."

"Well, what was it then?"

"Marcie, how about making some coffee, huh? . . . Or maybe we should just go to bed."

"Harry Nolan, if you think I could sleep. . . ."

"O.K., Marcie, O.K. But really you're going to think it's not worth waiting up for. Here in the kitchen it's going to sound. . . ."

"Never mind how it's going to sound."

"Well, we got to talking, you know. It was a real pleasure for me. Everything she said was interesting. And then finally she asked me what my work was."

"And?"

"Well, so I told her, and she'd never heard of it, of course. Didn't even know what skeet shooting is."

He saw Marcie glance at the newspaper.

"Oh, lots of people don't, you know—people you meet on planes. But usually they say 'how interesting,' or, 'how's business?' but to see how she took hold of this, just because she didn't know. So finally I asked her if she had never been to a carnival, never seen a shooting gallery. So then she said, 'You mean clay pigeons?' Well, that she'd heard of. This is where most people stop, if they get that far. But with her, why that was just the beginning. 'I never met a man who made clay pigeons before,' she said. "How do you do it?'

"Well, I gave her a quick rundown on the process, all the time feeling it could hardly matter less. And then she said, 'But what is the essence of it, Mr. Nolan? What is it you are trying for? I don't quite seem to catch on to what makes a superior one.'"

"Why, one that shatters quickest," I said, "into the smallest fragments. So people don't get hurt. So you don't have lawsuits."

"'Oh,' she said, 'how strange it must seem to spend your efforts trying to make something all the time more easily destroyed. It's a new experience for me. How does it feel?' Well, it's the truth. Marcie, I never thought of it before. She said she had known people who were striving for things that would last longer, and she had known quite a few who were concerned with destruction, but she had never met anyone whose concern was destructibility."

Marcie waited, but there wasn't any more forthcoming. Harry sat looking down at his plate, wrapped in a strange sadness. The silence grew between them till finally he raised his head and looked at her. "Don't you get it, Marcie? It didn't hit me all at once either. It just sort of settled down over me quietly."

"What did, Harry? What is it?"

"Why just that when you come to think of it, to be trying your best to make something that will break faster into smaller and smaller pieces—a man's whole life turned into that—it's pretty silly."

So at last Marcie did get it, what she had been waiting all these hours of false pathways for. "I never heard such rot," she said.

"The idea," Marcie went on. "The very idea a man that's worked hard all his life and been a good husband and a good father—a man it's fun to be with. Somebody says a few words in an airplane and you tell me all that is nothing? She thinks it's nothing for Helen to grow up in a good neighborhood, go to a good school, have an orthodontist if she needs one. . . ."

"Oh for Pete's sake, Marcie. It doesn't have anything to do with orthodontists."

"Why, it just burns me up," Marcie said, "and it isn't only Helen or me or you. There's 75 employees to think about and their families and their children."

"And their orthodontists," Harry said. He stood suddenly and carried his plate and cup over to the sink. "Oh, Marcie," he said, "you're wonderful. Really nobody else in the world could do it, take one of man's deepest philosophical problems and get it completely fenced in with a whole forest of crooked teeth. You know it's 5 o'clock in the morning? Let's go to bed."

"Go on," she said. "I'll be right up."

"Orthodontists," Harry said to himself as he climbed the stairs. He was still shaking his head over it while he undressed and put on his pyjamas, not even noticing when Marcie came in. There possibly he would have left it if he had not gone over to close the window. But outside were the stars, waiting. He stood there thinking how they had looked to him when he was littler than Helen even. And he had believed that by now he would certainly know all about them. Yet they looked exactly to him the way they had when he was five years old and if he could still see by then, they'd look the same to him at 80.

And that was the real injustice, he thought, that a man could desire to know what he had not the capacity to understand. In his life, Harry had heard quite a lot about injustice spoken, shouted, whispered. Even in those days when, as a young man, he had had all that time to talk and talk and endlessly talk, even then there had been this protest in him, this jagged rock of incoherency in his chest wanting to shout, "No, that's not it. That's not the real injustice." But he'd not been able to say it, then, let alone shout anything. He'd never been a shouter, Harry hadn't, though he'd known in his time people who shouted, even at God. Well, if he were the kind to shout at God, then at last he knew what he'd shout: Either take away the desire or give the capacity. Both or nothing. But to give a man a silly life, then to let him know it. . . .

"I can't bear you to be so sad," Marcie broke in on his thoughts.

"But I'm not, Marcie. Not at all sad. Not at all. In a way, it was a satisfying experience. And I'll tell you why. For the first time in my life I saw something I'd wanted to see and I wasn't disappointed."

"I don't understand," she said. She shivered and he pulled back the covers for her and moved so she could lie down.

"Why, because," he said, "they really are different, people like that, like Dr. Andrews. It isn't just that they work longer or try harder than other people. They really are different."

In the next room Helen turned over in bed and murmured some sleepy words and a flow of such tenderness spread out from the man toward the sleeping child that he felt drained to exhaustion. For there were two kinds, he knew now. The ones who got frightened and the ones who got excited about infinity. And they knew already which kind Helen was; they knew already. And there would be other fears ahead. He could tick them off for her ahead of time, just like a, b, c. He could make her a list. Right up to the moment of disappointment in herself when everything would get so terribly quiet.

You Will Remember, but Strangely

Peter and I were having breakfast. It was a fine spring morning, but not as fine as it would be the next day after because the next day would be Peter's day to get the breakfast and my day to be wan and languid and too delicate to lift a cream pitcher as Peter was pretending to be now. There are always two plates on our breakfast table, but three cups and that is because the mailman, Mike, always has a cup of coffee with us but he eats breakfast at home. We have it figured out so neatly that I can pour Mike's coffee when I first see him on the road and by the time he opens the kitchen door and comes in it's exactly at drinking temperature. Mike and Peter have a joke; it is the same every day. Mike accuses Peter of trying (with the coffee) to bribe the United States Post Office for an interesting letter at last and Peter accuses Mike of using the coffee for a pretext to rest his flat feet.

Well, this morning Mike came in and kicked the door shut behind him and threw a stack of letters at Peter (Peter always gets lots of mail; Peter is a writer) and one letter at me. I let out a squeak and Mike put his cap on the back of his head and drank his coffee standing up.

"What's the matter with Bo-Beep?" he asked Peter.

"Must have got a letter from Isabel," Peter said.

"Queen Isabel?"

"No, her sister Isabel. She always squeaks like that when she hears from her. Did you get a letter from Isabel?" he asked me.

"Yes!"

"She must be very fond of her sister," Mike said to Peter. They always talked about me as if I were in the next room.

"Oh, she is," Peter said. "They grew up together, you know."

"Well, well," Mike said. "Good-bye until tomorrow, same time, same situation."

"Sealed with a kiss," I said.

Peter threw his napkin at me, but I dodged it. Before Peter and I were married I used to write him long letters with pictures and I'd always put SWAK on the back of the envelope. I thought it was a very funny thing to do like the way Isabel and I used to stare into each other's eyes earnestly and break into a chorus of "Dear Old Girl," but I had forgotten that Peter didn't have any good old SWAK background where you go to public school, freeze in winter, burn in summer, take sassafras tea in the spring and go to the Wheat Show in the fall. Peter was always being dragged around to unfamiliar corners of the earth and about the first thing he said to me when we met again was "What is this swack? I've looked it up in all the dictionaries and I've asked everybody what it means, but nobody seems to know."

Isabel said, "You asked everybody?" and then she and I sat right down there in the railroad station where Peter'd met us and we had the giggles until we got all the porters and everybody in the station laughing. Peter was a little disgusted at first, but finally Isabel stopped laughing long enough to tell him and then he howled, too.

Well, it's been like that ever since and so you can tell just how I'd be likely to squeak at having a letter from Isabel and just how Peter would know without having seen the letter.

"You are excused," Peter said. Peter and I are always very polite to each other, partly because I am so romantic and partly because Peter has no office to go to and we spend almost all our time together. Peter never reads the newspaper at breakfast, but allows me the full view of his face and I save all the talk about my insides for the doctor and Isabel and we take turns getting breakfast, but Peter is always allowed to open a letter from his agent at any time it should come and I do the same with Isabel's letters.

Well, of course I hadn't read but about three sentences until I began to chuckle and finally Peter said, "Come on. Tell me," and

I read him a line. (I've told Isabel I do that and so it's all right. She reads some of mine to her husband, too. Isabel's husband, Leonard, is a marine biologist and they're always moving about from ocean to ocean on the trail of some fish. Once, for Christmas, Peter and I sent them all kinds of stuff to furnish a lighthouse.)

I read for about a page silently and then I said, "Peter, Isabel's going to have another baby!"

"Girl or boy?"

"A girl. Named for me."

"Doesn't it just take a load off your mind to have that all settled?" Peter asked. "And when is she going to have this baby?"

"Oh, in a year or two," I said, not looking up from the letter.

"I suppose," Peter said, "that she's just waiting around for a fine day."

"She's just made up her mind," I said. "She's been thinking about it for some time and now she's finally decided for sure that she wants a little girl. There have been times when Leonard wanted a baby but Isabel didn't and then times when Isabel did and Leonard didn't and. . . ."

"And times when Leonard and Isabel wanted one, but the Sea Urchin didn't, I suppose," Peter said.

"And vice versa. But now everybody wants one at the same time, Peter. Isn't that lovely?"

"Even the Sea Urchin?" Peter asked.

"Yes, only he doesn't know for sure yet if he wants a sister or a brother."

"Well, if he doesn't make up his mind pretty soon," Peter said, "they ought to make him have it."

"And besides, Peter, this is such a fine place to have a baby. Much better than when they had the Sea Urchin because they were at the University then and Leonard was teaching. Isabel was always having to entertain and go to faculty teas and where they are now, there's practically nobody and Isabel can be just as sleepy as she wants and wear those dear old shapeless Lane Bryant dresses and be unsocial."

"She could walk down to the sea every day and soak up a lot of prenatal influence and maybe it'll be a mermaid," Peter said. "Leonard would love that."

In February, when the big snows come, we don't have breakfast in the kitchen. We have breakfast in bed. And we don't take turns getting it either; Peter gets it every morning. We lie in bed until we're really just starving to death and then Peter jumps out of bed and puts on an overcoat and a stocking cap and fur-lined shoes and builds a fire in the bedroom fireplace. Then he shuts the windows and, while the fire gets going, he goes out in the kitchen and gets breakfast, still wearing the overcoat. In fact, Peter now calls all overcoats aprons. Peter has rigged up a sturdy cart with wheels and he puts the breakfast on this and comes riding it in as though it were a scooter. By this time the bedroom is warm and Peter can take off his overcoat and hat and we have breakfast in bed. You see, Peter really loves me a great deal.

Well, this morning, the snow was flying about outside like White Leghorn chicken feathers when Peter came in riding the scooter and threw a letter on the bed.

"Look what I found tucked under the door," he said.

"What about Mike?"

"Mike has a good wife," Peter said, "who gets up at a respectable hour and gets Mike's breakfast and sends him off to each new day with a fresh start."

"Yes, but Mike works," I said.

"So he does," Peter said, throwing a hot towel right in my face. "Mike works hard out in the snow and where are his good friends? Where are his good friends who give him hot coffee and let him put his feet in the oven?"

"They are in bed," I said, "for the winter."

"Mike is going to lose faith in us if we don't start getting up earlier. Mike is going to quit believing in us."

"It will be spring pretty soon," I said, "and then he can believe in us all over again."

"What a busy spring Mike's going to have, believing in us and the bears."

"And the new wheat."

"Are you going to read your letter?" Peter asked."Or shall I read it for you?"

"Why," I said, "it's from Isabel."

"I know it."

I read the whole letter through then I put it down. Peter handed me a cup of coffee. He left my breakfast on the scooter because he knew if I could get through a whole letter of Isabel's without laughing or reading part of it aloud that I'd need a cup of coffee right quick. Peter let me read the whole letter through again and then he poured me another cup of coffee.

"Is something wrong with Isabel?" he asked.

"I don't know, Peter. She doesn't say she's sick or anything, but something's wrong. I know it is."

"Is Leonard all right?"

"Isabel says he has to go away for ten days for a meeting, but he's all right."

"He's not going to be away when. . . ."

"Oh, no, Peter. He's going tomorrow and the baby's not due for two months yet."

"Maybe it's the Sea Urchin. Maybe he's got the mumps or something."

"No, he's had the mumps already and, besides, Isabel would have said. It isn't that she said anything, Peter. . . ." I handed the letter to him. Peter read it right through and he was frowning, too, I noticed.

"It doesn't even sound like Isabel," he said.

"I have to go see her, Peter. I have to go right now."

"I'll go with you," he said.

"No, Peter. Isabel loves you, but you'd be a guest. Isabel couldn't help fussing over you and . . . and I want to be alone with her. Let me go alone, Peter."

"I don't know if you'd ought to go or not," Peter said. "Couldn't you just call her up long distance or something?"

Now, Peter is neither selfish nor dependent and it wasn't because he couldn't spend ten days alone that he worried about my going, or it wasn't that he didn't love Isabel. Next to me Peter loves Isabel better than anyone. Peter was wondering if it might not make me miserable to be around somebody who was going to have a baby, with all the tiny garments and the talk and preparations.

When Peter and I go into town he always tells me something very interesting while we walk past the Tiny Tots Shop and also the store where they sell Klothes for Kute Kiddies. Sometimes he gets me clear past and I don't even notice.

We never do talk about it but I think Peter must think about it quite often because of the way he buys animals for the farm. Peter bought us a sheep and a cow and three dogs, but he always buys big dogs. He doesn't ever buy puppies. Then, too, we don't ever have to kill anything. The sheep and the cow and the chickens are all just going to die of a comfortable old age. Not that Peter and I are vegetarians; we eat fine, thick steaks, but they come from cows we didn't know personally and we can always imagine that the cows were sick, anyway.

Then, too, Peter always reads the reviews very carefully before we go to a play or a movie. I don't like to read the reviews because I don't like to know what's going to happen and some of them even tell you how it turns out. But Peter reads them all and we haven't seen a show that had a baby in it since "Farewell to Arms." Peter was awfully sweet to me the night we went to see "Farewell to Arms." He put me to bed and made me a pot of hot chocolate and then he gave me a manicure.

So I knew what Peter meant when he said he thought maybe I ought not to go to Isabel's, but I thought Isabel was more important than anything else right then and I thought I could keep remembering all the time I was there that I had Peter and that Peter was enough.

"I'll be all right, Peter," I said. "Honest, and you can come and get me and we'll ride home together on the train."

"All right," he said. "I don't suppose you remember where we put your luggage the last time we reorganized all the closets?"

"Oh, Peter," I said, "I'll have to take your bag."

"My bag?" he said. "What's the matter with taking your own bag?"

"Why, don't you remember? We buried the cat in it."

When I got off the train there was the Sea Urchin to meet me. When the Urchin was three he would for greeting look simply angelic and say "I love you" indiscriminately to anybody. When he was five he kissed me. Now he is seven and we shake hands.

"Hi, Urchin," I said.

"Hi, Brat."

"Nice fog you've got here."

"Gosh," he said, "It's like that per near all the time. Hey," he said, "Isabel couldn't come to meet you because Leonard doesn't like her to drive the car now on account of the wha-cha-ma-call-it . . . you know."

"Sure," I said, "how far is the house?"

"It's about a mile," he said. "You could leave your bag here at the station and one of Leonard's helpers at the lab will pick it up for you later. Here, I'll take it."

He lugged the bag into the little station, came back to me and we started walking up the hill. When we'd gone about a block he pointed over his shoulder toward the railroad station.

"The town's down there," he said. "There's nothing up here but our house and a couple of others and the lab."

"Are you right on the ocean?" I asked.

"Sure," he said. "It's swell."

We walked on a little way and then he said: "Of course we could have taken a cab up, but I thought since it was Saturday and I didn't have to go to school you wouldn't mind walking."

"I don't mind," I said. "I've got a stiff tail, anyway, riding the train."

"Well," he said, "I never will get a chance to talk to you after you and Isabel get started. It isn't so very much farther now."

"How is Isabel?"

"She's all right, I guess. She's pretty fat. Well, I don't know but what I'd better tell you so you won't be taking it personally."

"Tell me what?"

"Well, Isabel gets kinda cross sometimes now. Leonard told me before he went away that it was on account of the wha-cha-ma-call-it and for me not to take it personally. I just thought I'd tell you," he said, "just in case she might be a little sharp with you sometime."

"Thanks, Urchin," I said. "I won't take it personally."

"There's our house ahead," he said. There was so much fog I could only make out a vague bulk. Suddenly the Sea Urchin stopped right on top of the hill, spread his feet apart, took in a deep breath and yelled: "Hi, ho, Silver!"

I was just standing there with my mouth open when we heard, quite faintly, an answering "Hi, ho, Silver!", but, oh, it wasn't like the Sea Urchin's. It was Isabel's voice, but it wasn't right. It wasn't loud enough and it was sad. It was as sad as a train whistle on the prairie.

I began to run down the path to the house, stumbling because of the unfamiliar stones and my haste and my apprehension.

"Isabel," I said, "Isabel," and I had my arms around her and she was beating me on the shoulders.

"You don't mean to tell me," she said, "that you *walked* from the station!"

"Sure," the Urchin said. "She's got a stiff tail from riding the train."

"It's not very far," I said, and the Urchin wrinkled his eyes at me in gratitude.

Well, then I looked at Isabel and I don't know what I'd been expecting exactly, because she looked wonderful and radiant and I felt like a fool.

"My God," I said, "what a fog!"

"Makes your hair curly," Isabel said.

By this time we were inside the house and the place looked just like Isabel. Isabel and Leonard have lived in about ten different houses and they keep their possessions limited to a trunk and a couple of boxes, but still I could walk into any kind of house in any country and know if Isabel lived there. I don't know just what she does, exactly, but it works out that you could walk from one end to the other of the house and never trip or bump into anything. Peter says it's so she can take a deep breath without sucking all the furniture up her nostrils.

"Wouldn't you like to have a cup of hot coffee before you bathe?" Isabel asked.

I took off my coat and hat and we sat down before the fireplace. The coffee table between us was a low oval mahogany one that Isabel and Leonard had brought back from Saint Thomas. The Sea Urchin's nurse had had her lover make it for Isabel out of gratitude because Isabel had taught her children how to read. The coffee pot was the silver one that Isabel had found in a second hand store in Missouri someplace between trains once. It had just been polished I could tell and Isabel must have done it herself because even the veins of the silver leaves on it were untarnished.

"Hey, Urchin," Isabel said, "you'd better put your jacket over here by the fire to dry."

"This is the worst fog," she said to me. "It penetrates everything."

"Gosh, Isabel," the Urchin said, "I've even got fog in my ears."

He pronounced it fog to rhyme with cog. Isabel and I came from the Middle West; back home people say "fawg."

"What are you raising, Isabel?" I said. "A heathen? Listen to the way he says fawg."

"Sure, fog," he said. "You and Isabel don't talk like the kids around here."

"Doesn't even sound wet," I said. "They may call it fog, but it's fawg they get."

For some reason this sentence delighted the Urchin. He seized on it, repeating it over and over, louder each time with much laughter between times. "Ho, ho!" he'd shout, putting his face close to mine. "They may call it fog, but it's fawg they get" and then he would be convulsed with laughter. It soon began to get on Isabel's nerves.

"Go in your own room and yell," she said. "We want to talk."

Without stopping his chant, the Urchin glided into his room and shut the door. When the Urchin shuts a door he thinks he has shut out the whole world and now, safe in his own room he let his creative powers loose. He began to sing it:

> They may call it fog
> But it's fawg they get.
> They may call it fog
> But it's fawg they get.
> Fog, fawg; fog, fawg; fog, fawg.
> Oh, boy!

"Look what you started," Isabel said, and we both began to laugh. The fog, fawg; fog, fawg; chant, with a few "Oh, boy's" now and then began to have variations. It ran up scale and down, it grew loud and demanding, then soft and pleading and finally it stopped to give way to a large "Hi, ho, Silver!"

"It'll be like this till Monday when he goes to school," Isabel said. "You may as well make up your mind to it."

"It's all right with me," I said. "I can yell louder than he can."

"How's Peter?"

"Oh, he's . . . ," I said and then I stopped. "What's *that*?"

"Isn't it weird?" Isabel said. "That's the fog bell. It gives me the creeps."

"How long does it do it?"

"It goes on all day and all night, just as long as there's a fog," she said. "I wish it would clear. It's been like this now for a week. If the sun would just come out we could go for a walk, but my bones ache when it's like this. I thought this was going to be such a wonderful place. You know how I'm always beefing about seclusion, but I've about had my fill of it."

"Why don't you come back to the farm with me?"

"Oh, I couldn't now. I couldn't leave Leonard and I'd have to take the Sea Urchin out of school. There's no sense in my feeling this way. It's all imagination. I don't know why it should suddenly get on my nerves so. I've never been a sun lover."

"This ought to make you one."

"How'd you happen to come right in the dead of winter," she asked, "and not bring Peter? I got your wire and that's all I know."

It is not possible to look in Isabel's eyes and lie to her. "Well, Isabel," I said, "it was that last letter of yours. It . . . it scared me to death."

"Is it even creeping in my *letters*?"

"I'll say it is," I said. "I never had such a letter from you in my life I don't think, except the time the Sea Urchin had pneumonia."

"That's terrible," she said. "I don't know what's the matter with me I can't write a decent letter any more. Did you really come all the way East just because I had the blues?"

"It didn't sound like the blues to me. I didn't even have time to think about it. I just packed up my goose flesh and came tearing."

"I'll bet Peter could kill me," she said

"Do you ever get used to that?" I asked.

"To what?"

"That god damned bell!"

"I don't know," she said. "Maybe you will, but I never have."

"What do you suppose it is?" I asked. "It isn't as though it were deafening."

"It isn't really loud at all," she said. "The Sea Urchin makes more noise than that all the time. I don't know just what it is. I suppose it's just having it associated with dark days and fog and not being able to get out of doors. But, honestly, I wish sometimes if they're going to have a shipwreck they'd have it and get it over with."

"We'll be talking so much after a while we'll forget all about it," I said. "Remember the time I came to see you in Florida?"

"Wasn't that awful?"

"There I walked right in in the middle of a party, having forgotten to tell you when I was coming. . . ."

"Remember how we just sat right down and started to talk?"

"And about three hours later we looked up and all the guests had gone?"

"I don't suppose Genevieve McGuire will forgive me for that as long as I live," Isabel said.

"I've got to have a bath," I said. "I'm filthy. Have you got a robe or something I can put on?"

"Didn't you bring any clothes?"

"Sure, but I left my bag at the station. The Urchin said some friend of Leonard's would pick it up this afternoon."

"You don't suppose he actually asked somebody to do it? The men are all overworked now that Leonard's away."

"Well, he certainly made it sound convincing," I said.

"Ever since we got your wire he's been worrying about how he'd get you to himself without having me under foot."

"Suppose I take a bath," I said, "and we can worry about the bag later."

"It's mighty quiet all of a sudden. Have you noticed?" Isabel went over to the Urchin's door and knocked. Getting no answer, she called and finally opened the door. "Why, he's gone!"

"Look, Isabel." I pointed out the window. There came the Sea Urchin up the hill pulling my bag in a little red wagon.

Isabel opened the door and we stood waiting for him. Peter always buys great big bags and the Urchin was puffing and red in the face from the exertion. He looked up and saw Isabel and me. "Well," he said, "I said one of Leonard's helpers would get it for you."

After I'd had a hot bath and brushed my hair and put on the wool robe that Peter got me for Washington's Birthday, I felt better about the whole thing. Isabel and the Urchin and I had dinner and after the Urchin had gone to bed Isabel and I had coffee by the fire. A Mr. McNaughton from the laboratory came over with his wife and Isabel made a hot drink called Nelson's Blood, which is supposed to protect you from the fog. Mr. McNaughton carried in a great stack of logs for the fireplace before he left. We talked about Leonard most of the time they were there and whether he'd be elected president of the society or not. Mrs. McNaughton shook hands with me when she left. She was a pretty little woman, but rather intense I thought. She clasped my hand tightly and over long and said, "I'm so glad you're here so that Isabel doesn't have to be alone while Leonard's gone."

"Why, Isabel's been alone lots of times," I said.

"Just the same," Mrs. McNaughton said, "I'm glad you've come."

After they'd gone, Isabel said, "The McNaughtons were bent on having me stay with them while Leonard's away."

"Why? Is the fog any less at their place?"

"No, of course not," Isabel said. "It's just the same. The bell, too."

The telephone startled us both when it rang. "You answer it," Isabel said. "It's sure to be Peter."

It was. "Hello, Brat," he said. "Miss me?"

"Pining for you."

"Did you find out what's wrong?"

"Gosh, Peter, I. . . ."

"What's the matter? Is Isabel there in the room with you? Can't you talk?"

"No, it isn't that, Peter."

"Well, what's wrong? I've got all the fingernails bitten off one hand."

"Well, it's nothing, Peter. I think it was just my imagination."

"You mean everything's ALL RIGHT?"

"Well, no. Not exactly."

"My God, are you trying to keep something from me or can't you talk or what?"

"No, Peter. Isabel just had the blues when she wrote, I guess."

"The *blues*! You mean you deserted me and took my one decent piece of luggage to go half way across the country because Isabel has the blues?"

"I guess so, Peter. I mean I think that's all. Well, anyhow, I'm glad I came. Isabel looks wonderful and the Urchin's swell and I'll write you a letter, Peter. I'll write you a letter tomorrow."

"Didn't you write me one today?"

"No, Peter. I just got here this afternoon."

"I'll tell Mike on you. I'll have Mike for a witness."

"How is Mike?"

"He's got his ear frostbitten."

"Which one?"

"The left one I think. My God, I don't know. I'm not going to spend a fortune in long distance calls to talk about Mike's ears. What I want to know is what's the matter with Isabel?"

"Well, nothing, Peter. Oh, nuts! I'll write you a letter."

"I love you, Brat."

"Good night, Peter."

"Good night."

"Good night, Peter dear."

After I answered the phone Isabel left the room and now I

could hear the bath water running in the bathroom. I went to the door. "You want me to wash your back?" I called.

"Sure," Isabel said. "Come on in."

The bathroom was warm and the steam had collected on the mirrors and the window glass. I had a curious floating sensation, the way I imagine deep sea divers feel.

"How's Peter bearing up?" she asked

"Bravely." For some reason I didn't mention Peter's concern over Isabel. I reached for the soap and began to scrub Isabel's back.

"I hate to desert you like this," she said. "We've always stayed up and talked all night before, but Little Sister has changed all my habits. Honestly, by nine o'clock at night I'm just stupid for sleep. I've got to go to bed."

"That's all right. We can talk tomorrow."

"Do you and Peter still stay up half the night?"

"Sure. You know me. Peter says it's because I was born after midnight and I just got started off wrong."

"Leonard just ordered us a lot of new books. I put most of them in your room. I hope you haven't read them all. You still read in bed, I suppose?"

"Sure."

"I fall asleep before I can even find my place."

After Isabel had finished her bath we went into my room. It was next to hers.

"You want to make the most of this room," she said. "You'll probably be the last guest to sleep in it. Two more months and it'll be a nursery."

"Are you going to change it any?"

"I meant to," Isabel said. "I've planned so long on this baby and I meant to have new curtains and reupholster that chair there, but somehow I don't seem to get anything done. I thought I'd have plenty of time, but I haven't done a thing. I suppose the week before this baby's born I'll drive everybody nuts by insisting on making curtains.

"Maybe we could do it together while I'm here."

"If this fog would just lift," she said, "maybe we'd feel more like shopping. There's only one store in the town and I don't know if they've anything decent or not. Mrs. McNaughton has been dying to shop for me or sew or something, but the woman chatters until I could throw something at her head."

"She seemed pretty protective, all right."

"She's just one big bundle of concern," Isabel said. "Really, it's kind of flattering. It's only lately that it's got on my nerves." Isabel went over to the table by my bed and got a cigarette. I noticed they were the kind I smoke and I marvelled at how she had got them there on such short notice, having as much on her mind as she did. When she held the match for her cigarette the little blue patches under her eyes showed very plainly and suddenly I remembered the sound of her voice calling through the fog: "Hi, ho, Silver!"

Isabel closed her eyes and inhaled deeply on her cigarette. "It's just so silly of me to be talking about nerves," she said. "I never have nerves."

"You do now," I said. "You'd better go to bed."

"You're right there." She smiled at me and said: "I'm glad you've come, Brat, blues or no blues."

"So am I," I said.

"Say, if you go in the bathroom, don't turn the light off. We leave it burning all night for the Sea Urchin."

"O.K."

"Good night," she said.

"Good night, Isabel."

Despite the fact that I had had a long train ride, drunk two glasses of Nelson's Blood and met two new people, I was not sleepy and while I had a cigarette I looked over the new books Leonard had ordered from the city. Some of them I had read already and it amused me to see how much Leonard and Peter were alike. Leonard had chosen them "to keep the expectant mother cheerful" just as carefully as Peter reads the reviews before we go to a play.

I chose a book finally and adjusted the bed lamp. I felt a little thrill of pleasure to know that the book was a new one. I like to be the first person to read a new book. I like to cut the pages and open the book right so it won't squeak. I like the way new books smell, too.

The page numeral, thirteen, caught my eye and I suddenly realized that I didn't know what I was reading about. I put the book down for a moment and lit another cigarette. The house seemed abnormally still. I supposed my feeling of great wakefulness to be caused by the fact that I could very plainly hear the waves of the sea hitting the shore, a sound I had not heard for a long time, but after I had started the book over again I realized that I was becoming more and more aware of the bell. I shook my head to get the sound of the bell out long enough to try to concentrate on the book again, but it was no good and finally I decided to try listening TO the bell. When Peter and I used to go to concerts a great deal he told me that I would not mind the applause so much if I would applaud, too. I tried it once and it worked, so now I thought I'd try listening to the bell instead of attempting to ignore it.

It was really a curious bell I noticed when I paid attention to it. We used to have a song in grade school, I remember, with a chorus that went "Ding dong bell; ding, dong; ding, dong; ding, dong," but we always sang it with the first word accented: DING dong, DING, dong and I suppose most bells sound like that, but this one was very clearly ding DONG! ding DONG! with the second sound accented and followed by a distinct pause. I remembered feeling that I had stumbled onto something really significant, but somehow, paying all that attention to the sound of the bell worked the trick and I went back to my book and found it really fascinating.

I forgot all about the bell and read the book clear through to the end. It was a very pleasant book and I put it on the bedside table with a slight regret that I could never again read it for the first time. Nice and drowsy now, I put out my cigarette very carefully and was just reaching over my head to pull out the bed light when I heard Isabel cry out in her sleep.

"Wait!" I heard her say. "Wait!" and then she was sobbing pitifully.

I jumped out of bed and I remember being aware how painfully cold the floor was to my bare feet. I was unfamiliar with the room and didn't know where to turn on the light, but I opened the bathroom door because Isabel had left the light on in there and it made just enough illumination in the bedroom so that I could see Isabel quite plainly.

"Isabel," I said, "Isabel!" but I didn't touch her. "Isabel, wake up."

The sobbing stopped and Isabel sat up in bed and pulled on the light. Her hair was disheveled as though she had been turning her head back and forth on the pillow. Her eyes were very wide open and her face was wet. She looked at me and then she closed her eyes very tight and shivered. "Get me a cigarette," she said. "Please."

I got a cigarette, lit it and give it to her and then I put her robe around her shoulders.

I have shared a room with Isabel and I have seen her bathe and brush her teeth and I have seen her be sick, even, but I had never felt then as I felt now. I felt as though I had been indelicate somehow, as though I were observing something that I should not see. I felt as though I had walked in on Isabel and caught her talking with witches.

"Shall I go away?" I asked.

"No," she said, "only put something on. It's awfully cold in here." I went back to my room and got my robe.

"You'd better crawl in Leonard's bed," she said. I did just as I was told and for some reason I remembered the day Mamma took me in the bedroom, shut the door and told me the facts of life and I giggled, slightly off key.

"Be careful," Isabel said. "You'll wake the Sea Urchin."

"Sorry," I said.

"Would you mind getting me a handkerchief out of that top drawer?" Isabel said. "I seem to be all over tears."

I remember being conscious as I walked across the room of the bell's ringing: ding DONG! ding DONG! but the sight of Isabel's dresser drawer, always in such perfect order and smelling faintly of rose geranium, and the fact that at last I was doing something with my hands made everything seem normal again and I took the handkerchief to her and said, "Do you do this often?"

"It's just lately," Isabel said. "I have the damnedest dream."

"The same one?"

"Yes, it's always the same. There's nothing so very terrible about it either, only I always wake up crying and cold."

I lit a cigarette for myself and as I blew out the match I asked, "What's it about?"

"Well, there's nothing much to it," she said. "It's just that I'm running like mad down a long hall or a tunnel or some place and there's something terrible going to happen when I get to the end."

"Only you never get there?"

"No, I never get to the end of it," she said. "I always wake up first."

"Is it always the same?"

"Yes, I'm always running down this long tunnel or hall or whatever it is and I'm just about to see something or hear something horrible or. . . . Did I wake you up?"

"No, I'd just finished reading one of the new books."

Isabel put out her cigarette and yawned. "Was it any good?"

"Yes," I said, "pretty good. There was a guy in it like Peter."

"You always say that," Isabel said. "You say that about every book you read."

"Well, the nice thing about me is," I said, "that I don't say it about Peter's books."

"No," she said, and she yawned again, "I'm the one that says it about Peter's books."

"Would you like me to sleep here?" I asked.

"Uh huh."

I remembered that I had left the light on in the guest room and I started back to turn it out.

"You know," Isabel said when I was at the door. "You know, I just remembered something about that dream. There was something . . . something in my right hand."

When I came back after I'd turned out the light Isabel was asleep. The next morning she woke me and the first thing I remember was that she was looking at me and she was smiling. "Look," she said, "the fog's gone."

I don't think I have ever seen such a day. I got out of bed and looked out the window. The sea was calm and blue and oh, I wanted Peter to be right there with me and I wanted us to have a foot race down to the beach and I wanted to beat him.

"Aren't you ready for breakfast YET?" and there stood the Sea Urchin in the door.

"Are you waiting on me? I'm sorry. I forgot all about breakfast."

"Well, hurry up, Fog-Fawg."

"Don't you ever forget anything?"

"Wash your face, Brat. I'm starved. I've been all the way down to the beach already. There's a dead turtle washed up almost as big as the rug and boy! does it smell terrible!"

"That's a fine thing to tell me before breakfast."

Isabel was beautiful that morning. There was a kind of scrubbed glow to her cheeks and the sunlight hit one side of her hair. Everything was shining and new.

"We'll take a walk after breakfast," Isabel said. "It's a shame it's Sunday and all the stores are closed. I wouldn't mind shopping on a day like this."

"Hey," the Urchin said. "Isabel said that Peter brings you your breakfast in bed. Is that so?"

"Yes sir, that is so. Well, that is, in the winter time anyway."

"I would have brought you your breakfast in bed," he said.

"No, you don't, " Isabel said. "Peter can spoil her all he wants to when she's home, but when she's here I want some company for breakfast."

"Well, gosh, Isabel," he said. "I could bring you yours in bed, too."

"Bless your heart, you did once, didn't you?"

"You know," Isabel said to me, "Leonard and I always sleep late on Sundays and one time when the Sea Urchin was only five years old he slipped downstairs very quietly, made toast in the oven, fried bacon and squeezed orange juice. When Leonard and I woke up there he stood just beaming with everything all neat on a tray."

"And she didn't even know," he said to me (and he wrinkled up his eyes the way Leonard does) "that I knew how to light a match."

"I'll bet she was surprised," I said to the Urchin.

"That isn't all," he said. "She was s-c-a-r-e-d to death." He caught me with a mouthful of coffee.

"Want to go for a walk?" Isabel asked when we had finished breakfast.

"Sure," I said, "only first I have to write to Peter."

"We can mail it while we're out," Isabel said. "There's ink and paper and everything over on the desk."

When I started to write to Peter there in that pleasant room with the sunlight forming a parallelogram on the rug and the sound of Isabel's humming "A Woman is a Sometime Thing" as she dressed, it seemed to me that the day was real and constant. I could not have sworn but what I and not Isabel had had that dream. The night seemed very very far away and trivial. I was not even sure that what I remembered was true and I felt sure that if I did put it down on paper I would exaggerate its importance. Once the thought crossed my mind that it was somehow too intimate to tell Peter about my sister and I shivered and got up and went to the window. I looked out at the sea again and then I came back and wrote Peter a love letter; I didn't mention the dream at all.

We had a fine walk and that evening Isabel and I both got

special delivery letters from Leonard and Peter (it being Sunday with no regular mail delivery) and something about the man who delivered the letters got me to thinking about Mike, so I told Isabel all about Mike. I slept in Leonard's bed again that night and I had had so much fresh air and such a good work out with the Sea Urchin that I didn't need to read in bed at all. Isabel and I went to sleep about the same time I guess and we both slept right through until there was the Sea Urchin holding the alarm clock in his hands and asking us didn't we realize it was a school day and he'd be late if we didn't hurry and get up and get some breakfast.

The school bus came by and the Sea Urchin went tearing out and was up the two steps and inside the bus before I'd hardly got the good-bye out of my mouth.

"Pretty soft," I said to Isabel, "going to school in a bus. Makes me feel like a pioneer."

"Wasn't that awful," Isabel said, "the way we used to tear out about half dressed?"

The sharpest little prickly of cold ran up my spine then, but I hardly had time to notice it before Isabel said, "What do you say we do down town this morning and see if there's anything in that store we could make curtains of?"

"Such ambition, Isabel!"

"If this weather just holds long enough," she said, "I honestly think I could get something done to that room. I'd be so pleased if I could get it done before Leonard gets back."

We went down town and found some quite lovely marquisette and by the time the Sea Urchin got home from school we had all the curtains cut and two of the hems basted and for a wonder they were the same length.

The clear fine weather held for a week and by that time we had all the work done of transforming the guest room into a nursery except for the actual moving of furniture and Isabel wasn't going to do that until Leonard came home to help her anyhow.

I'd had three long distance calls from Peter and a letter saying if there wasn't anything wrong why didn't I come home. I was beginning to get pretty homesick for Peter by this time and for the dogs and the sheep and the cow and even for Mike, but Isabel and I were having such a wonderful time together that I thought I'd stay until Leonard came back.

Then one evening, two days before Leonard was due home, Mr. McNaughton came by on his way home from the laboratory to see if Isabel needed anything from town and to ask if he couldn't bring in a good supply of wood. "The weather's changing quite fast," he said.

I had promised the Sea Urchin to help build a model airplane after dinner and Isabel said she thought she'd lie down a while and maybe take a nap.

In no time at all I had glue up to my wrists, not to mention one fine spot in my hair and one on my skirt and by the end of half an hour the Sea Urchin had broken one piece of balsam wood and I'd broken three.

"Leonard is the one," he said, "that can really do it without busting anything."

"Well, after all," I said. "I haven't had much experience with airplanes; Peter builds sheep pens."

"What for?" he asked.

"For sheep. What do you think?"

"Have you got *SHEEP*?"

"A sheep," I said.

"You never told me," he said, "that you had a sheep."

"Sure," I said.

"It's nine o'clock," Isabel said, coming out of her room, "and you have to take a bath, Urchin. Better put your airplane away for tonight."

"O.K.," he said, "just as soon as I get this propeller cut. Boy, wait till Leonard sees this. Say, did you know Peter had a sheep?"

"Yes," she said. "Come on, now. Take your bath."

The Urchin went into the bathroom and Isabel sat down in a chair by the fire. I went into the kitchen to clean the glue off my hands and when I came back Isabel was sitting with her elbow on the arm of the chair, her hand supporting her head.

"Did you have a nap?" I asked.

"No," she said, "I couldn't sleep."

"Maybe we made too much noise."

"No," she said, "you were wonderful to keep him so quiet. I'm just restless, or something. I feel like going to a movie."

"Maybe we ought to go to one."

"It's too late," she said. "I don't really feel like going to one; I just wish I could be at one without going."

"Maybe we ought to play some solitaire," I said.

"Oh, that's wonderful," she said. "I'd forgotten all about solitaire. I wonder if I could find my cards." The last time Isabel and I played solitaire was when Peter sent off the manuscript of his first novel. Peter was quite calm about it, but Isabel was visiting us then and neither of us could stop waiting, so we just played solitaire constantly until the letter came.

I cleared off the coffee table while Isabel hunted for the cards and then the two of us sat down and played double solitaire and for a while it was quite exciting and we felt as though we were waiting for good news. We played about ten games and Isabel looked up at the clock and said, "We ought to stop this and go to bed."

"I know it," I said, separating the cards out of the middle and giving her her deck.

"One more game," she said.

"Maybe it'll come out this time," I said.

We didn't get stopped this time and we played clear to the end. Isabel got all her cards out first and it was pretty exciting there for a couple of minutes and then we started in to play another game without making any apology. We must have played five or six more games and I noticed Isabel was slowing down quite a bit.

"Let's quit this," I said.

"It's not much fun, is it?" she said.

"Not even when you win."

We didn't even have enough energy to put the cards away, but left them on the coffee table. Isabel tried the front door to see if it were locked and I saw her look out and shiver.

"I think I'll take some luminal," she said.

We turned out the lights and after a while Isabel went to sleep. I couldn't sleep for some reason and I didn't feel like reading. Besides, I didn't want to turn on a light and waken Isabel. I heard the clock strike a couple of times and I kept feeling as though I were waiting for something and after a while I knew what it was because the bell started: ding, DONG! ding, DONG! ding, DONG!

The sound of the fog bell began to pervade everything in the room. I could feel the bed beneath me rising and falling in time to it and I found myself counting: one, TWO; one, TWO; one, TWO. It seemed to me that the bell began walking clumsily up the cliff toward the house and that now it was coming into our room. It was a lame bell and it lunged forward every other step and that was why it went ding, DONG; ding, DONG, ding, DONG. Now it was standing right by Isabel's dresser and it got the clock doing it too so that the clock began ticking in a lame rhythm: tick, TOCK; tick, TOCK; tick, TOCK; and then I began to hear my heart beat right with the bell: la, bump; la, bump; la, bump. Now the bell and the clock and the bed and my heart were all lunging together in that crippled rhythm and I became aware of the sound of my own breathing. I kept trying to stop it for fear it would waken Isabel. I was lying on my back and I suddenly had the idea that if I were to roll over on my face I could break the spell before the bell should absorb me a little at a time, beginning with the feet. I rolled over on my face and buried my head in the pillow and I thought: think of Peter, think of Peter, real hard. And then I went to sleep.

Just at dawn I woke up suddenly with my head feeling very clear. That is unusual for me, because ordinarily I am one of those people who comes up a five hundred rung ladder, taking a fond farewell of each tread and bitterly resenting every forward step.

All through the morning I had that detached, unreal feeling that I had had in the bathroom the first night when Isabel was bathing and the mirrors and window glass were clouded. I felt as though I were just about to discover or remember something and, at the same time, I seemed to be withdrawn and unobserved like a cobweb growing quietly and secretly in a neglected corner.

I felt this way all morning and when the Sea Urchin came in at noon from school he and Isabel stood by the fire discussing the fog and the dampness of his clothes and their voices seemed to come to me from a great distance, but when we were all sitting at lunch the good, hot soup brought me back close to them again and there for a moment the fog seemed to be pushed away and the three of us were real and together.

"Say," the Urchin said, "maybe I'll have the measles."

"The measles!" Isabel said.

"Yeah. Billy Marks is in my room at school and he's got the measles. He's got a quarantine sign on his house. I went by there today to see it and it's a big red sign with black letters and they won't let anybody in."

"You stay away from there," Isabel said.

"And hold your breath while you go by," I said.

"Why?" asked the Urchin.

"I haven't thought of that in years," Isabel said. "Who was it told us that?

"Told you what?" asked the Urchin.

"Oh," Isabel said, "when we were going to Schenley Street School somebody told us to hold our breath when we went past a quarantined house so we wouldn't catch the disease."

"It was Nora Peterson," I said. "She was always scaring the hell out of me, anyway. What do you suppose ever happened to her?"

"Something violent, no doubt," Isabel said. "You know, I used to do that religiously and one time when the Andersons and the Petersons and the McIntyres were all quarantined at once I nearly choked to death trying to get by all three houses without taking a breath.

"When I remember Market Street, Isabel, it seems to me that somebody was always quarantined for something."

"Honestly," she said, "the way we used to go tearing down Market Street to Schenley every single morning with our coats half buttoned. . . ."

Just then the fog bell rang again and I said, "Isabel." Isabel looked at me and the two of us just sat there motionless for a second suspended and static while outside the wind dashed around corners and clocks ticked and clouds hurried through the sky. The two of us opened our mouths together and said: "Schenley Street!" for that was the answer to the dark cloud that had hung over Isabel these weeks, the cloud that had finally begun to stifle me, too.

How it was the janitor of Schenley Street School had leaned on the rope to get that particular sound out of the bell, I don't know, but there was no question about it: the tardy bell had exactly the same accent and warning tone and promise of punishment as the fog bell.

And suddenly Isabel began to laugh, the way I had not heard her laugh since I'd been there. It was a wonderfully free and hearty laugh and hearing it I knew that Isabel was all right again and the two of us weren't apart any more.

"Why do you suppose," she said, gasping for breath from her laughter, "why do you suppose that we didn't get up on time just once and WALK to school?"

"I don't know," I said, "but if I'd known then it would make you have nightmares now I would have got up at dawn."

Just then the phone rang and it was a telegram from Peter saying he'd be there that night at midnight.

"Peter's coming!" I said.

"Is Peter going to sleep in the nursery?" the Sea Urchin asked.

"Oh, yes, oh yes," I said, "and so am I."

After the Urchin had gone to school I started getting in a dither about Peter's coming. I couldn't decide what to wear when I went down to the train to meet him and Isabel finally chose for me and she pressed my dress while I washed my hair. It was just like when Isabel and I used to be at home together dressing to go out in the evening. We'd always mean to help each other and talk too long and Mamma would be stuck in the living room with one man and sometimes two while they waited for us to quit giggling and find two whole pairs of stockings and come downstairs.

"You'll have to do this all over again tomorrow for me," Isabel said, "when Leonard comes."

I had at least twelve hours in which to get ready, but of course I had to run all the way to the station, but it was all right because the train was late and then suddenly there was Peter and he had a new hat.

Peter doesn't like to kiss people in public and so I just stood there twitching at the mouth for a minute and then I said, "You've got a new hat."

"Yeah," he said. "I lost my other one. I couldn't find it anywhere."

"But, Peter, it's in my closet."

"Your closet? What's my hat doing in your closet?"

"Well, Peter, one day you were gone all day and I took your hat in and hung it by mine and then I took your shoes in and put them beside mine."

"Oh, My God!" he said. "I bought new shoes, too."

"I'm sorry, Peter. When you came home I forgot all about it."

"Let's go," he said. "Let's not stand out here on a train track all night."

"Sure, we'll go. Only let's walk up to the house because I want to tell you all about Isabel before we get there."

"O.K. How far is it?"

"About a mile. Listen, Peter, you know. . . ." and I started to tell him all about how the cloud had hung over Isabel and finally over me and about the fog and the bell and Isabel's dream and then I told him how we'd recognized the sound of the bell to be the same as the Schenley Street School bell.

"We used to go dashing out of the house, Peter, and Isabel'd be in front pulling me along by the hand and we'd keep thinking the tardy bell would ring any minute." And while I was telling him about it I stopped walking and I could see the two of us so clearly. I could see Isabel bent forward running, with her long yellow curls bobbing up and down on her shoulders and I could see the ribbing in Isabel's long cotton stockings. I have never remembered anything in my life so clearly as the ribbing in Isabel's stockings. Suddenly, while I was telling Peter about us and seeing us so plainly under the great dark trees arched over the sidewalk on Market Street, we looked so small and so vulnerable . . . vulnerable as a sleeping face. I took hold of Peter's hand and the two of us began running very fast back to the house.

"Where's Isabel?" Peter asked when we got inside.

"She's gone to bed, Peter. It's so late and she wants to be all rested for tomorrow when Leonard comes home. She said to tell you 'hello' and she'd see you at breakfast.

"Oh," he said, "sure." And then he kissed me. It was lovely to be inside a room with Peter again and having him kiss me. I was shaken and disjointed all over again at the great miracle of our being together, until finally we sank back to the fact that we were in a room and Peter had on a wet coat and we'd better go over to the fireplace.

Of course it was true that Isabel had wanted to be rested for Leonard tomorrow, but also I knew that she had gone to bed so that Peter and I could be alone these first few moments.

I made Peter some hot coffee and we sat drinking it in front of the fireplace and Peter told me all the news. Peter was talking in a low voice so as not to awaken Isabel and after a while he quit talking and sat listening.

"That is a curious bell," he said, "but it's not unpleasant to me. I see what you mean, though."

We sat there staring into the flames and listening to the bell that was powerless, now, to frighten Isabel or me any more. I could not get the picture of Isabel and me out of my mind. I would close my eyes and then when I looked into the flames again there would be Isabel running very fast just ahead of me, with her long thin legs in those ribbed cotton stockings.

"Oh, Peter," I said, "I think I can remember what it was like, but I can't really. I can't really remember what seven years old was like."

"I know," he said, "I wish I could write all the time, write everything down and try to hold on to it."

"Oh, Peter," I said, "I will forget this year, too, and this night . . . and the day you bought your new hat."

I knew I couldn't hold it for sure and I thought about Peter's new hat getting familiar and of my sometime not being able to remember which day he'd bought it and I started to cry. When I cry I bellow; it sounds terrible.

Peter came over to my chair and took my head in his hands and held it tight. Peter's hands are very big and you know the bones are all there. It was like not having any hair or skin; it was like having his good old bones, white and clean and solid right on my skull.

"Poor Brat," he said. "You cry just like a child. So sudden . . . and so hard."

A Young Man Found It

I think it will be tomorrow I am going to die, because it can be any day now and I think I will make it tomorrow. It is only a little matter of a few eggs and some milk that is keeping me alive and it is strange to think of it as so many eggs equals so many days, but it is a nice definite knowledge to know that I can make it be a day, a week or two weeks so simply. All I have to do is to stop the eggs and milk. Within a short limit I can do it anytime and I think I will do it tomorrow.

I am not really an old man sitting here in this room that is, I suppose, a poor room and a cold one. I was never much able to care about the rooms I have lived in because you have to be in them a little while before you can see what it is it will take to make them better and that little time you are waiting to see how you can make the whole room better at once has always defeated me. No room I had lived in for two days could ever look to me the same as it did when I walked into it. Once I had a house, but that was years ago and I never felt at home in it. It is strange that this is so and that after the first two days in any hotel room I never see it any more and I can rest.

Some things, no matter where the room is or how often I change rooms I always put in the same place. My own home—the land and the house where I was born and grew up and first learned to take care of myself—I put on the ceiling so I can lie in bed and look at it, and my son, who has been dead so long I can't remember now about his face, him I put in a chair by the window. I have never yet had such a bad room that it did not have a chair and a window. I put him there because of the light.

There are other things, too, but they don't matter to anyone else and they're not very unusual and besides, that isn't why I'm writing this at all.

It seems to me that I have not lived all these years without having come onto some knowledge and it seems to me that they are good things to know because I got to know them the hard way. And by that I mean that I tried everything else first that was stacked up on top of them and, then when I got clear to the bottom of the stack, I found these things and they were good things.

If you have had all the time to think that I have had to think, then you ought to come out of it with something pretty good.

Sometimes I have wished that I was a little famous, so that people could ask me questions and I could tell them these things I know in the answers, because when it gets to the place where you have to write it down for a scrubwoman to read and even have to ask yourself the questions, why it sounds a little egotistical, that's all.

But there is no other way for it, because I don't want to die without having somebody, even a scrubwoman, know that I really did learn something at the end of all this staying alive and so, these are the things I learned.

I learned that the greatest motivating force in human lives is loneliness. I do not mean that loneliness is the worst thing or even that you are more aware of it than of some other things. All I mean is that this is the thing that is responsible for the greatest number of human actions and in that respect it is stronger than money and more powerful than sex.

I learned that ritual, routine and habit are the most effective weapons against loneliness, but I also learned that if you will not let yourself have any weapons against it that ultimately you have a choice between two things and it is quite a gamble to watch and see which of them is going to happen to you at the end of your waiting. One of the ends is madness or some form of complete debility, but if by some chance you escape this, then there is only one other thing that can happen to you and that is a wonderful thing.

That is the realization that, self-functioning and self-nourished, lives in the very inside of you a piece of strong real stuff. It is better than power and it is different from chemistry.

I learned that the worst thing there is is the certain knowledge that you cannot erase anything you have done, and, no matter if it is only for fifteen minutes, you cannot go back and do it over again and do it better, or differently.

And I learned that of all the fine things there are in any world the finest of these is courage and that surprised me some because I thought it would be love. And it also surprised me that there is no other word for it.

I know perfectly well that, no matter who finds this tomorrow or the next day, it cannot possibly do anybody any good because if you are ever going to know these things you have got to know them of yourself.

I even know that I am not the first man or the only man to have got this knowledge in the way I got it, but STILL I am proud to have known it and glad to have it in words my own.

Duress

Duress is a little town sitting in the west of Oklahoma like a piece of cold beef in the middle of a plate while the diner has been called to the telephone. Have you ever seen a woman lying waiting in a bed with the sheets all fresh, no wrinkles, and all day the woman has been home alone and all afternoon she has been walking about the house saying tonight is the night? All day she has been waiting for the night and then at last she is lying in the bed with the sheets all fresh and everything is ready, but her husband is in the bathroom washing his teeth. She can hear her husband washing his teeth then she can hear him spit for the last time and put away his tooth brush and close the door of the medicine chest and maybe he stops and looks in the mirror for a while and maybe he feels of his face. All the time the woman is lying there ready, ready. And then she can hear the door knob turn and hear the door open and now he is coming over to the bed and the woman is ready and she reaches up her hand to pull off the light. Her husband sits on the edge of the bed and he takes off one shoe while the woman is saying over and over to herself *take off the other shoe, take off the other shoe,* and then the man says, "My God! I forgot to shut the garage door," and he walks down the stairs and never comes back. Well after a while the woman begins to breathe again and she breathes slower and slower and pretty soon she rolls over on her side. That's the way Duress is now.

Duress is a woman with her lover gone down to shut the garage door and never returning.

Duress is a town without a highway.

ONE

"This town was like a dead house on
a hill
Solitary, quiet.
And though you leaned against the
wind
And felt the sleet upon your face
And though you saw the windows
open
The curtains of that house hung
still. . . ."

So had Luke Cummins begun one of his poems and so had it remained, as they all did, only a beginning.

Many a man might walk by such a house again and again, feeling each time a slight jog—a little incongruity, just as a man will say of another, "I remember something about his face—something not quite right," and only years later, perhaps riding on a bus in another city, would he say to himself: "That man had a blind eye; that man had a scar."

So could a stranger drive through Duress in a car along the now discarded highway, past the depot, the Peebles Hotel, the filling station, the five and ten, and, being thirsty, stop at Ramsey's Drugstore.

Back in the car again and on his way to the city he might realize only after a hundred miles or so that he had drunk a lukewarm Coca Cola out of a bottle, while he leaned against a dusty, unused soda fountain. He might remember no one went in or out of the Peebles Hotel. He might remember the train only whistled and did not stop at the depot.

A man who saw the curtains of a house hang still when the wind was blowing would someday realize the house was deserted. A man might know with a shock, a hundred miles down the road, that when the little colored streams of syrup do not spout from the only soda fountain of the town—that town is dead.

Luke Cummins, though, was not any man; he was a poet and though the drawers of his desk and the bottom cupboards of the china closet were stuffed with his manuscripts—all of them unfinished—he would not have to pass such a house twice. He would not have to go two miles down the road. He would see the curtains and the soda fountain the first time and know.

Doctor Romig was not any man; neither was he Luke. John Romig's hair was gray and neat to his head; Luke's was thick and wild and black and, though it was brushed often and furiously, it was never combed. John Romig's eyes were large and kind, changing and gentle; Luke's eyes were gray. They looked one way and had no compromise in them. John Romig wore a size six glove; Luke's hand covered a dinner plate. John Romig lived in the only brick house for a hundred miles; Luke's house was frame and full of boarders.

John Romig would see the house with the still curtains all right, as he had seen Bart Ramsey's soda fountain—as, dear God! he had seen Luke Cummins' wife, Gracie. And he would store them all away at the blurred bottom of his brain until they pinched and tickled and cried out in the dark nights and then began to swell slowly like an evil thing mounting the staircase. Step after step they would climb—and just as they reached the landing John Romig would take a drink of whiskey. He never failed to get it in time.

The whiskey had come only after the flute had gone. When John Romig had had his flute the whiskey had never been necessary. It had been pleasant, but not necessary.

When you take the highway away from a town even the rustling of the trees becomes a boisterous racket. If the butcher beats his dog, if the midnight train is late, if Luke Cummins has one of his headaches, the whole country knows it.

John Romig played his flute just once after they changed the highway and the jagged hole that he made in the darkness so frightened him that he put it away for good.

Suppose you were old Mrs. McCandless lying with your head in a window, propping yourself up on pillows to breathe, and you with a bad heart and a pulse like a silk thread knotting itself into snarls—suppose you were lying there awake and afraid in the night in a house with no telephone and you heard Doctor Romig's flute! Wouldn't you say, "I am an old woman and my heart is crumbling inside me and I can't stop it. This is the only heart I've got and there is no one to watch over it but a flute player!"?

Suppose you were Luke Cummins writing a poem and having to be defeated once over, once more, for the furious, blinding, maddening pain in your skull, while the wail of a flute grew louder and louder! Wouldn't you bash your skull open on a stone, though? Wouldn't you let the pain be free at last and splash over the window sill?

But a glass of whiskey, now, it makes no noise; it disturbs nobody.

So quietly can one slide the fluid out of a bottle and down the side of a glass—so gently can the lips meld with the rim of the glass, that, for all its warmth and fire, it makes no crackling, no popping—no sound.

There had been Irish whiskey the day John Romig's mother died taking with her his last excuse for staying in Duress, and Scotch the last time he had refused to sell his house for enough to start a practice in the city. Scotch there had been while he kept remembering that no new doctor would ever come now to a town without a highway, while he thought of Mrs. McCandless dying alone with no telephone in the house, and of Luke, maddened by the pain in his head and no doctor for a hundred miles, and of Luke's wife, Gracie, and Gracie's child Erma. What if Erma should have the croup or pneumonia, and Luke not seeing for the mist he walked in and Gracie with only the egg money in the house?

Bourbon there had been the day he should have made Gracie go into the city for an operation and he let her talk him out of it.

And rye . . . there had been rye the night he sat with Grace while she died.

"Gracie," John Romig said that night, "let me take you to a hospital now. Let me take you into the city."

"You know I've waited too long," she said.

"Maybe it's not so, Gracie," he said. "Maybe there's time. Let's try."

"Even if it worked now," she said, "I would be sick for a long time. I would not want Luke to be around sickness day after day. He could not stand it, John."

"Then you can stay in a hospital till you're well. Then he wouldn't have to see you if you didn't want."

"What would we do for money, John? How could I stay in a hospital?"

"Damn the money," he said. "Mortgage the house. Sell it . . . sell my house. What difference does it make?"

"*Sell* the house?" she asked. "Sell the *house*? How can he live without a house, John Romig? How can he write without a desk or read without a lamp? How can he be clean with no place to wash?"

"Christ, Gracie, what does it matter if he's clean so long as you live? Let me take you away now while there still might be time."

"I do not mind to die, John Romig," she said, "but I will have my love. I will not let it go."

"Mother of God," he said. "I'll not argue with you, Grace. I'll not disturb you further. Would you like me to give you something to make you sleep now?"

"Not yet, John. Not yet."

"Mother of God," he said and patted her hand.

"You never had a love like this," she said, "or you'd know."

"I never even touched the outside edge of a love like this," he said.

"You never asked for it."

"No," he said, "it seems to me I was always a little blurred—just a little smeared. I never quite came into focus. You know, Gracie, when I was in medical school in Chicago I used to have to ride the street cars every day. When the cars stopped at a street I used to look out the window and see young women standing by a shop window or on a corner. Sometimes two of them would be talking together and I could not hear what they said, though I could see their lips moving neatly over their teeth and the dimples in their elbows. I was afraid of them, even then, of their wonderful efficiency. There they would be standing so neatly corseted and their faces so clean under their hats and they would be having opinions, Gracie, with little nods of the head and quick smiles and shiftings of the feet.

"But the thing underneath all this—the thing that scares the hell out of you, Gracie, is that they keep the night and the day separate, the living room from the dining room. Their knives and forks and spoons are partitioned off. They put the roast in the oven, and feed the baby. They dress and undress and right in the middle of it all—*they know what time it is.*"

"John," Grace said. "John, I was forgetting—I was forgetting about Erma."

Even while she said it her voice was so different that John Romig reached for the little white tablets he had brought with him so that when he had to call Luke in, everything would be nice for him to look at, for Grace had asked long ago that Luke should not hear her cry out in pain—nor see her face twisted.

"Erma will have to take over the house," she said. "She's fourteen now. I've told her already. I've told her we have to keep the boarders. I've told her how to get along with them. But John . . ." she said.

"Here, Gracie. Drink the water now." He helped her to sit up and he put his hand around hers to steady the glass.

She looked dully on him and smiled.

"John," she said, "you tell her, you tell Erma . . . a little later on. You tell her I had a fine time."

The Wonderful Rich Billboard
of Kingston

Paul so often heard his mamma say they were too poor to do this, too poor to have that, that he always thought of himself as being poor.

"You know, we are poor," he often said to Mr. Hossenpeffer. Mr. Hossenpeffer was the man on the billboard across the street from Paul's bedroom window. He was the last thing Paul saw every night because Mr. Hossenpeffer stayed lighted until midnight. Every night before Paul went to sleep, he would lie in bed watching Mr. Hossenpeffer.

Mr. Hossenpeffer's elbow moved back and forth and, from behind it, a big ham jumped out. Mr. Hossenpeffer always smiled, but not too much.

One day after school Paul went home with his friend Joe.

"You know, Joe," he said on the way, "we are very poor at my house."

"Oh, no," Joe said. "*You* aren't poor. Wait till you see my house."

Joe's house was much smaller than Paul's and after he had seen it Paul began to feel very rich. The main thing was that catercorner from Joe's house, not even visible from Joe's bed, was a man on a billboard who was far inferior to Mr. Hossenpeffer. Joe did not even have a name for him. He just called him Him. This man sat on a bicycle and he held a hat in his hand. He never put the hat back on his head. The bicycle wheels never went around. In the basket was a loaf of bread. It just stayed there. Nothing moved at all. The man was supposed to be smiling very wide but instead he looked as though he had just found a cockroach in his soup.

Paul and Joe played marbles. They had a good time.

When Paul went home he said to his mother, "Mother, we are rich."

"Oh, no," his mother said. "We are relatively poor."

Lying in bed that night, Paul told Mr. Hossenpeffer about it: "I was wrong," he said. "I told you we were poor. We are only *relatively* poor; Joe is poor."

Mr. Hossenpeffer moved his well-lighted elbow. The ham jumped out. Mr. Hossenpeffer smiled—not too much; just right.

Next day, after school, Paul went home with his friend Volodya.

"You know, Volodya," he said, "I am relatively poor but Joe is awfully poor."

"Ha!" Volodya said. "Poor? Wait till you see my house. Maybe you are poor and Joe is quite poor, but we are *horribly* poor."

It was a long walk to Volodya's house. The house was very small and full of Volodya's brothers and sisters and you walked right on the boards of the floor with no rugs between. But worst of all, practically on top of Volodya's house was an old billboard full of printing. It had no light. It had no men on it at all. Only printing. Even the words were all wrinkled and covered with soot.

Volodya let Paul blow on his harmonica. They had a fine time. Paul did not mind any more that Volodya also loved Nancy Halliday.

That night Paul looked a long time at Mr. Hossenpeffer. How bright he was! How wonderfully he moved his arm so the ham could jump out.

"I was wrong again," he said to Mr. Hossenpeffer who was smiling just right. "We are relatively poor. Joe is quite poor. But Volodya is *horribly* poor."

One day his mother said, "Someday I must take you over to see your Aunt Clara in Kingston."

"Where is Kingston?" he said.

"Oh, Kingston is clear across town," his mamma said. "It's the very nicest section where the rich people live."

That night he got clear out of bed to talk to Mr. Hossenpeffer. He sat on the floor and leaned his elbow on the windowsill. "Sometime I'm going to Kingston, Mr. Hossenpeffer, to see my Aunt Clara. In Kingston the people are rich."

Mr. Hossenpeffer had a light bulb out tonight and the darkness cast a shadow over the ham.

"But do you suppose," Paul said, "that my Aunt Clara is relatively rich, or just quite rich, or only horribly rich?"

"I have never been to Kingston," Mr. Hossenpeffer said.

And then came the thought that was to stay with Paul for weeks and weeks. It burst upon him suddenly one night when he was sitting leaning on the windowsill, the night that Mr. Hossenpeffer's light bulb was replaced: *Think* what billboards they must have there!

If Mr. Hossenpeffer was so much better than Joe's bread man and Joe's bread man was *so* much better than Volodya's dirty old printing, what must there not be in Kingston?

It seemed to him that his mamma would never make up her mind to take him to his Aunt Clara's so night after night he would sit by his window looking at Mr. Hossenpeffer and dreaming of the wonderful billboards of Kingston. First of all they would be big, twice as big, two hundred times as big, as Mr. Hossenpeffer. The lights would not be just white lights standing still and sometimes burned out at that. They would be blue and red and yellow and purple and they would chase one another around all the time and they would be on all day. Boys would jump out and play baseball games and then they would go away and lots of girls would come out all looking like Nancy Halliday— only they would have on long dresses. On the bottom of their dresses bells would be sewn in and when the girls jumped up and down or shook their heads, the bells would all tinkle.

And when you went up to the billboard and leaned against it

and put your head back and reached your hand up to touch the billboard, it would feel like fur. Soft, soft fur.

Every night he would have a new addition to his dream billboard to tell Mr. Hossenpeffer but Mr. Hossenpeffer did not much like the conversations. He began to get dim. His smile began to fade. The ham began to slow down. Mr. Hossenpeffer had nothing to say.

Finally one day his mamma put Paul in the bathtub and scrubbed him hard every place. She put his most uncomfortable clothes on him. She put toilet water on his hair. Then they got on the streetcar and started for Aunt Clara's in Kingston. When they got off the streetcar Paul put his hand over his eyes and asked his mamma to lead him. He wanted to see the billboard all at once. He wanted to be surprised.

"We're here," his mamma said, letting go of his hand. "This is Aunt Clara's."

It was a house. He turned his back and looked across the street. There was another house. He looked catercornered from Aunt Clara's house. There was another house. Wherever he looked there were only houses: relatively rich, quite rich, and horribly rich.

"Where is the billboard?" he said to his mamma.

His mamma laughed. "Why, there are no billboards in *Kingston*," she said.

"Not anywhere?" he said.

"Not anywhere in Kingston," she said.

He could not believe it. He turned his back on his Aunt Clara's house and looked across the street again.

"There is no rich," he said. "There is no rich in Kingston. There is no rich anywhere. There is only horribly poor and quite poor and relatively poor and then just poor."

Well now, he had it straight and he could hardly wait to get back home tonight and tell it to Mr. Hossenpeffer who would be waiting.

No Smoking, No Spitting

Every morning she took the 8:15 street car and by now she knew everyone that rode on it and she hated them all. When she had first started going to work, she had felt very companionable toward them. She had stood and looked around and felt that it was rather fine and wonderful the way they had all made it over the edge of one more day, the way they must all have had to get up separately groping around in the early morning dark and hating together the shock of the electric light and wandering sleepily into their bathrooms. There must have been a great number of them brushing their teeth actually in unison if they had known it and perhaps even in rhythm. Once it had seemed to her that they were all together swimming against the stream, like salmon. But that had been a long time ago when she had liked them. That had been right at the beginning when she thought of them as salmon.

Now they were cows. Once she had got a place in the back end of the car, a step lower than the main part, and she had seen a line along their legs. The wide spread of the feet for balance, the weight shifting, the anticipation of the curves and sudden stops, looked exactly like what she had seen through the side boards of a truckload of cattle. And as intimately as she had grown to know them all, as many times as she had had their elbows in her ribs, as many times as she had bumped their bottoms and stepped on their feet, she knew that if she were to speak to a single one of them, he would turn and look behind him.

It was certainly strange the way the car was always exactly full. Surely they didn't all of them make it on time every single day. You'd think now the way they were packed in that if one of them died it would leave a hole. You'd think that if one of them had the flu or took a few days off to get married that it would certainly leave a vacant place that you could notice. But if anybody had died there must have been someone right there to take his place because the car was always exactly full and every morning when the motorman yelled, *Back in the car, Back in the car,* not one of them moved an inch. He kept on yelling it every morning and afterwards he slammed the door harder than ever and stamped his foot on the bell.

It probably was the same ones over and over that never had any change. The motorman must have known for years that if he sold tokens a dozen for a dime, there would still be some bastard pop a five dollar bill on him at a diagonal intersection with a green light. She doubted if the motorman had had any surprises for years. She herself had not been surprised by any of them for a long time, not since the religious fanatic had started coming down on Tuesdays and Thursdays. It was a good six months now that the R.F. had been riding the car and she pulled the same trick every day. She was an elderly woman and her clothes, though very good, were always either too long or too large for her as though she could never really believe in her own limitations. She always wore flowers on her hat whatever the season and she wore the hat at a right angle to her face. There was nothing at all remarkable about her except for her eyes, which were very clear and innocent and gray with long black lashes. She would stand by a seat that held a woman by the window and a man on the aisle.

"Young man," she would say in her clear ringing voice, "don't you think you're better able to stand up than I am?" The young man always looked up very startled and then looked around him and then he always got up and slunk to the back of the car. Then Mrs. Straight Hat would sit down. She asked only for a support for her bottom, however; she never rested her back. Sitting in a vertical Z, like Cassiopeia's chair in the heavens, she would wait two full blocks before she pounced on the unsuspecting girl by her side.

"Well, the last days are upon us," she would say, "the last days are upon us." The girl would turn toward her then, startled to hear the voice, startled to think the R. F. was speaking to her.

Don't turn around, she wanted to say to each new victim. *Just keep on looking out the window. Just count the houses or the automobiles or the store buildings. Don't leave yourself open like that.* But the girl always turned around. She never had to say anything, just turn around in her seat, just prove she could hear. *You'll get a deaf one some day my little fanatic, my Little Straight Hat.* But so far, they had always turned.

"Yes, it's hot when it should be cold and cold when it should be hot. That's what the Bible says. When the last days are upon us, you can't tell summer from winter. Why, I see they're having floods in Arizona. Oh, anybody with his eyes open can see what's happening. And snow in Texas. Who ever heard of snow in Texas? And all these wars everywhere. Why, it's plain to see the whole world's in sin. Everything is upside down. Why, look there," she'd say, pointing straight at a bill board, "flowers! Why, there should be ice on the streets this time of year. Flowers in February. Oh, the last days are upon us. You can't tell summer from winter when the last days are upon us.

"Why, I see in the paper where a mother, *a mother*, took her two little babies and covered their heads with a pillow and smothered them, actually smothered them. And why did she do it?"

Maybe she didn't have anything to feed them, my Little Straight Hat.

I'll tell you why," she'd say. "It's the devil, that's what. The devil got into that woman. Oh sin, sin everywhere. The last days are upon us."

But not on you, Loose Clothes, are they? Not on you. You're strong as an ox; you'll last forever. Did you really think the man was better able to stand than you? You, who can lean on God? Isn't it always easier for a woman, anyhow. Doesn't she always have the solace that it is only temporary? The man on the street car, does he not know he will work as long as he lives, but the woman, does she not say one year, two years, until Bill gets his raise, until the car is paid for, until we have a baby, until . . . until?

But the girl now, by the window. She is making the worst, the fatal, mistake. She is looking out the window and she is smiling. She is showing the rest of them that this does not disturb her, the Straight Hat did not come with her, is nothing of hers.

Ah, now you've smiled. Now you'll get the works.

"I see the devil has been working on you, too," says the R. F. with pleasure. "When you get home tonight, you look in the mirror, you'll see the devil there. You wash that red stuff off your lips and get down on your knees and beg God to save you. That vile red stuff—that's the devil's work."

Oh, Darling, My Sweet Red Lipped Darling, don't raise your eyebrows. Don't look bored. That's going to let all hell loose.

"You smile," says Straight Hat. "You'll take that smile off your face some day. I saw another woman smile like that once. But I saw her on her death-bed, too, and she wasn't smiling then, I can tell you. She screamed and she said, *'I'm burning in hell, I'm burning in hell'* and she put her hands out and tried to hold on to the wall and BLOOD came out of her fingertips."

That's right, Darling. You just turn your pretty red lips right out the window. You read every letter of every single sign. It's only five more blocks till you get off and you can tell them all about it at the office, how you never heard of such a thing and they will never have heard of such a thing either and it will carry you right straight through to the lunch hour.

"That's right, smile," says Never Tired. "You with your painted Devil's lips and your fur coat and your slave bracelet. You'll burn in hell and then you'll wish you'd listened to me. Then you'll wish you'd got down on your knees right in the street car. Why, there was a rich man went to hell and he was right on a hot fire all the time and he couldn't move and there was a little stream of water just out of reach. He would lie there and pull and stretch with his mouth open, but the stream of water kept moving back, moving back. Why, he would have given all his lands and all his cattle and all his money and all his houses just for one DROP of that cold water. But it didn't do him any good. No sir, it didn't do him any good."

Why are you so happy about it, Straight Hat? What makes you so glad he never got it? Does it make it up to you, then, not to have the houses and the cattle and the land?

"I know," she said, her grey eyes full of flame, "you listen to me, you devil's pawn. I know, because I am very close to the right hand of God."

You and God can have the seat all to yourselves now. Don't trip Little Red Lips when she slips by your bony knees. Little Red Lips is leaving. Little Red Lips is going to work for a man who has not only houses and lands and cattle, but a cold stream of water flowing right through his mouth. What do you think of that?

But the R. F. could have been speaking behind glass for all you could have told from watching the others. The girl and Little Red Lips were the only ones who had any reaction to sin or the rich man's thirst, apparently, and perhaps the girl's own reaction did not show. Perhaps her own face had only one expression like Miss 39th Street's or young Mrs. Neat-Tidy's, or, at the most, two, like J. B.'s.

She did not know, of course, if he were really called J. B. or R. E. or O. D., but certainly he was a two initial man. J. B. had a well-run house and a wife who sent his clothes to the cleaners and kept the buttons on his shirts. He certainly owned a car, but he hated all that fuss of parking and, besides, he liked to read the newspaper going to work and then, too, if you drive to work, you're always having to give the neighbors lifts and wait on them to get ready. J. B. hated to wait on anybody. He hated to wait until he got to the end of the column before he could begin reading the next.

He was more prosperous than most of the passengers. He had both a lightweight and a heavyweight overcoat, four suits of clothing, a clean shirt every day, eleven different neckties, a fine gray Homburg and last year's brown for the rain. He wore pince-nez glasses which had by now marked a deep channel on either side of his nose. He lived south of 59th, where the girl lived, but not really suburban because he never had a seat. He ate breakfast at home with plenty of time for it and was never nauseated by the street car. "Your eggs are ready, J.B., Now don't let your coffee get cold, J. B."

It's always Your eggs, isn't it, J. B.? the girl thought, *Your coffee. Never my eggs or our eggs. They all know jolly well whose eggs those are, don't they, J. B.?*

J. B. had two ways to stand—one, with his feet parallel, left hand holding onto the strap, right hand holding the newspaper, and the other, toes pointed out for balance, his left hand in his pocket. And he had two expressions. He either had or had not been to the bathroom after breakfast. The days he had, he would change the newspaper to his left hand and run his right smoothly down the five vest buttons and then on the sixth he would pause and give a little encouraging pat, a little reward of a pat. The days he hadn't, his fingers would catch slowly on the vest but-tons. He would hold his newspaper upside down and stare out over it with a little frown, sometimes even he would shake his head and purse his lips. *Yes, J. B., you have to watch these things. Can't let them run on, you know. Makes all the difference.*

Miss 39th Street also had her breakfast before she went to work. She wore no wedding ring, lived with her mother and spent all her money on her clothes. Unlike the girl, Miss 39th Street always wore a hat, a new one every two weeks, and fine hats they were. Several people woke up when Miss 39th Street got on. She was a triumph of organization. Of all the work-faced, work-ready people on the car, she alone could have gone straight to a night club without going home for anything. Oh, she had everything she needed right with her. No cold water splash on the face and a run for the street car here. Miss 39th Street has had time for everything. Ten whole minutes for the thick, sweet-smelling cold cream to flow into the thirsty pores, just like Elizabeth Arden says, and then off with that and on with the astringent and a thorough face slapping for the circulation and two whole minutes for the foundation cream. Then the good, expensive, heavy odored powder and the mascara. *Steady now, take your time. Get every single lash. Don't let them stick together. Now the eye-shadow for the lids and the pencil for the brows and a small brush to brush them with even. Now rest yourself a little. Take your time and let's begin with the lipstick. You're working in stone now, you know. Can't make any mistakes.*

And all this Miss 39th Street surely must have done sitting down. *How is it, then, you have such leisure, Miss 39th, that you alone stand on the street car perfectly poised for the day or night, unconscious of your stocking seams, your shoulder straps, the taste in your mouth, the heels of your shoes? How is it then that you and your furs and a new hat every two weeks are always, always in constant repair? Is it that you get up in the middle of the night. Oh, your mother. How wonderful, your mother. Every night when you come home your dinner is ready and your mother stands there, waiting, tentatively, lest you be displeased. Because it is your food, isn't it. And even as little as you let yourself eat, it still would buy a hat in a week, wouldn't it. So did she once wait for your father to come home, but he gave her something back, you know. He gave her something back.*

Friday nights, of course, dinner is an hour later. Fridays your have your hair done, but you don't comb it out. You sit all evening, in that glued up state, so that Saturday night it will be perfect. If you go out in the evening everything is laid out for you on the bed, isn't it, in a neat row? And when you step into the bathtub you drop your clothes on the floor and later they disappear just like magic and reappear again, all clean, all pressed, all mended. In the morning, they are there, too, waiting for you. Even all the things for your purse are in a row on the table: your clean handkerchief, your cigarette case full. Even your street car token lies waiting by the door so that you, in your fine and furry elegance, with both gloves on, can board the street car and stand among the motley, sleepy, cow-like crew, with perfect poise, completely finished, without having to fumble in your purse. Finished, crystallized, done to a turn and eternally constant, what work do you do and what happens when you open your mouth to speak? You do speak, don't you, Miss 39th Street?

And your mother, now when she is doing her work, when she is synchronizing all the perfect machinery, constantly caring for the clothes, every piece of which she has memorized, every piece of which is admirable to her, what does she wear?

Does she not always wear service weight instead of chiffon? Does she not always eat for lunch what you have left over from dinner? Does she not sometimes (while you are away) stand with her head over the teakettle so that the steam will give a little life, a little curl, to her hair? Is she not always eternally and forever concerned with buying and eating and doing what will wear, what will last the longest, she who has such little time to last?

And do you really think, Miss 39th, that with what it takes to feed and clothe her, you could buy a car?

BACK IN THE CAR, PLEASE, the motorman called, and then, almost in a yell, GET BACK IN THE CAR, PLEASE. None of them moved, of course, and he wondered why he bothered, why he kept on trying. There was absolutely no goddamned sense in it, them standing back there with their feet spread a yard apart and him up here with six high school kids on his shoulder blades. Well, he'd show them, all right. He'd gather up a good speed and hit the next red light just as it turned. Knock a few of them on their ass, by God, that's what he'd do, the stone deaf, blind, dumb, feeble-minded jerks. When he got to the end of the line he'd have a cigarette, too. He'd smoke it right down till it burned his fingers. The hell with the schedule.

He hit the red light just as he had planned and Miss 39th

Street felt a heavy foot come down on her elegantly shod toe. She glared with instant hatred upon the woman ahead of her and the woman said, "Oh, I beg your pardon." *Ah, Mrs. Neat-Tidy, you couldn't have picked a worse one to step on. She hates your kind worse than all the rest of them put together. And it's not just a toe mark you made or a heel mark. It's the print of the entire broad crepe sole of a walking shoe.*

Mrs. Neat-Tidy took good care of her feet because she wanted them to last a long time. She was very efficient about everything. She kept a hat box at the office so that her pale blue sports felt would be out of the dust. She and her young husband kept a budget so that they would know just where they were. They lived in an efficiency apartment so that their utilities would be paid and she was working two years more so that the refrigerator and the stove would be theirs before they had a baby. Everything Mr. and Mrs. Neat-Tidy did, they did so that they could do something else.

Mrs. Neat-Tidy's underwear was as clean as Miss 39th Street's, but it was entirely different. It was the most efficient kind you can buy and it was approved by Good Housekeeping. Her stockings were dry when she put them on this morning and her blouse was fresh and had been pressed the night before. The blouse was called The Business Classic. Mrs. Neat-Tidy's face was clean and her lipstick was mildly pink and she and Mr. Neat-Tidy had had a breakfast that gave them all the vitamins they needed.

Now she looked Miss 39th Street up and down, carefully, and she changed hands to hold on to the hanging strap so that her wedding ring would show. She stood in a consciously good posture, hips tucked in, belly tucked in, feet together. She was telling Miss 39th Street, telling her every second that she consciously held her belly in, that you don't have to be beautiful to get a husband. You can even be slightly thick in the calf and thick in the waist. It's being sensible that counts, and simple and having good taste.

Like Mrs. Neat-Tidy, the girl also had been knocked off balance by the car's jerk, but she did not mind it as she used to. Earlier, when she had thought of them all as salmon swimming upstream (herself included), she had resented the motorman's treatment of them, she had thought him brutal and without feeling for mankind, but now, now that they were all cows (herself not included) she was on the motorman's side. She, too, would have liked to stamp her feet needlessly, furiously on the bell; she, too, would have liked to yell, GET BACK IN THE CAR. She and the motorman together could have made plenty of space in that car. She could start from the back and he from the front, each with a big club and they could knock them on the heads like still-live fish in a boat, stack them up on the floor and meet each other in the middle of the car. Then, standing on the seat backs, he on one side, she on the other, their hands clasped across the aisle, they could have danced up and down the car, up and down, faster and faster.

But the jolt had put her two feet further back and here she stood over Miss Incorporated and she was easily able, from this position, to read Miss Incorporated's magazine over her shoulder. Like Mrs. Neat-Tidy, Miss Inc. was also concerned with Good Taste. Pencil in hand she was taking the Good Taste Test reprinted in the *Reader's Digest* and she was being very careful to keep the answers covered up so that she would not cheat. There were a great many lesser Miss Inc.'s in the car, this being the time of day when they flourished, but the one the girl had given the name to was the end result, the ultimate triumph of them all. Miss Inc. had arrived. She was the head of the department, the oldest employee, the secretary of the Business and Professional Women's Club, Queen of THE FILES, guardian of THE BOOKS, and one of THE GIRLS.

THE GIRLS all read the *Reader's Digest* to keep up with each other and, in time, they came to see that this was all they had to read. Miss Inc. did them one better, though. She went to book reviews (free with the thirty-five cent lunch at the club).

The girl stared at Miss Inc. in a kind of forbidden fascination. *You're the only one I really hate, Miss Inc., because you're the one I'm scared of. I won't be Mrs. Neat-Tidy or J.B. There's no chance of my being Miss 39th Street. Let us trust there is no danger of my being Straight Hat, the fanatic. But in you, there is real danger; you're logical, you're what comes of beating the boys in arithmetic. You're the slow accumulation of being patted on the head day after day; you're the infinity where all the tiny lines of triumph meet. And stop.*

Miss Inc.'s husband was dead, divorced or else he traveled and "came in" on week ends. But no matter if she had one husband or five, if she had children in high school or not, she was always called Miss, because they had got used to calling her Miss long ago, and no matter what happened to her after hours, there was no apparent change in her at the office—no change except the gradual, slow polishing, the minutely accumulative sophistication, the piece by piece substitution of the smart for the pretty, the gradual slipping away, drop by drop, of the vital juice. *The juice, Miss Inc., that's it. The juice is gone. Remember the juice, Miss Inc., the lovely golden juice that used to make the little hairs by your temples curl up on hot days and tickle your forehead, that used to make soft, damp lovelocks on the back of your neck? Remember the juice that used to well up in your eyes when you were pleased and when you would put your hand up to cover your eyes a dimple would show in your elbow? Soft and round your elbows were then, like your knees. You had such round knees, then. Remember the day you bought the bonnet that did not "go with" anything you had, but made your eyes so clear that you wore it anyway, wore it with that gold-washed locket on your neck below it? Remember your voice? Remember your laugh?*

You're going to get the blue ribbon, Incky, old Sport, old Girl. You're the very top. You don't sweat; you don't smell. There is no wax in your ears, no stray hair on your coat collar, no lint on your lapel. Nor any down in your arm pits, either, no hair upon your legs, no milk in your breasts, no rumbling in your guts, no juice anywhere, except in your hands.

You've got a flair for hats, now, just like THE GIRLS are always saying and under this one is your very distinguished coiffure, of which you are by now so confident that you never need to touch it. Swirled and waved in a way it never grew, it is without doubt elegant, but also, it is dry. Your skin is dry too now, no matter how much you spend on it. So are your eyes even after the three dollar herbal pack every Saturday afternoon. The juice has all slipped down, down into your hands.

The hands of business are a beautiful thing. Long wristed, velvet skinned and coral tipped, they flit about all day, almost by themselves, never dirty, never rough, never still, picking up and putting down. And yours, Miss Inc., are so fine and so practiced that you can wear a ring as big as a saucer on you middle finger and get away with it. I know where you got it, too, the girl thought, *in the antique shop near the office, the antique shop that is so successful that the articles are clean, even, and they gave you a good story to go with the ring. It was the story you paid for, wasn't it, paid such a terrible price for? But it was worth it. After you told it to THE GIRLS it was worth it, all right.*

Miss Inc. had made a perfect score on the Good Taste Test (that would be one to show THE GIRLS) and was now turning the pages of the *Reader's Digest* to find another short article, turning the pages with her elongated, sharp-pointed fingers. She loved sharp, neat things: newly sharpened pencils, her own personal letter opener (antique), clean fresh paper, a special staccato sound achieved on a typewriter by leaving one edge of the paper loose, the click of the automatic lock on the filing cabinet, the rows of neat, small figures in THE BOOKS, the sound of her own voice, clear and precise and exact.

Now she looked up from the *Reader's Digest* and out of the window to see how near the car was to her destination. *Take that one on Unusual Careers, Incky, old kid. That's just the right size. That one will come out even at Twelfth Street and leave you time to put on your gloves by Eleventh.* She herself was going on to Tenth. It was the last block, really, that got her every day, as the car began to empty, as she came nearer and nearer to the office, the way they could all sit there absolutely dead for forty minutes and then get up and walk out at the right place. Because if they knew where to get off, they ought to know other things, too, and it ought to show on their faces.

It must be something special about the 8:15 car, about the people with five minutes to spare, because she didn't hate street cars, really. She use to like street cars, especially the Sunday afternoon street cars with papas and children on them and beautiful colored girls with purple sashes showing where their coats were open and the white haired blind man whose wife took him to church. The two of them walked together like a set of perfectly balanced scales. The old lady never led him by the hand, apparently never touched him. He would walk very close behind her, and when she came to a vacant seat she would stop and he would slide in very quickly and sit by the window and she would sit on the aisle. When she would start to get off the car, he would feel the weight shift on the seat and get right up and follow her out, walking very close behind her. Yet if someone got in front of her and she had to pause, he would always feel it, because he never bumped into her and he did not hold on to the backs of the seats. It was like watching two people dance. The girl had seen them many times on Sundays in the old days and she always wondered at them because they never talked to each other. She had always liked the Owl cars, too, late at night. There would be as many different hats as there were men on the car: caps with bills and round hats and stocking caps and fur hats with turned down ear muffs. Almost every man carried something: tool boxes and lunch boxes and folding rules in their pockets and pipes to smoke.

Well, she had to do something. She couldn't spend forty minutes of every day hating the same people and none of them even noticing it. She had to think of something besides hitting them with clubs or smashing in all the car windows or spitting in a beautiful arc on the No Spitting sign. Tomorrow, she decided, she'd change the car, anyway. She's take the 8:20. At least it would be another set of people. It wouldn't be the people who had five minutes to spare. It would be the people who hit it right on the nose, who opened the door just as the minute hand shifted. Maybe they would be a little different, not needing the extra five minutes to look in the mirror or dust off their desks with their own private towels (middle drawer, left side). Maybe they would be enough different that they would just go right to it and start in working, putting their forearms flat on their desks, dust or no dust.

She could tell right away that the 8:20 was going to be better, even though she still had to stand up, because of the woman with the sack. She was a middle aged woman with brown skin and light eyes. She wore no make-up and her coat had once been a man's overcoat, though the alterations she had made were rather skillful. It was in the way the woman sat and it was in her jaw. For this woman, there was only one way to sit and that was the way she sat at home—solidly. No matter if the house had been knocked upside down, no matter if she had to go to work sewing in the factory, no matter if even now she held onto a large, brown paper bag containing her lunch, held it by the rolled top in her fist, held it firmly on her stomach, no matter if everything she did nowadays was foreign to her, she was not going to learn a new way of sitting. And she was not going to change her jaw line, either, especially now that she needed it more than ever. Come hail, come drought, come locusts, bad lunch and pneumonia, eventually they would hit that jaw and glance off. If she could just always manage a place to sit down solid, she could wait it out.

That was the first day the girl saw the man. He was square.

She had never seen a square one on a morning car before. Oval ones, long thin ones, short ones, round ones and lots of triangular ones, but never a square one. Square ones you run into if you are about late at night. Particularly in the park she had seen square ones, walking alone with great, heavy heads bent forward on short necks. Square ones are in oyster houses, too, picking up crackers with their whole fists. Square ones stand and watch the trains, stand and watch the rivers, stand and watch the weather. They never go to business on the early morning car. She was standing a little behind him and she could see the back of his large head, now turned toward the window. The man had thick, coarse, black hair, cut very short and stiff all over his head. His coat seemed too good for him and it did not fit well. The distance across his shoulders was almost equal to the car seat and a very scrawny little woman perched on the edge beside him had difficulty keeping her place, though the man was trying to do all he could, she could see that. He was trying to hold himself in. He had turned his head as near the window as possible and he was sitting perfectly still. But he did not fit; he simply dwarfed everything around him, made it look confining. Now he turned his head, so as to be looking directly out the window and the girl could see the heavy masses of his face, piled against each other without order, and she could see the muscles of his jaw moving.

After a while she realized that he was gritting his teeth to-gether—not making any fuss about it or any noise. He was just sitting there quietly staring out the window and gritting his teeth together. There was a definite rhythm to it and after a while the girl began to feel hypnotized by it and to try it out on her own teeth once, experimentally, so as to find out how the muscles would feel pulling at the temples, but once she had started it she could not stop and she kept on, in the same rhythm as the man, until in desperation she turned away from him and began to read the advertisement placards. She could not concen-trate on them and they did not seem funny to her, the way they often did, and finally she looked back at the man. When she remembered that he was sitting down, she began to realize how big he must be. The car went around a curve and the man put his hand on the seat in front to keep his balance. The hand was absolutely huge and it also was square. There was no fat on it; it was just a large, powerful, square hand, but it was the wrong color. The whiteness of it was as startling as a blue eyed Indian.

The car cut through a park here and then it began the long uphill climb past the small outlying business sections, the apartment buildings, the hospitals and the railroad station and then it took the slope down, down into the old part of the town. In the old days, apparently, they had been afraid to make the street wide lest it should crack down the middle and split the two sides apart. Through all of it, the stopping and starting, the changing of the scene, the man sat frozen and immobile, staring out, only the muscles of his jaw and temple visibly beating like an auxiliary pulse.

On the flat bottom of the slope there is a place where the sides of the street close in like the middle of an hour glass and the buildings suddenly begin to get taller and it was there, as the car entered the neck of the town, that the man suddenly turned and took one wild look at the people standing in the car and then began to scrub his face with his hands. Without regard for the lines or features the man washed his face, violently, without water or soap, with only the stale air of the street car and the harsh friction of his hands to cleanse away the fog and the freezing, to bring the necessary awareness and warmth and identity so that he could arouse himself, so that he could get off the car, so that he could tell where he was. And though the girl could not hear it over the noise of the traffic, she knew that this violent scrubbing and washing of the face must make a sound to the man, a sound that he could identify as his own above the noises of the city.

Then, as though he had just thought of it, as though he had sat there the last moment he could endure, he lurched forward and was up and out of the car and gone. She would never have thought a man that big could have got out through that solid pack, but they had made a path for him easily and quickly, for what they will never do for a bicycle, they will always do for a steam-roller. This is the thing that keeps them alive, this is the one thing they all know for sure, and that is their own size. They know when to pull back in time.

All through the day she would suddenly be reminded of the man's scrubbing his face and, though she was up in time the next morning for the 8:15, she let it go by. She was so relieved to see him on the 8:20 that she felt sure it must show, that the man must feel it, but he was sitting as before, staring out the window. While she stood a little behind him, as she had the day before, she began to feel a great tenderness come over her for the back of his head.

Day after day, as she stood in what now seemed to be her place, as she felt the great waves of tenderness go out from her to lap against the broad back of the man, the other people of the car began to fade away. She ceased to watch or hate them or to find counterparts for Miss 39th, Mrs. Neat-Tidy, J. B., Miss Inc. She would stand there watching the man, feeling the apprehension rise in her chest, feeling, as she watched the muscles of his jaw move in time to the beating of her own heart, as though the moment would soon come when the man would fly apart, when the tiny threads that held his great bones fastened to a center, would all snap, sending his jaws and his shoulder blades and the bony arches over his eyes flying off in all directions. As the car approached the curve every day, she would feel this excitement rise in her until he put out his hand on the seat before him and then she would relax for a moment. But it would begin to build up again and she would hold her breath, waiting for the man to feel that bottling up, the closing in of the neck of the town, waiting for him to turn and stare for a moment without recognition before he scrubbed his face with his big hands and shook his head and lurched out of the car.

When he was gone each morning, she would feel very tired and it seemed to her that if he should ever delay his going by one block, that she would crumble apart or begin to scream. It seemed to her that the street where he got off was the last moment she could have held in her excitement. But after she had been through this every morning for two weeks, it no longer satisfied her, and she began to wish that the man would notice her, that he would not be continuously unaware of her knowledge of him, her tenderness of him, and she began to plan how she could make him see her. Every day when he would give that wild look around before he scrubbed his face, she would be completely concentrated in attention, but there was never any recognition in his eyes, never any focusing even, and she was almost sure that he saw them all together, that she was to him only a part of that mass that stood in the aisle, and that even the mass to him was blurred.

Finally, one day at the office it came over her how she could do it, how she could be standing there in that crowd and suddenly moo like a cow. The more she thought about it, the better she thought it was, because that one sound would say more to him than any moment of conversation. Surely that one sound, so foreign and startling on a street car, would cut straight through his unawareness. It would tell him everything at once about how they were like cows and how she knew they were like cows and he knew they were like cows. Oh, she would only have to do it once. It would cut straight through his back like a pain between his shoulder blades and it would turn and run up the back of his neck. Surely then he would turn from the window. He would focus his eyes and look around to find who had made that sound. She would be waiting for him, waiting for his eyes and after that . . . after that he could take care of it. All she had to do was make that one sound, that moo.

Once she had got the idea she was suddenly full of panic for fear he would change street cars or buy an automobile before she could get through to him and she was already looking around hunting for him while she dropped her token. He was in the same place and she was so relieved that at first she didn't notice how different he was. It was going to be much better than she had expected and the moo would now be doubly effective because the man was not staring out the window this morning. He was reading a government department of agriculture bulletin on the Purchasing and Care of Dairy Cows. She was very pleased and excited and it was only necessary now to decide when to do it. She was debating whether to do it right away or to wait until the crowd was heaviest, after 31st Street, when suddenly all the people on the car came back real for her.

All this time she had been concerned with the man, the other people had been receding and fading in a group. It had been not only that they had ceased to irritate her, it had been almost as though they weren't there, as though she and the man were the only ones on the car. Now that she had thought of mooing, of projecting a sound into that mass, a sound of her own making, they had all magically become individuals. Each one was suddenly real and separate from the others and each one had just that morning acquired a brand new set of ears, a bright new pair of eyes to turn on her, in focus. She looked back at the man reading his bulletin and she pursed her lips experimentally to form the m, but no sound would come out. She could not do it. Even by closing her eyes, she could not do it. She realized they were almost to the man's destination already, though it seemed to her that she had, just a minute before, got on the car, and she saw that she would have to put off the mooing until the next day.

But something had happened to the man, and he was not acting according to schedule. As the sides of the street closed in on them, he turned and looked out the window and suddenly he said, "Ha!" and smiled. Then he got up and slowly threaded his way out of the crowd and he was still smiling.

She was puzzled and depressed all through the morning, but, going home that night, she began to work herself up again. She began to be certain that she could moo on the street car the next day, but the next day the man was reading a fence and implement catalogue, and she could not get the sound out of her mouth. She would get her lips all ready and she would close her eyes, but the people would come to life and she could see them there behind her eyelids, each one separate and alive, dressed differently from the others. Even with her eyes closed she could see them all standing there with their brand new ears and she could not get the sound out. Every evening she would work herself up to believing positively that she would be able to moo just once so that the man would hear her, but every morning she would be defeated, every morning while the man read progressively through agricultural bulletins on cattle, poultry, hatcheries and fruit trees, and made heavy, thick marks with a chewed-up stub of pencil beside the items in his fence and implement catalogue. He did not scrub his face with his hands anymore, but each morning would look out and up at the buildings closing in and smile. Sometimes he would nod his head.

One morning while she was waiting for the 8:20 she was so certain that she could do it this time that she began to practice while she was standing there on the street corner. She did it several times out loud and one for good measure while the car was approaching. She mooed very loud, and she was still laughing to herself when she got on the car in anticipation of how easy it was going to be, but the man was not there.

It was not only that he was not in his usual seat; he was not on the car anywhere, not seated or standing in the aisle or talking to the motorman or down in the back of the car. He was not there, and the girl was suddenly panic stricken to think that this day, when it was going to be so easy, she had got on the wrong car. But the sitting woman with the paper sack was there and the rest of them with their new ears, they were the right ones. Every morning for two weeks she thought of him as missing before she thought of him as gone. That was the day the bulletins and the catalogues and the end of face-scrubbing all added up for her. That was the day she quit taking the 8:20.

Unlike the people on the 8:15 who have five minutes to spare, or the people on the 8:20 who hit it on the nose, the ones on the 8:25 are five minutes late every day for the privilege of sitting down and they do not give a goddamn. There are a few people who are late by accident, these keep looking at their watches and sitting forward in their seats, but their faces change from day to day. The steady ones are relaxed and seated. They look out the windows and wear strange hats.

The girl wore no hat at all and sat alone on a seat by the window looking out, but she did not see what was out there. She did not see that it was the middle of March already and that soon would come the yellow forsythia blooming in the little park, and that after that the tiny crocus, blue and white, and after that the yellow jonquils. She did not see anything at all from 59th to 17th where the broad arms and shoulders of the town give onto the neck, where the way gets narrow and the buildings close in. She saw these; she saw the buildings. When she did, she put her hands up to her face. She closed her eyes and began to rub her face hard, hard enough to hear the sound of it over the traffic.

And it was like a thing that had been with her always, like something she had known all her life.

Overture and Beginners

"Naturally, I found all this quite disturbing," Mr. Mallory said.

"I can well imagine," agreed Doctor Crane. He watched his new patient carefully, taking note of the man's healthy skin, his good muscle tone, the picture marred a little by signs of sleeplessness (though this, Doctor Crane thought, was probably temporary and recent) and the signs of nervousness which, under the circumstances, were unremarkable in view of the man's embarrassment.

"And finally," Mallory continued, "as there did not seem to be any obvious explanation, I was forced into believing either there was something wrong with me, or that a group of strangers had spontaneously conspired against me."

"And you were reluctant to believe in such a conspiracy?"

"Certainly," Mallory answered. "After all, why should they? They had never even seen me before. What reason would they have?"

"Exactly," Doctor Crane agreed, smiling at Mallory. "But tell me, what made you come to me? I'm not a psychiatrist; I'm sure you know that."

"I suppose it was because of Sarton," Mallory said.

"The painter?"

"Yes. I was reluctant, after I had calmed down somewhat, to discuss a thing like this. One hates to appear a fool . . . or worse. But I did mention it to Sarton, simply as a baffling mystery, and it was he who suggested that. . . ."

"I understand," Doctor Crane said. "I am a great admirer of his painting. And I'm glad that he did suggest you come to me. Did Sarton happen to mention anything to you about the Tuesday meetings that some of us attend?"

"Tuesday meetings? No, I don't recall. . . ."

Circumspect, as always, Doctor Crane thought, with satisfaction. You could count on Sarton to keep his head.

"Well, Mr. Mallory, I think, from what you have told me, that you do not need to feel alarm for yourself. It is unusual, I grant you, but it is not unprecedented. I have heard of some rather similar cases and, so far as I know, they weren't accompanied by any progressive deterioration in personality, and usually there is not even a repetition. I'm not prepared to speak with absolute assurance on one interview and I should like to see you soon again."

"I'm glad to hear you say that," Mallory said with obvious relief.

"After seeing you further, Mr. Mallory, it might be that in my opinion you should be referred to a psychiatrist. What would your attitude be to that?"

"Well, I don't know," Mallory said. "I suppose I'd take your advice. After all, that's what I asked for."

Perfectly logical, Doctor Crane thought, with satisfaction, as he had expected. "I find," he said, "that this attitude in itself is a very good indication, just as your rejection of the possibility of conspiracy was, even though many indications pointed to it."

"I won't deny," Mallory said, "that I got sore and yelled about a bit and probably I did some fist pounding. But when I cooled off, I had to admit that, as I told you, it didn't seem reasonable that it was all planned and staged. I mean, what for? What would be the purpose? Why, I had never even been in the place before that night."

And rarely had he been in that neighborhood. He had been to call upon an old friend of his father's who was ill and, finding himself far from home at the dinner hour, had stopped in the restaurant. It was an ordinary sort of place, not elaborate enough to be too expensive for him, nor yet so humble but that he might expect a reasonably quiet corner booth and linen on the table. He did find these and ordered the pot roast, which was served, as it had been cooked, in an individual earthenware pot. It gave off a good honest savory odor, undisguised, just as he liked it. But it was quite hot, so he decided to eat the salad first. The dressing had a pleasant tang to it that he could not quite identify, some herb, arresting but delicate. . . .

It was then that he saw the girl. She was sitting at the counter, the corner seat, so that she was perhaps eight feet from Mallory with no tables between them. In her left hand she held a book which had a red binding and in her right she held half a sandwich which she would raise toward her mouth and then lower to the plate, but from which she seemed never to take a bite. Mallory found his own fork going up and down with the girl's sandwich until his cheated salivary glands demanded attention.

The girl's complete absorption in what she read had an hypnotic effect upon Mallory and he found himself smiling because the girl was smiling. He shook himself and wished that she might change her position a little so that he could make out the title of the book. It was quite exasperating the way that he could almost but not quite read the title. He devoted himself to the pot roast for a few moments and when he looked again, the girl's face was suffused with sadness. She had put the sandwich back on the plate and was holding the book with both hands as Mallory, feeling swept with the same sadness, watched a slow tear slide down her cheek. She had an extraordinarily mobile face and Mallory, trying to break the spell, opened a Parker House roll a little savagely and was amazed to see there, like a jewel, one of his own tears glistening.

"I just stared at it," Mallory told Doctor Crane. "It seemed to me that it stayed spherical an extraordinary time. And I simply had to know the name of the book. I thought it must be the most wonderful book in the whole world, all absorbing, the way that you are always hoping a book will be."

He changed his position then, squirming about in the booth,

trying desperately to make out the title. It was in gold lettering, he could see it now. But from this distance it might be in Arabic or Russian. Certainly he could not read it. He ate the roll with his own tear in it ("feeling rather like a cannibal," he said to Doctor Crane) and finished the pot roast while he considered going over to the girl and asking her the title. But there were people in the other booths now and his progress over to the counter would be conspicuous and misinterpreted. He knew that he could not carry it off without embarrassment and decided against it. The only thing to do was to walk near the counter as he left and hope to be able to read the title.

He was so impatient to find out that he refused dessert and asked only for coffee. He waited for the waitress to finish pouring the coffee, for she blocked his view, and when he had had the first, cautious, temperature-testing sip and put his cup back on the saucer he was already reaching in his pocket for the tip. But when he looked up, the girl was gone.

"I was stunned," he told the doctor. " Absolutely stunned. I simply couldn't let her get away. I never in my life felt such a need for anything. I *had* to know what that book was."

He left his topcoat and hurried to the door, for she couldn't have been gone more than a moment, he thought, and must surely be in sight. But in the street outside there was no sign of her. In fact, there was no one on the street at all. He came back into the restaurant and spoke to the cashier.

"Where did she go?" he said.

"Who?"

"That girl. That girl with the book. It couldn't have been more than a minute or two."

"I'm sorry, sir. I don't remember any girl."

"But she was right there sitting at the counter. You must have seen her."

"I'm sorry, sir, but at the dinner hour we get pretty busy. . . ."

"But—" Mallory said, and kept on saying it as the waitress

appeared holding his check, as someone reminded him of his overcoat, as more and more diners began to turn their heads in an effort to understand the commotion.

"I'm the last person in the world to make a disturbance in a restaurant," Mallory said, "but I couldn't seem to stop. I even demanded that the counter waitress be called and questioned and she swore there had been no girl there."

The manager of the restaurant had come by this time and, with Mallory's own waitress and the cashier, it seemed to him that he was surrounded with people, all trying to placate him, get rid of him, until thoroughly shaken and angry, he found himself outside on the empty street again.

"Vanished," Mallory said. "She simply vanished. And I can't seem to get over it. At first, of course, I was angry but one can be in the wrong and get angry, or even be in the right and get angry, and simply write it off. It was the feeling of loss, of irreparable loss, that hung on."

"Tell me, Mr. Mallory," the doctor said, though it was only a formality, for he knew the answer, "what is your work?"

"I am a writer."

"Well, Mr. Mallory, as I said, I don't think you need be unduly alarmed. I would like you to return on Tuesday. In the mean time, go on with your work the same, eat whatever you enjoy and try to increase your amusements a little—the theatre, or a concert. Maybe a nightcap before turning in."

When he had shown Mallory out Doctor Crane asked the receptionist not to bring in his next patient until he buzzed for her. It was Mrs. Wheatley again, for whom he could do nothing, really, except a little gentle fencing while he managed to deny her, without making her feel denied, what it was she wanted of him.

Alone, he turned from his desk and opened the doors of a small, inconspicuous cabinet. For relaxation, the doctor did a little sculpture and here in the cabinet was a rather delicate and not too amateurish small figure. She was, in fact, a replica of the girl that Mallory had seen in the restaurant. The goddess of anticipation, Doctor Crane called her to himself (for he had never shown her to anyone) who ruled over the next, the new, the promised.

"And so you have shown yourself to another one," he said, chidingly, as though She had been up to mischief. He had no doubt that Mallory would be back on Tuesday, when he would meet Sarton, to whom She showed not a book, of course, but always the new canvas, stretched and waiting, or the brushes, cleaned and soft against her fingertips, and for whom She surrounded Herself in the odors of fresh pigments and turpentine.

And at the Tuesday meeting Mallory would meet Gavingole, the playwright, to whom She appeared seated before a theater curtain and to whom She had confided Her preference for velvet over other curtain materials and the scalloped folds of the vertical risings over center partings. She was waiting (and all around Her were the movements and babble and restless twittering of the expectant crowd) for the play to begin, the play that would never for one moment step its foot out of enchantment.

And there was Mortane, the mathematician, to whom She showed the beginning of a significant mathematical equation, elegantly expressed. It was written in pencil on a scrap of paper and partly obscured by Her wrist.

And there were the others that Mallory would meet (there would be nine of them now, Doctor Crane realized), the stubborn throwbacks in a jaded world, who had in common this powerful and hopeful appetence which could not be killed or diverted or ground into a cynical foreknowledge.

Yes, Mallory would meet them all on Tuesday. And himself, of course, though he had never told them, for he knew he served as their necessary anchor of safety, as indeed they served as his.

"He didn't even notice the color of your hair," Doctor Crane said to the little figure. "But then we mustn't think him unobservant, really, because of course he was paying attention to the book, while I. . . ."

He closed the doors of the cabinet gently, emptied Mallory's cigarette butts out of the ashtray and buzzed for Mrs. Wheatley.

No, you couldn't say Mallory was unobservant, not when you remembered that roll. He himself would never, he thought, open another Parker House roll without looking for that tear.

"Nothing really seems to help," Mrs. Wheatley said. "For a while, I thought, but then. . . ."

Mrs. Wheatley had chronic lower back pain and a feeling of tiredness, even on awakening. But what she wanted today was for Doctor Crane to say the right thing which would somehow satisfy both her conscience (which was formidable) and her relatives who were threatening to visit. She herself could not tell them her dread of their impending visit. She could not tell tomorrow her dread of it, nor tonight, nor even the next hour, unless of course Doctor Crane could somehow give her the word, the phrase, the necessary reason why she should stay forever, as she wished to, in today. For nothing was, to Mrs. Wheatley, *promised*; all things were impending.

There were no more patients after Mrs. Wheatley and as Doctor Crane prepared to leave his office he smiled apologetically toward the cabinet in embarrassment that he had done so poorly with Her. He knew that behind the doors of the cabinet was only a crude and amateurish version of the radiant vision that had been given him, but all the same he was glad he had tried to capture a fraction of it.

How she had looked that day, running up a hill where there was no hill, her lovely red hair flying in the wind, her butter-scotch blouse coming loose from the band of her chocolate-colored skirt, her lips parted with laughter. She was chasing one of her children, the little one, the toddler, and when she caught up with him she snatched him into the air and held him above her head and laughed. And then, bracing herself, for the hillside (which wasn't there) was steep and the heavy child had threatened her balance, she turned and looked directly at him.

"I never have that pain any more," she said. "I'm free of it. And I'm only tired with good reason to be. What you did for me made all the difference and what you said to me was of real importance in my life. Why, do you know, even the food I eat, the simplest thing—a piece of bread or fruit—it has such savor and I relish it."

So had he seen Her first, before he had known about the others and learned of Her amazing versatility in appearing to the unrepentantly expectant, the curiously zestful ones. He had not called Her "goddess" then, but only tomorrow's patient, the one that he would really help.

Chu Chu

In the village of Sandski by a smelly sea there were two foci: fish and the train. The fish could be caught, bought, sold and eaten; the train could be met every day at twelve noon, when it stopped for seventy-nine seconds.

In time this life becomes dull, even if you like fish and trains. The people of Sandski, going about their errands from the east side to the west side of the village, between the sea and the railroad track, felt a need for something more: some luxury, some unnecessary thing, for a warmth beyond comfort.

All the things none of them had, they found in Chu Chu. Ah, Chu Chu! He was their bad boy. He was their wicked, clever darling. He was the devil in a soft woolly blanket. Before he was a grown man he had a hundred names and as many legends. There was a phrase about him in the native dialect that he was born with the sun on his face. And another, that he picked the pockets of the gods. They called him the little boy with the mountain chest.

But the name that stayed with him longest was Chu Chu, which he had earned from the first of his pranks. It was when the train had first started coming to Sandski. Every day at high noon when it blew its great whistle, all the people would run out of their houses and the men would leave their boats and go to stand in wonder and admiration for the seventy-nine seconds, while the train took on fish and water.

One morning about six o'clock the whole village was awakened by the train's whistle, and an earthquake could hardly have caused more consternation than this mysterious deviation from the routine. Men ran across the sand in their bare feet, not having taken time to put on their sandals. Women came out without their kerchiefs, and one arrived at the tracks still holding a frying pan in her hand. And what did they see, these three hundred people? Had the president, then, come to buy a fish? Was there a hurricane warning? Was there even a train?

No. There in the middle of the railroad track, no more than five years old, stood Chu Chu with his head thrown back, singing out this tremendous sound, exactly like the train. And then he laughed at their mouths hanging open, at their sleepy-eyed disbelief, and made the sound of the train again, for he had only discovered that morning what there was inside his tremendous chest. He had just found out what his throat was for.

Right after that he began to sing, as he was to sing all the days of his life. And by this wonderful voice doors were opened to him everywhere. At night he would go into the wine shop and the men would stop playing cards and everyone would set his glass down softly and wait. Chu Chu would lie on the floor in the middle of the room, close to the stove, perfectly relaxed like a piece of heavy silk fallen on its own folds. He would lie with his hands under his head and only the great toe of his right foot moving freely in his sandal, and when he was warm all through he would look up at the ceiling and begin to sing. No one ever asked him to sing or to stop singing. No one ever thanked him directly.

Yet, always, they gave him the best they had. All his life he never bought himself a meal or a drink or a pair of shoes. When he had errands in the shops, the people would give him in change the new silver pieces, shiny and clean, for the sight of his bronze throat, unmarked and shining, astride the open wings of his collar, was truly heroic and his smile was constant testimony that delight lives somewhere in the world. He lived upon the fat of a very lean land and never knew it. He kept his hands clean; the people kept them full.

And what did he do for all this homage? He sang and scrubbed himself clean and strode about the village looking at things and smiling. Every day he would make the rounds and in each house or shop, and by each boat, among people who saw him every day and who had known him always, he was a choice guest. They saved their best gossip for him, their most amazing confidences, their odds and ends of treasured information. He would lie sprawled in the sun or sitting in the best chair with his feet up, listening with wonderful, amazed attention to their wisdom and their ability for conversation, and the most he ever said, wiggling his great toe and giving his hand a quick jerk, was, "Ah, God. Ah, God."

Even when he was over six feet tall, he had the face of a young boy. His was the face that pregnant women everywhere carry with them. He looked the way all women believe their children are going to look. There was no thing his eyes would turn away from, and his mouth was shaped with trust. There was no evil in him, only a gigantic mischief. And never the same trick twice. Once he caught a small fish in a net, wired a tiny gold ring into its fin and put it back in the sea. He had to wait weeks before it was caught again in the nets and discovered. He let them talk about it, theorize upon it and take it to the priest. They had made a religious omen out of it before he laughed and told them. Once at a marriage feast when the cover was lifted from the "tureninvaal," or bridal pudding, six small kittens jumped out on the table.

The sandals the Chu Chu wore were made by Penantro whenever he noticed that Chu Chu's were wearing out. They were carried by Penantro's son in the dark of the night and placed on Chu Chu's doorstep where he would find them in the morning. Penantro's shop was built half under the ground and his house was set on top of it. Now he looked up from his work as his son came down the stairs almost falling in his hurry.

"Chu Chu's coming," he said. "Chu Chu's coming *here*."

Penantro did not go toward the door which Chu Chu would enter, but ran to the back of his shop and called up to his wife:

"Mamma, Mamma, Chu Chu's coming." Then he ran back to his bench, wiping his hands on his apron.

At this message, which came perhaps twice a month, Mrs. Penantro left her ironing with a petticoat still spread out on the board and started for the back stairway, but at the head of the stairs she turned back, changed her apron for a clean one and smoothed her hair before descending to the shop. There she found her son and sent him to wash his face, after which she sat down on a bench and tried to recover from the breathlessness caused by her hurrying. There was no need for her to sit on the bench for there was a large, sprawling indented chair there, but this was left purposely empty, conspicuously waiting.

Chu Chu came down the little front stairway from the street, bending over to save his head and smiling at everyone. He sat down in the empty chair, leaned back and stretched out his legs. Penantro made a few taps with his hammer to show that he was going right on with his work.

"Would you have a little glass of wine, Chu Chu?" asked Mrs. Penantro. "Go," she said to the boy who had reappeared with one side of his face carefully washed, "go get the wine for Chu Chu." Then she went after the boy herself, lest he bring Chu Chu a chipped glass.

Along the front of Penantro's shop was a window which gave onto the street and Chu Chu, when he came here, would lie back in the chair, a glass of wine in his hand, and identify the villagers by their feet. Sometimes he would boom out their names and then he and Penantro would watch the feet hesitate while the villager would be hunting all about him for someone who had called his name. Penantro and Chu Chu would be smothering with laughter.

"Penantro," Chu Chu said, with his eyes on the window, "whose feet are those?"

"But you don't know?" Penantro asked. "Haven't you seen her?"

"No," Chu Chu said, not moving his eyes from the window.

"But surely those shoes don't hold real feet in them?" As though
to give Chu Chu a good look, the two shoes had been detained
by something and stayed there before the window in doubt, one
of the heels not touching the ground. They were an amazing
sight to see in Sandski. First they were about half the size of
Sandski women's shoes. They were elevated at the back end and
made from fine soft grey leather with two small grey bows poised
over the pointed toes.

"If you could bring yourself to lift your head a little, my
friend," Penantro said, " you could see the ankles that go with
those feet and perhaps even a little more."

"Tomorrow, Penantro," Chu Chu said. "Tomorrow I will lift
my head. There should not be too much pleasure in one day."

Now this sentence did not mean to Penantro that Chu Chu
was lazy. "Mamma," he said, for Mrs. Penantro had just returned
with the wine,"did you hear? Chu Chu will be here tomorrow."

Mrs. Penantro smiled upon Chu Chu. "I will make gemordelind,"
she said, very definitely, "and you will eat with us."

"Gemordelind!" Chu Chu said, for this is a festive dish, a kind
of great stew made for weddings and christenings. Gemordelind
is not only a stew; it is a social advantage, a distinction. And
why? Is it because it contains only the hearts of humming birds
or because it is difficult to make or because only a few have the
secret recipe? Not at all. It is easily made. It has no rare sauces,
contains nothing that cannot be bought in Sandski. It is so
wonderful simply because it contains no fish.

"Yes," Mrs. Penantro said, "you come tomorrow and I will
make gemordelind."

"With absolutely no fish," said Penantro. "Positively no fish."
And here they all laughed at the memory of Mrs. Delurgos. Mrs.
Delurgos wore a hat instead of a kerchief, her table was covered
with oilcloth from the city and, before her daughter's wedding,
she had bragged for weeks that there was to be gemordelind. Oh,
how she had bragged, how she had patronized, until all the

women were sick of the sight of her, but at the last minute, poor Mrs. Delurgos, looking at the tiny piece of veal floating in the gemordelind had had to face the fact that, though it was all she could afford, it really would not be enough to go around, so she had ground up fish after fish, very fine, praying while she did it that the taste of the veal would somehow come through it all.

"Ah, God," Chu Chu said, enjoying it all over again, "Ah, God, that was a thing," for Mrs. Delurgos had started a whole saga of jokes. People would buy a little liver in the butcher shop and ask the butcher to take the fins off it for them. In the wine shop the men would look into their glasses in consternation and say, "What's this in my wine—a fish head?" While pretending to pull out a large, repulsive object. The poor groom, whose marriage had been entirely overshadowed by the false gemordelind, had had to stand a thousand jokes about the possible piscine characteristics of his firstborn.

There was one restaurant in the village where the single men of no family ate. The proprietor, not being a native of Sandski, and hearing their gossip, had thought to make a name for himself by advertising gemordelind. He found out the recipe and, not knowing it was used for special occasions only, simplified it somewhat in order to be able to afford it. Then he put a placard in his window:

GEMORDELIND
15 zloros the bowl

After this, the men transferred their jokes from Mrs. Delurgos and her son-in-law to the proprietor. They refused absolutely to eat any of it, saying they had heard it had fish in it and not only fish, but snurgs, which are vile black blobs that fasten onto the bellies of sick fish. In vain did the harassed proprietor change his placard on successive days to read:

GEMORDELIND
10 zloros the bowl

TRUE
Gemordelind

TRUE Gemordelind
absolutely no fish
POSITIVELY no fish

---

until at last he had thrown it all out and given up the whole idea.

Chu Chu held out his glass and Mrs. Penantro filled it. When he looked up at the window the little grey shoes were gone. "They're gone," he said to Penantro in mock tragedy.

"Mamma," said Penantro, "what do you think? Chu Chu didn't know about the one who paints."

"No!" she said. "You mean you haven't seen her, Chu Chu?"

"No," he said, "of course not. Where would I see her? Where has she been?"

"But at the train day before yesterday. Surely you saw her get off the train at high noon?" Chu Chu smiled as he got up to leave, for day before yesterday he had taken advantage of the general high-noon exodus and, while the whole village had been watching Grey Shoes get off the train and look about her shyly at the staring crowd, Chu Chu had been in the wine shop, filling with vinegar a fine old bottle which he had just emptied. As he went up the stairs to the street they called after him: "Don't forget tomorrow."

"I won't," he said. "I'll wear my Christmas shirt."

Everyone in the village knew about Chu Chu's Christmas shirt, for it was the only one of its kind they had ever seen. At

Christmas time the year before, the priest had got out his yellowed score of the Mass in B Minor. He had played it over for Chu Chu, not very well, on his violin and asked Chu Chu how much of it he could sing on Christmas Eve.

"Oh, all of it," Chu Chu had said. "All of it." He had sung almost the whole night through, while the villagers sat silently in the cathedral, forgetting sleep, and the tears rolled endlessly from the priest's eyes at the beautiful ease and honesty and tirelessness of the boy's voice.

"Well, Chu Chu," he said, "I shall have to get you a Christmas present. What would you like to have?"

"I want a new shirt," Chu Chu said, "a shirt that doesn't scratch." The priest had got him the shirt, all soft, white satin with great full sleeves. Chu Chu wore it rarely to preserve it longer and he wore nothing under it so that when he pressed his hand on it he could feel its smoothness both inside and out.

The gemordelind, savory and steaming, sat waiting a full twenty minutes before Chu Chu arrived next day in his Christmas shirt, for on his way to Penantro's he had seen the rest of Grey Shoes and the sight of her had kept him standing rooted where he was for half an hour. Chu Chu was very gay at the Penantro's. He ate and ate of the gemordelind and Mamma filled his glass again and again. He picked the littlest Penantro boy up and swung him over his head, laughing and singing to him. Quite out of the air, apropos of nothing, he said, "Where does she live, that one?"

"Who?"

"Grey Shoes," he said. "Where does she live?"

"But at Mrs. Delurgos'. Everyone knows that. In the room her daughter used to have."

"Ah, God," said Chu Chu. "At Mrs. Delurgos'?" Well, Mrs. Delurgos, he thought, you do not know it, but you are going to hear a serenade tonight, such a serenade to make your precious oilcloth curl up at the edges. And then he left them, for he had a new song coming in him and he wanted to go out alone in a boat and try it.

That night outside the window where once Mrs. Delurgos' daughter had knelt dreaming of her lover and her wedding feast, Chu Chu stood singing his new song. He sang very softly, pitching the notes carefully one at a time, so as to make them go directly through the lighted, curtained window. It was a wonderful song about the bottom of the sea and how a small grey shoe had been found there. All the great, shining queen fish had tried to get in it, but it would not hold the farthest tip of their tails. Smaller and smaller fish were allowed to try and the least important fish were even given a chance, but none of them could even begin to get into it. A thin and sickly oyster had got part way in and begged to be pulled free from the pinching. Then a little minnow, dwarfed from birth, had managed to get its head clear in, but no more. At last, a beautiful woman, all white and shining, naked except for one grey shoe, came riding triumphantly down the sea on the back of an immense turtle and stepped into the shoe easily. But at the sight of that bare, white foot with its perfectly curved arch, all the fish were instantly blinded and, turning their white bellies heavenward, floated off to their death.

Though Chu Chu had sung the last note of his fine song there had been no sign behind the curtain: no shadow, no drawing back of the shade at the window's edge, no winking light signal.

"Maybe I ought not to have had her be naked," he said to himself. "I never thought. Maybe she's religious." So he began to sing the Mass in B Minor and, when there was still no sign, he began to sing in crescendo, continually in crescendo without regard to the context, until he was singing constantly fortissimo. Though there was no sign behind the curtain of this house, there was, in almost every other house, a young girl kneeling by a window in the dark, shivering with delight at the love in Chu Chu's voice. They would think of flowers they had never seen growing and, lying in these flowers, Chu Chu, warm and golden. Dazed by their own wantonness they would shiver and bury their faces in their hands, never noticing the faint, clinging odor of fish.

At last Chu Chu, cold, downhearted, depressed, went slowly homeward, crawled in his bed and pulled the covers over his head. But when he awoke he was more cheerful. It began to seem quite logical to him that he could have got the wrong room. After all, it might be that Grey Shoes did not live there at all. It would be exactly like Mrs. Delurgos to brag that Grey Shoes was in her house when she might be living at the other end of the village. Or, perhaps she was gone! Maybe she had not thought Sandski good enough for a picture after all. At this thought Chu Chu was so frightened that he jumped out of bed, dressed and washed and ran all the way to Mrs. Delurgos house, which he entered without knocking. He burst into the room outside which he had sung the night before and, in blessed relief, he saw her standing before an easel, painting.

"Well, hello," she said. He had not really expected to find her and he was so surprised and so out of breath that he sat down on the first chair he could find.

"What's the matter?" she asked. "You're all out of breath."

"I thought you'd gone," Chu Chu said.

"What made you think that?" What had made him think that? Chu Chu looked about the room, confused now, embarrassed. His eyes came to the window and then he remembered. Now he was angry at her calmness, her tolerant, friendly watching.

"Say," he said, standing up, "what's the matter with my voice? Don't you like my singing?"

"Why, I don't know," she said. "I never heard you sing. Where do you sing?"

"That was me," he said, "last night. That was me outside your window. I stood right there and sang for hours. I sang you everything I know."

"Oh," she said, "I'm so sorry. I didn't hear you."

"That's not true," Chu Chu said. "How can you say that? The whole town heard me. Why my voice is the biggest voice in Sandski. I can stand on the railroad track and sing and you can hear me half a mile out to sea."

He realized he was shouting at her while she stood very close to him looking friendly and attentive and he stumbled back a few steps and blushed. It's me, he thought. She doesn't like me. He wished he had worn his Christmas shirt.

Grey Shoes went over to a table, fastened a piece of white paper onto a board and sat down with a pencil. She looked at Chu Chu over the top of the board.

"You see, my friend," she said, "I can't hear you. I'm deaf."

"You're deaf!"

"Completely."

"You mean you can't hear? You can't hear anything at all?"

"No," she said, "nothing at all. Not any more."

Now this might have fooled some men, some dull fellows, some clod of a fisherman perhaps, but not our clever boy. Not that devil of a fellow Chu Chu. He wasn't to be taken in by any such tricks. He looked up at the woman craftily. "Then how can you answer my questions? How can you hear what I say?"

"I read your lips," she said.

Chu Chu had never heard of such a thing. He was avid for information and completely without tact. He asked question after question. He was amazed to know that his lips made a pattern, a kind of picture that meant something.

Finally, the woman went over to the window, turning her back on him, so that she should not see any more of his questions. Chu Chu followed her as far as the easel and there he saw on the board a sketch of himself. He left while she was still standing at the window and the first place he went was Penantro's.

"Hey, Penantro, look. Look what I got," and he showed him the sketch. "Pretty good, huh?"

"Mamma," Penantro called, "Mamma, come and look what Chu Chu's got."

Mrs. Penantro would look at the sketch, then she would look at Chu Chu. "Why," she said, "how are such things possible? Did she give it to you, Chu Chu?"

"Well, no, not exactly, but I'm going to take it back. I'm going to take it back tomorrow," for there of a sudden he was ashamed of having taken it. He did not tell Penantro that the woman was deaf, either, though when he came in he had been bursting with the wonderful knowledge that lips can be read. While he stood there holding back the information, he knew for the first time in his life what it is to protect another human being. No one he had ever known had ever needed it.

This was a terrible, a shaking, thing. This was no slap on the broad bottom of a village girl bending over a fish net. Chu Chu took back his picture and walked down to the sea to think of it. There, sitting alone on the sand, looking out to sea, his simple faith came back to him. Chu Chu believed that questions have answers, that problems have solutions, that tomorrow will come.

He sat until dusk, while the sea calmed him and then he got up and stretched himself. "I will make her hear," he said. "I will break her ears open." That night he slept soundly and trustingly, not even stirring when the tide came in.

Next morning, early, wearing his Christmas shirt and carrying his picture, he called upon the woman.

"Well," she said, "you're up early."

"I brought back your picture," he said. "I didn't really steal it. I just wanted to show Penantro. He says it's very grand. Penantro says it looks just like me."

"Oh, that," she said. "You can keep it if you'd like."

"Do you mean it? I can have it?"

"Yes, surely. It's nothing. It's just a sketch."

"That wasn't all," he said. "I mean I didn't just come about the picture."

"No?"

"I want to take you out to the island," he said. "I want you to go with me in a boat. You could take your things out there and make a picture. You could draw the island."

"Well," she said, "I don't know."

He had thought it out so carefully there by the sea. It surely was not possible that she would refuse to go. He was in a panic and about to beg her desperately, when suddenly he stopped, relaxed and smiled. "Please come," he said.

"Well, all right. I'll come. Wait till I get my things together."

When they had arrived at the island and secured the boat, Chu Chu waited until she was quite settled.

"Now," he said. "Now. Now I am going to make you hear. Oh, I was so afraid you wouldn't come."

"Is that why you have brought me all the way out here?" she asked, for certainly there was nothing on the bleak island she cared to paint.

"That other," Chu Chu said, "that time I sang by your window, that was nothing. That was whispering. Out here I can really sing loud."

"But I told you," she said. "I told you I can hear nothing. Absolutely nothing."

"But we have not tried yet. You wait. You'll see. You'll be able to hear this all right." For he did not really see how she could have drawn him so beautifully if she had never heard him sing. He did not quite believe in all this lip-reading talk. Perhaps she could hear only a little—only a very little—but something.

So he stood up before her and began to sing. "There," he said. "Did you hear? You can hear that, can't you?"

"No," she said. "I told you. Why don't you believe me?"

"Because you must hear me," he said. "You MUST. Because this is all I have to give you."

He would walk over to her again and again and put his hands on her shoulders, tilting her head, her fine small head, so that she would be looking directly at him. "Now," he would say, "try again." He would walk back a few steps and take a deeper breath, swelling his chest further yet and begin to sing with his mouth wide and wider open. "Try again, try again, try again," he would say, until he had worn her out, until she was tired, tired to tears.

Oh, she had had it all. She had had kindness and sympathy and consideration and impatience, but never had anyone blamed her for being deaf. No one, no one, had tried to MAKE her hear. She could hear each single beat of her own heart, but nothing more, and all this preoccupation with something which no longer bothered her, she had thought to leave behind her for a small time. She had come for vacation to this desolate place to be alone and to paint in freedom among strangers. She had not come for this.

"No!" she said, pushing him away. "I will NOT try again." And she got to her feet and stood facing him in anger and hatred. "I cannot hear you or anybody or anything, do you understand? And I will not endure this any more." She gathered up her pencils and sketch pad off the ground and jumped into the boat.

"I'll send it back for you," she said. "I'll send someone back with the boat."

Chu Chu stood there, one man alone on a small island, stunned and silent, watching her going away from him, getting smaller, rowing the boat in a furious, erratic course. He knew how tired her arms must be and how her back must be hurting, yet he was powerless to move after her. He stood there on the small island looking after her and his simple faith was quite gone. While he could still see the boat, his inertia turned to rage and he felt powerless and thwarted and burning with impotent fury. He took his picture, his beloved picture, and holding it in front of him, spat on it. Then he threw it into the sea.

And now he wished to take out his voice, pull it out of him, tear it from his throat and spit on that, too. He wished to defile his voice, to violate and crucify and utterly destroy it. He wished to shame and debase it and he began to curse with it and to befoul the air of the desolate island, but finally he gave off words altogether and roared and raged and screamed in a violent fury until he thought to break his throat open, cleave it with roaring and destroy it, destroy it.

But he could not annihilate his genius altogether, not forsake his destiny, for even in his horrible roaring there was a kind a cadence, in his rage a rhythm, and through it all a certain, great, bellowing beauty.

My Walks with Confidence

It can't be true. The newspapers must be wrong. Last week I read that President Truman had spoken with Confidence and that General Eisenhower had exuded Confidence in Paris, but how could Confidence have been in Washington and Paris last week when all the time I've had him right here locked in the cellar, where I hope he starves to death? I have put up with his eccentricities all I'm going to. There was even a time when I loved Confidence, at least I had a very tolerant affection for him. Why, when I think of it now—I even *mothered* him and I used to go around explaining him to people. Honestly, I don't know how I could have been fooled like that. But it's the last time. This time he's gone too far. Let him whimper down there in that cellar. Let him try his tricks on that damp cement. I've listened for the last time.

How old do you suppose he is? He doesn't seem to change any. Only now he seems like an evil old man to me and I can remember that when I first met him, why I thought that he was just a boy.

"Want to help me burn the trash?" I asked my nephew who had recently arrived for a visit on the Colorado Desert.

"Take the flashlight," his mother said. "It's dark now. Watch for snakes."

I didn't hold with flashlights on the desert because they blinded your side vision and made you stupid about catching movement. "All this talk about snakes," I said. "Don't let it make you nervous. Everybody talks about rattlesnakes down here. I've lived here for two years and I've never seen one yet. The thing to do," I said, "if they worry you, is get some high boots and then just put your heels down hard and walk with confidence."

"Hey, what's that noise?" Buck said, putting down his bundle of trash on the ground.

"I don't know," I said. "Flash your light in the creosote bush. Sounds like a giant cicada."

"Awful loud for a cicada," he said, flashing the light over the bush.

"Must be big as a bird," I said.

"Maybe we ought to look on the ground," he said.

Well, after all the times I'd heard it described, it certainly was easy to recognize. There came a sidewinder, sure enough, flapping the coils of its belly straight toward us. Even though its head was going at right angles, there was no doubt but that it was certainly getting closer and sounding for all the world like a great big cicada.

Buck moved through a quarter circle and held the light in its eyes and the sidewinder just sat there motionless except for his tongue going in and out.

"Hold the light just like that," he said. "I'll get the hoe."

He was back in a minute with the hoe poised over his head. "This is no time to be half-hearted, I guess," he said, giving me a devilish smile. Then he slashed with the hoe and there lay the sidewinder in two pieces.

I exhaled.

"Where's Confidence now?" Buck said.

"There he goes," I said, "right behind that bush. I can just see the red feather stuck in his jaunty green hat."

That was the first time I ever saw Confidence and only part of him at that. But I came in time to be nauseatingly familiar with the whole costume. He was only three feet tall and I suppose that's why I thought of him as a boy for so long. He had all his clothes custom made, of course, and he was always immaculate. He wore highly polished riding boots and carried a riding crop, though I never knew him to ride a horse. He had quite an assortment of rather snappy jackets and he always wore yellow pigskin gloves. He was a real dandy and terribly vain. I suppose he was really a midget but everything about him was in such perfect proportion that I never thought of it until just now.

He finally moved in on us with an inordinate amount of expensive luggage and yet it was hard to take offense even at this. He was so ingratiating and his mischief never seemed to be planned. Only he was always missing just when you needed him. He would hand me a stack of tortillas and a guitar to hold for him just as the *immigrantes* came looking for wetbacks. After we moved to the city and I tried to get accustomed to traffic again, it never failed but that when the traffic cop would descend on me, the other seat would be empty and, after I had the summons put away in my purse, there would be Confidence just emerging from the nearest saloon.

Then for a while in the city I lost track of him altogether and, much as I hate to confess it, I missed him. I really did. I read in a book that you could sometimes get in contact with him again through friends. The book didn't say whether to try his friends or my friends, but I was pretty sure Confidence didn't have any friends, so I tried mine. I had dinner with a friend of mine who had brought along a friend of his named Jack and when I had told my friend about having lost track of Confidence, Jack said, "Describe him."

So I did. "Why?" I asked. "Do you know him? Have you seen him?"

"Well," he said, "I'm not sure. I haven't seen *him* exactly, but I'm pretty sure I've seen something that belongs to him."

"His gloves?" I said. "His hat?" For these I was sure I could identify.

"No," Jack said. "It wasn't clothing. And it wasn't recent, either. Maybe it was too long ago to do you any good. You see," he went on, "my father knew him. At least he knew a lot about him. He also knew a lot about airplanes and he taught me how to fly. Well, he tried, anyway. We cracked up and my father got me right out of the hospital, still with a cast on my leg, and he said that I had to go right back up again or I would lose Confidence."

"You, too?" I said.

"Take my word for it," he said, "that guy is better off lost. Well, anyhow, we flew around a while and my father said, 'Tell you what we'll do. The hangar's empty. We'll zoom right down here, go in the hangar, go straight through and come right out the other side.' I really began to sweat. Just so you get the picture, this was soon after the First World War and it was an absolute crate we were in."

"What happened?" I asked.

"Well, everything would have been all right," he said, "if somebody hadn't left a motorcycle right at the end of the hangar."

"Did it have a sidecar?" I said.

"It did."

Well, there's no doubt about it. I can practically see the yellow gloves tossed carelessly in the sidecar seat. This was the first time I got the idea that Confidence was no boy.

I had plenty of chance to check on this later, for he kept popping in and out of my life so that I finally just kept the guest room ready and got over using it for a sewing room. When I really paid attention, there was plenty to notice. Confidence was getting gray at the temples and one time he showed up smoking a Corona-Corona. When he had those yellow gloves off you could see the skin was really getting quite crepey.

And yet there were times when the illusion would be overwhelming that you were having a carefree conversation with a healthy boy. Like the time they kept telling me on the radio to shop with Confidence in my neighborhood drugstore and I thought, why not?

Why not, indeed. My God, I told the police I had no idea how I happened to have a whole bottle of Seconal tablets in my coat pocket and no prescription for them. I told them and told them, and where was Confidence? Making a great to-do at the other end of the store about getting his foot stuck in a bedpan. And he cried, he *cried*, over the scratches on his riding boot.

I know it was weak of me, but I bought him a new pair to shut him up and I got him a one-way ticket for a long sea voyage. I hoped I would never see him again. Then, last week, he walked in, twice as arrogant and three times as insufferable, wearing, of all things, an army uniform.

"Listen," I said, "you can't be in the army. You're only three feet tall. I'm going to call the FBI."

"It's a diplomatic assignment," he said. "I'm a military advisor to the United Nations in Korea. I shall need a new briefcase."

That's when I sprang. I dragged him to the cellar door and I kicked him down the stairs and I locked the door. He finally pushed me too far. Other people can fight and donate blood and subscribe to Care for Korea but, take my word for it, the greatest service I could possibly do my country is to sit right here and hold tight to this . . . .

I know I put the key to the cellar in this very pocket not over an hour ago. Now, *where is it?*

The Little Green Velvet Park

Trains were bad luck for him; he had always said so. And now here he was once more stranded in the unfamiliar hospital of an unimportant town only half way to his destination.

Even as they had carried him from the train to the ambulance, and while the ambulance had crawled in that ever rising circle to the town's one hospital, he had begun, with what consciousness he had, to set in motion that familiar mechanism of *holding on*. He had begun already those first steps toward convincing himself that he could not die.

Weeks later, able to sit up, he congratulated himself on having been right once again and it was with real eagerness that he looked out of his window for the first time upon the town of Basilanda.

To a well eye, even, the sight of this town occasioned a sharp surprise. But his eyes had for weeks now been seeing the threads of his counterpane as so many minute, white bumpy tubules interlaced, while the face of his nurse was a triangle capable of becoming a square and the ceiling over his head throbbed toward him and receded like the tip of a great white plaster heart.

He saw the town for the first time as few people have ever seen it, that is he first looked down upon it and it is from a height that one is most aware of its unusual quality.

Most of the buildings of Basilanda are made from a native stone which changes from grey to white with exposure to the sun and rain. Because of the different ages of the buildings all the variations between grey and white are represented, so that there is often produced, even in the full sun, the effect of many shadows.

The town is built against the side of a hill, so that from a distance and in certain lights it seems to have been made from stiffly beaten egg whites and thrown there. It has a kind of fluidity about it, particularly when seen from above, by which one can imagine it's not staying so stiffly in place always, but sometime coalescing and sliding softly down upon itself.

It was the looking down which made him lean far over the side of his chair, clutching the window sill and forgetting completely his illness, for there, almost at the bottom of the town, was a little square park of a greenness which he had only seen before in the lining of Easter baskets.

When they made him go back to his bed after half an hour he carried the green park with him and while he lay there like a piece of wet cement, grateful for his increasing heaviness, the thought of actually going down into the little park warmed and soothed him and made him really happy.

Now as he grew stronger the total of his days began to focus upon this one desire: to get to the park. He began to embrace passionately his routine and his treatments for the insurance of that hour each day spent by the window. The image of the little park came to be almost constantly with him, gently blotting out his former unpleasant awareness of the room's details in relief. Once in the afternoon he fell asleep and dreamed that he reached out his hand to touch the park and that it felt soft to his fingers like velvet.

But as the vision of the park and the memory of it away from the window began to grow in importance he became aware of something else creeping in around the edges, something old and familiar and futile.

He was conscious of it for days—days in which he realized it must be well into summer by now, days in which they told him he could go out and walk a little within a week—before he remembered all of it at once, remembered it perfectly and completely after ten years.

First, there had been those glowing letters from Richard, his one great friend, Richard, so expansive, so voluble, so robust and healthy and excited in his new marriage.

"But now you must come to live with us, really, and Eleanor [Richard had always pronounced it El-e-a-nor, saying all four syllables clearly] says so too.

"I am sure there is no one there to take care of you as well as I have and I shall be even better at it now, what with the gentling influence floating about these days."

And again,

"My God, we have got a house and such a house you never saw. I have had to lower my voice a little, it is so impressive and grand, but it suits Eleanor perfectly. *When* are you coming to see it and us?"

But he had never seen Richard in his house, for Richard had been struck down by lightning and killed, with the new strawberry plants scattered all about him and never planted.

He, with the telegram still in his hand, had put his feeble carcass on a train and started to Eleanor. Then, as now, they had taken him off the train, still five hundred miles from her and even while he was in the ambulance he had begun to hold on to Eleanor. All the days in hospital in a strange town he had clung fast to the belief that he had to reach her, so as to have a reason why he could not die.

As soon as he was able to demand anything he had his nurse write to Eleanor, but she did not answer the nurse, but wrote directly to him. So much had Richard talked of him, so carefully had their plans included him, that she began, even in her sorrow and from a distance, to nurse him.

Every day for the six months he was ill she wrote to him, until in his illness he fastened upon her as he was later to cling to the little park. He would recite to himself what she had for breakfast and what flowers were blooming then in the garden and sometimes he put himself to sleep by repeating the names of the dogs: Hedda and Curtis and Hans.

Toward the last, in his excitement at the promised release, he would forget Richard for a whole day at a time. He would even forget Eleanor herself. It was not Eleanor, but the getting *to* Eleanor that mattered. That was what he had started to do; the doing of it now would be proof of his recovery. It would be the picking up of an old, old faith.

And at last, out of a blinding sun, he entered Eleanor's house and until then he had forgotten Richard's words: My God, we have got a house and such a house.

For he had never seen such a room as this one and falling into it out of the harsh sunlight after his long, slow journey so stunned him that he forgot even to see Eleanor for that first minute which, even in ten years' memory, still seemed to him to have lasted for hours.

He felt as though he had suddenly entered a great, deep, cool forest.

The floor was completely covered to the walls with a carpet of such a deep green that it showed spots of black under the chairs and the low round tables. All of the walls and the ceiling and even the folds of heavy cloth hanging at the windows were of a green only a little lighter than the carpet. These were about the color of English ivy leaves, not the new leaves at the tip ends, but the older ones near the roots where they are darker and thicker.

Against these walls the furniture showed all shades of living green, the blue greens and the lemon yellow greens and before the fireplace was a large circular rug lying on the carpet and this rug was the lightest imaginable green: the white green of a newly peeled live twig.

Across the room from him, as though separated from him by miles of fallen pine needles and moss and silent trees, Eleanor, in a pale yellow gown like the accidental dappling of the sun in a secret forest place, Eleanor rose and began to move toward him silently across the green softness, the pale unearthly whiteness of her bare arms reaching toward him.

"I am so proud you made it," she said and he remembered being shocked at her courage to speak out, to make a sound in this quiet place.

"I knew," he said, pausing and trying out his voice, "I knew all the time that I would finally get here."

"Sit here," she said, "and rest and I'll make tea. Or should you lie down at once? Your room has been ready for weeks and it's on this floor, so you won't need to climb any stairs."

"No," he said. "Sitting in this room must be twice as restful as lying down any place else in the world."

"I have so prayed that you would like it," she said, "because it has meant so much to me, but it's too strong for some people. It simply depresses them."

"Most people," he said, "have never been weary enough to know the need of it."

"Yes," she said. "Yes, I suppose that's it."

She went across the room from him then and began to make the tea. A long time after, he would think of how if she had had to go out of the room for the tea things, or if *he* could have escaped that room only for the time it takes a kettle to boil, how differently his life might have gone. He thought of all this years later in Basilanda and of how, but for a few moments to get a kettle or a sliced lemon or a tea cup, he might not have been alone in Basilanda, craving the sight of a little park like a crazed and thirsty man.

She sat beside him while they had tea and once as she reached out to the table before them her white arm brushed his knee and he had the illusion for a moment of hearing music like the thin low sound of a distant violin in a high room, but it was gone almost instantly and Eleanor was saying, "Richard always wanted you to live with us, you know. I remember one day he went all over the place pointing out what you should have when you came. I mean you to have them now," she said, "those things, and tomorrow we'll go over the place and I'll show them all to you."

He was on his third cup of the good hot tea now and as he put down his cup he looked about him at the room, which had grown a little less large now and he looked at Eleanor.

"You know," he said, "I feel fine. I feel better, I think, than I ever felt in my life."

"That's wonderful," she said, "wonderful. Oh, this will be a fine place for you. Richard always said that if you could just get here, he was sure you would be well."

"Poor Richard," he said, "he was so wonderfully alive. It is I who should have. . . . Oh, I am a beast, Eleanor. You must forgive me. So long ago I started out only to bring you condolence in your sorrow and when I at last arrive I sit and speak only of how good I feel. No one is so truly selfish as the. . . ."

"Hush," she said. "So many months have gone now. Even I . . . I don't know what I'm doing here. I, who never so much as sent Richard to take the dogs off for a walk without weakening and going after him, I certainly never meant him to die alone. I don't know just why, but I always thought somehow that he would die in the winter time and that I would just go out and sit by him in the snow. That would have been quite easy, I think and quiet, but I could never do anything violent or noisy like guns or poison."

The afternoon light had begun to change and soften and the black circle of shadow under the table stretched into an ellipse. Eleanor's voice dropped with the light. She was staring straight ahead of her.

"I never once thought of his dying in the spring," she said, "and now . . . now I don't know what it is I'm waiting for."

"Eleanor," he said, "dear Eleanor. Don't speak so." He took her two hands in his. They were quite cold.

"I'm so glad you've come," she said. "I've been so dreary.

Several times I thought I should come down to see you, but it sounded such a hole and I didn't know what I should do with myself outside visiting hours and then I hated to leave the dogs. They grieve so now."

"Hedda and Curtis and Hans," he said. "How are they?"

"Oh, fine now. Shall I let them in? Would you like to see them?"

"Don't go," he said, "don't go just yet, Eleanor. I am still trying to believe that you are real." He felt her hands, still in his, turn suddenly warm.

"It's almost dark. I should turn on the lights. And dinner," she said, "I had completely forgotten about dinner. You must be starved."

"No," he said, "no."

And with the coming darkness the two of them fell silent. They did not look at each other, but watched with a kind of fascination the furniture of the room melt piece by piece until even the color of Eleanor's dress was gone and he was aware only of the faint light from her bare arms.

There in the soft, black-green darkness their great loneliness became almost embodied into a breathing thing standing near them in the room, breathing and breathing for want of a voice.

And as the music that he had heard earlier came back to him and the swelling pounding of his heart beat in upon him he became aware of her as he had never been aware of another human being in all his life.

There was no more than an inch of space between them and it diminished by millimeters like the melting away of the furniture in the dark and their meeting dissolved that breathing presence which had hung over them in heaviness and oppression and loneliness. Their meeting was a clean blue light in a dark place, like the sudden free odor of pine needles trod upon in a green forest.

His hand in the dark was rounded already to touch her breast, cupped for the holding of their hungered peace, when Eleanor cried out and struck him away from her and, standing, turned knives of light into the room.

"Oh, how could it happen so soon, so soon?" she cried. "Richard, Richard. Oh, it's obscene . . . obscene."

Completely stunned by what he saw he stumbled away from the sight of her standing crying under the bright light, her thin fingers tearing at her breasts.

Days later he identified the last sound he heard as he went out into the street as that of the dogs, Hedda and Curtis and Hans, scratching and crying at the door to be let in.

"Now, tomorrow," his nurse said, "you are to be allowed an hour's walk."

"Can I make it to the park, do you think?"

"The park?"

"Yes," he said, "the little park down there."

"Oh, yes," she said, "I should think you could. You have only to walk straight down this road here, but you must certainly sit down there for a while before you start up again. Would you like me to go with you?"

"Thank you," he said, "but I think I'd like to go alone."

"Look," she said, "it's coming up a storm."

"Does that mean I won't get to go to the park?"

"Oh, no, I don't think so. This time of year the storms are over soon, but they're quite violent while they last."

"Then you think it won't keep me from going?"

"This one won't. But of course if there's another one tomorrow, you couldn't go out *in* one."

"No," he said. "No, of course not."

"I must see to the windows in the other rooms," she said. "It's coming up fast now." But she had hardly gone from the room before he could see the great trees begin to bend in the wind and while the whole building shook with the thunder he stood by the window watching and willing the storm to go away and leave tomorrow and the park in safety.

On the next day he could see from his window that the rain had only left the park more beautiful, softer, greener and he began to dress in eagerness.

This thing had never paled for him, this wonderful release and freedom, this first day out of hospital. It was always, time after time, new and exhilarating. Always with the first steps in hard soled shoes upon the stern pavement, the old, old faith came back to him, the wonderful belief that he could not die.

Now that he really had it within his reach, he did not hurry, but put off by seconds the pleasure of actually being in the little velvet park and when at last he came to the bench that months ago he had marked for his own, he laughed out loud that the sun should be shining on it so exactly right. He sat down slowly, physically glad to be sitting, and let the sun wash over him.

"That's him," he heard. "He's the one." Turning, he saw two little boys standing near him.

"Aren't you the man they took off the train, sick?" the taller of them asked, stepping nearer him to stare the better.

"Yes," he said, "I'm the one."

So preoccupied had he been with his illness and his struggle to achieve the park that he had not realized how he had become the center of interest for Basilanda.

Here in this small town he had taken on more importance than he would ever have again and for days there had been talk of little else than his increasing appetite, his being able to sit up and stand up and his desire to see the park. It was only by the greatest self control that the natives had not turned out in a crowd to watch him sitting in the sun. He had become their celebrity, their common interest and their struggle.

"I told you," the boy said to his companion, "I told you it was him. Say," he said turning back to the man, "what did you do all the time? Did you just lie there? I said I bet you played some kind of games, but lots of people said you just lay there and didn't do anything. What do you do all the time?"

"Oh," he said, "I think."

"You think? Well, what do you think about? Different things or just one thing all the time?"

"Oh, different things," he said.

"Well, what things?"

"Oh, I think about the park and about what there's going to be for lunch and whether I'll get any mail and . . . ."

"And what else?"

"And I think about a woman," he said, for he was suddenly so tired now at the thought of walking up hill to the hospital that he did not care what he said to the boy so long as the boy didn't notice his knees shaking, "a woman named Eleanor."

"My sister's name's Elinor," the boy said (he pronounced it Elner). "She's funny. She's scared of thunder and lightning. You should have seen her last night in the big storm. Oh, she cried and bit her knuckles and hid under the bed."

The Way Things Are

She was sitting there in the little car with her hands on the steering wheel and the engine going and Jennifer stood outside with one foot on the running board.

"If you left anything," Jennifer said, "I'll send it to you."

"I always do leave something, don't I?" she said.

"But if it's that same goddamned brassiere with the crooked hook, I'm going to burn it up this time."

"You know you won't," she said.

"Did you pack the presents for the children?"

"Yes, the last thing."

"And Rick's?"

"Sure," she said, and they both laughed then, for the picture of Rick using his new present: the crazy heart shaped bar of spiced soap with a cord to go around his neck, so he wouldn't lose the soap in the shower. And then they stopped laughing because it was not funny, really, their saying goodbye, but horrible the way it always was for them.

"Please stop over, Darling. Don't try to do anything wild and make the whole trip in one day."

"Well, maybe I will," she said.

"I'm so afraid you'll fall asleep, driving."

"I won't sleep," she said.

"Well," Jennifer said, taking her foot off the running board and standing back a step now so that the early morning sun hit her hair, making it red. "Well, Darling. . . ."

She started the car then, still looking at Jennifer and Jennifer could see her lips moving in the goodbye, but she could not hear her over the sound of the motor.

Driving down the street now away from the house, as long as

she could see anything, she could still see her sister in the rear view mirror, see Jennifer raising her right hand to brush the heavy hair back from her thin face.

When she came to the corner she turned to be out of Jennifer's sight and stopped the car, for the tears were there now, one hanging on each wide open eyelid, making the street wave in front of her. If she closed her eyes now, the two tears would fall and spot her dress, but if she kept her eyes wide open, kept on staring, the street would come back to her.

Then she closed them and let the two tears fall and more after and finally she put her head down on the steering wheel, still holding tight with her hands, crying now, really crying, for thinking of Jennifer.

For there was grey in Jennifer's hair for the first time and that meant that Jennifer was getting old and if Jennifer was getting old, then she was, too. And the years were piling up and still they were living six hundred miles away from each other, seeing each other on visits—they, who had loved each other all their lives before anyone else, before friend or husband or child.

"I keep hunting for someone a little like you," Jennifer had said, "but whenever I find anyone they either die or move away."

It seemed so stupid to her that she, who loved Jennifer more than anyone else on earth, should let the years pull her on, should be meeting and parting and parting again from Jennifer. And while they were living on with miles between them, the years were slipping, one on top of the other, quietly, in measure.

Because of this she was not very excited to be going home to Rick and the children, though they would be terribly glad to have her back and though she came with presents, with Rick's soap and the hundred piece model farm for the boy and the sewing set for little Jennifer.

It had been such a terrible mistake to name the child Jennifer, for she was going to look exactly like Rick and there was nothing, nothing at all, of the real Jennifer in her. So she had taken to calling her Janey now in the last year, now that it was certain that she was going to be like Rick.

Oh, it was absurd that they should be going about the streets of separate towns, she and Jennifer, being taken for responsible young matrons, that they should have houses of their own to keep and care if the chickens were fat or lean and lie with strangers in strange beds.

And she thought of the big old bed at home in the room that she and Jennifer had always had together and of how, when Jennifer, being the older, had started to go with boys she would lie awake waiting for her and give her the warm place in the bed. She could feel again how delicious it was to be rolling onto the cold side, having Jennifer so pleased she had stayed awake, putting her warm feet on Jennifer's cold ones. Jennifer's feet were always cold.

She could smell the sheets again that had been dried out of doors and see the blue curtains blowing into the room. And she could see the wallpaper now, wild and ugly and somehow violent in its design, yet having come by this time to be almost beautiful, almost the very essence of safety.

"Isn't it awful?" Jennifer had said this time, "I don't have a single thing from the house, do you?"

"No, not a thing," she had said, "but if you could have something now, what would you take?"

"Oh, I don't know. Something of yours, I think, or something we used together. Maybe the footstool."

"I'd take Laughing Boy."

"Oh, God!" Jennifer said, "I had almost forgot about him. Why do you suppose we never got ourselves a proper ashtray?"

"It was because we always had our money spent a week ahead, if you remember."

She wished now that she could find Laughing Boy again and send him to Jennifer, but he would be gone now, surely, with the house or thrown on some alien trash heap. She had forgotten now which relative had left him there (or had he been a souvenir of the fair?) this huge iron ash tray, holding on one edge, as a kind of handle, a hideous little iron Pierrot playing a guitar.

They had called him the little man with the big guitar and the animated handle, but finally they had settled on Laughing Boy and she had seen him once so that she would never forget him. That was the day Jennifer got married and she had sat there alone, after Jennifer had gone, staring at Laughing Boy until suddenly she had seen him in all of his hideous ironness, standing up to his knees in cigarette butts, playing his guitar and smiling, smiling.

And she knew now as she wiped her eyes with the back of her hand and started the car going that she was tired clear through, that she had been tired for years.

As she drove into the filling station the prospect of driving six hundred miles on the highway, hearing Jennifer's words and Jennifer's laughter, was more than she could bear and she said to the attendant: "Isn't there some other way to get to Reading besides Number 24?"

"Well, yes Ma'am," he said, "there is, but the roads aren't first rate and it's a couple of hours longer."

"Well, here," she said, taking out her maps, "show me how to go." For a change of scenery, a different set of billboards, even a bad road, would help. Anything, anything at all that would demand attention, that would keep the surface thinking until she got there.

"Well," he said, "this is the way you go, but if I was you, Lady, I'd stick to the highway."

If you was me, she thought, you'd scream.

"It looks a little bit like rain," he said, "and part of them roads is dirt."

"That's all right," she said, "I don't care." She liked the rain, though Jennifer never had.

She had gone almost two hundred miles before she ran into it though, and she was glad to see it, even though she was by that time on the dirt road, for it made her feel better, less tired, more aware.

But neither she nor the attendant had reckoned on a cloud-burst and very soon it became no longer a diversion, but a serious and essential matter to get to a shelter.

Though it was only noon, it was night dark out and she was almost hysterically thankful to see the lights of the little town burning ahead and feel the wheels grip the pavement of its main street.

She had not eaten since she had left Jennifer that morning and then she had only had coffee and so when she saw the hotel sign ahead with the globes of the H gone dark, she stopped and went in to lunch. It was dark in the dining room even though the electric lights were turned on and she was the only person there. The food was not very good and after she had finished lunch she went out into the lobby and stood watching the storm.

"How soon do you think I'll be able to go on?" she asked the proprietor who also stood by the window watching.

"Oh, you wouldn't get two miles in this, Miss," he said. "This is the worst one I've seen for years. You'd best stop the night anyway."

"I suppose there is nothing else to do," she said. "Would you get my things out of the car for me?"

It was a very old hotel and her room rather pleased her. Lying on the bed looking up at the high ceiling, she felt quite good now, almost as though she had found a day, for Rick was not expecting her until tomorrow and there was nothing she had to do and no one she had to see.

She had an almost hot bath in the antiquated tub and then she unpacked her bags, taking out first the presents for the children which she had put in last: the model farm (one hundred pieces) and the sewing set. Then she took a nap. When she awoke some one was knocking on the door and the first thing she heard was the howling of the storm outside, really violent now, really menacing. She opened the door on the proprietor whom she had seen that afternoon.

"Mrs. Curtess," he said, "the cook would like to know what time you want dinner."

"It doesn't matter," she said. "What time do you serve?"

"Well, Mr. Frazier eats at six," he said, "and the cook thought, if you don't mind, since you two are the only guests in the hotel, if you'd eat when Mr. Frazier does. . . ."

"Of course," she said. "you don't want to stay up all night just to feed two people."

"Thank you, Mrs. Curtess. You see, it's such a bad night that we're not likely to have any trade at all from the town and the cook would like to try to get home tonight if he can make it."

"That's all right," she said. "What time is it now?"

"It's five."

"That's plenty of time."

"And the cook would like to know, if there's something in particular you'd want to eat. He could be preparing it now, you see."

"Oh, I'm very agreeable," she said. "I'll just have whatever Mr. Frazier has."

While she was dressing she recaptured the feeling that the room had first given her. She thought of what a fine letter she would write to Jennifer about Mr. Frazier. She knew quite what he would be like: a little fat man, very annoyed at being delayed in the storm, very concerned with the weather, having to have his dinner at six o'clock sharp. She only hoped that he didn't have a taste for liver and onions.

Mr. Frazier would probably have a cigar after dinner and grow chatty about business, so it would be best to take something to read with her, but she had no books, so at six she picked up her cigarette case and stuffed the directions to Janey's sewing set in her bag. If Mr. Frazier were like she thought he'd be the sewing directions would be an improvement over his conversation.

She arrived very punctually in the dining room (not for the world would she have kept Mr. Frazier waiting), walked clear through to the end of the room and sat down. Mr. Frazier was late.

She drank two glasses of ice water while she was waiting and when she heard his footsteps she looked down at the table, lest she in the slightest way encourage him to sit with her. She could hear him walking now clear through the room as she had walked and when he sat down at the table next to her she looked up.

And there was between them an almost instant spark of recognition, though neither one of them ever realized why and possibly only Jennifer could have told them had she been there that though in all their other features they were dissimilar, their eyes were exactly alike.

It is amazing that though people have only two eyes and these even have to be placed in a rather limited space, yet almost none of them have eyes alike except for an occasional father and son. The expression, also, was almost identical, though in the man it was more pronounced, a look of profound, but dispassionate, realism.

"Good evening," he said to her.

"Good evening," she said, wondering if there could have arrived in the last hour still a third guest. Surely this man, this could not be her little Mr. Frazier, whom she had known so intimately, so well, between five and six.

They were each given a rather good soup and an omelette which they ate in silence. Once he said "coffee" to the waitress and she repeated it after him.

They both lit cigarettes at the same time and, looking up at the first exhalation, they saw each other and both of them would have spoken then but that the woman suddenly looked down at her lap and began to fumble at her handbag. Her hands were shaking now, violently, and when she felt the little folder of sewing directions she clutched on it in desperation and began to read to herself:

Lay the pattern on the cloth and pin it down so that it will not slip. Then cut the cloth around the pattern and cut from A to B, being sure to follow all the notches.

She could not go on reading it forever and finally she took a drink of water and looked up again. He was sitting just as she had left him and there was a moment there when they were looking at each other and no turning away now and then the room went black. While they heard the sudden curses of the cook she could still see the after image of his eyes upon the dark. It was so still that they could hear each other breathing and finally he said,

"Just because we can't see is no reason why we can't talk, I suppose."

"No," she said, "no reason."

"Any minute, now," he said, "some fool is going to come in here and tell us that the lights are out. It never fails."

She laughed then, easily and gladly and her hands were no longer shaking.

"You don't look like some one who has to have his dinner at six," he said.

"Neither do you."

"What did you say?"

"I said, 'neither do you.'"

"Well, I'm not," he said. "What made you think I was?"

"The proprietor told me," she said. "He said, 'Mr. Frazier eats at six.'"

"And the cook thought," Mr. Frazier went on, "if you don't mind, since you two are the only guests in the hotel, if you'd eat when Mrs. Curtess does. . . ."

"Did he tell you that, too?"

"Oh, that lying bastard," he said. "Are you responsible for the omelette?"

"No, are you?"

"I simply said 'what's good enough for Mrs. Curtess is good enough for me.'"

"Oh," she said, "how easily we fell into it. What do you think we'd have got if we'd asked for squab?"

"We'd have got omelette," he said. "That omelette was ordained years ago."

The proprietor came in then carrying a dusty and wavering lamp. "All over the place," he said. "It's not just here. All the lights in the town are out and they say the river's rising a foot an hour." The proprietor stood there holding the lamp in his hands not knowing which table to put it on. Frazier got up and walked over to her table and the proprietor, much relieved, set down the lamp.

"I will have a light put in your rooms," he said, "and when you are ready to go you can take this one with you."

"Thank you," the woman said.

The proprietor stood there, a little tentative in his manner and quite excited still about the drama of the storm. "Well," he said. Well, I'm sorry about the light."

"I'm not," Frazier said, when he had gone. "Are you?"

"No," she said, "no."

"And what are you doing in Milton, Mrs. Curtess?"

"I was on my way to Reading," she said. "I was trying to avoid the highway; I was trying to find a new way. And you?"

"You'll never believe it," he said, "but I came here on purpose. It seemed a good place to think because I don't know anyone here."

"And what are you thinking about?"

"I am thinking about not going home."

"NOT going?"

"Yes . . . not going. I am trying to talk myself out of it."

"I have just been to see my sister," she said, "and all day I have been wallowing in the most horrible nostalgia."

"Nostalgia?" he said. "Christ, don't I know it?"

"Then why don't you go?"

"Because I just made a thousand dollars."

"I should think that would be a very good reason to go," she said.

"Oh, no," he said. "If I go home I shall have to give away the thousand dollars because they need it very badly and I will not be able to look at it."

"Well?" she asked.

"Well," he said, "if I give away the thousand, I shall have to go back to work and if I have to go back to work I cannot go to Africa and if I cannot go to Africa I cannot paint the great yellow lions and if I cannot paint the great yellow lions lying in the fat sleek green vegetation again this year, I think that I shall die."

"Are you going to live a year on a thousand dollars?"

"Yes," he said.

"How?"

"Why, last year I lived on eight hundred. That is, I think I did, but I was afraid to count it." And she knew it would be better not to say anything, anything at all just then.

"So you have been to see your sister?" he said.

"Oh, yes," she said.

"And what is her name?"

"Jennifer."

"Jennifer? And is she beautiful?"

"Oh, yes," she said. "Jennifer is very beautiful."

"And what do you do," he said, "when you go to see Jennifer?"

"Well, we laugh, mostly and talk and sometimes we giggle."

"And what do you laugh about?" he said.

"I don't know. As soon as I leave her I can never remember because they're not jokes, you know. They're just our things, our language."

"And are you never sad," he said, "with Jennifer?"

"Before we have babies, we are," she said. "Jennifer always comes to me and I always go to Jennifer and we say 'Of course nothing is going to happen. Of course everything is going to be all right and this is melodramatic, but, really, if I should die this time, would you take care of my child? Would you bring him up?' and we always promise and we never die."

"How many children does Jennifer have?" he said.

"Two."

"And you?"

"Two." And she hated for him to know as he surely must that she was older than he.

"I don't have any," he said.

"Yes, I know, but perhaps you will in Africa."

"Do you really think I can get to Africa?"

"Yes," she said, "yes, I know you will."

They sat there not speaking then, looking at each other across the yellow wavering lamp and she kept hearing idiotically over and over the sentence from the sewing instructions: *Lay the pattern on the cloth and pin it down so that it will not slip.*

"I cannot go on calling you Mrs. Curtess," he said. "Not if you believe I can get to Africa."

"My name is Penny, Mr. Frazier."

"Penny?"

"Yes."

"Mine's John," he said. And they were silent again, seeing each other's faces change from yellow in the lamp light to green in the lightening.

"Are you afraid of the storm, Penny?"

"No," she said. "I should love to go out in it."

"All right."

They got up then from the table and walked the length of the dining room, together now, and went out into the storm, not stopping for wraps, never believing it could be as fierce as it was, but they had not gone more than six steps before Penny was blown right down hard on the pavement.

And there in the storm John knelt beside her, frantically calling the name he had only just learned, but by the lightening he could see that she was unconscious and he picked her up in his arms and went stumbling into the hotel and up the stairs in the dark, somehow not falling. And he could have kissed the proprietor for the light burning in his room.

Penny moaned a little when he put the wet towel on her head and then she opened her eyes.

"That's a real storm," she said.

"You've cut your head, Penny girl. It's bleeding. Should I get you a doctor?"

"Get me the mirror, first," she said and, when she had seen the cut, "It's not very bad, John."

"It will be black by morning, I'll bet you."

"Well," she said, "then let it."

"Penny," he said, "Penny, you scared the hell out of me."

"I'm cold, John."

"Your clothes are wet," he said. He took off her clothes, very deftly, very easily, so that there was no question about it between them and then he rubbed her skin all over with a towel until she was warm and then he wrapped her up in a blanket.

At dawn when she woke up John was holding her on his lap, sitting in the big chair by the window, but almost before she remembered where she was she knew that it was still raining.

"How's your head?" he said.

"It's all right. Have you been sitting up all night?"

"Yes," he said. "The storm was wonderful in the night. It was green."

"Are you tired?"

"No," he said, "no. I feel fine."

"So do I."

When they went downstairs to breakfast, she stopped at the desk.

"Is there any way I can send a telegram?" she asked the proprietor.

"No, Ma'am, he said. "I'm sorry. All the wires are down. Where did you want to send it?"

"To Reading."

"Oh," he said, "south? Well, maybe by tomorrow we might be able to get one through. It's west where the wreckage is the worst."

"Oh," she said. "I suppose the roads are impossible, too?"

"Completely," he said. "All the bridges are out and the trains have stopped even. The river's over its banks, now. It will be right in here by night if it doesn't stop raining."

"In the hotel?"

"Yes, Ma'am," he said. "This is a real flood." And he seemed very proud of it.

Rick will not start to worry until tonight, she thought.

After breakfast they went to their rooms, but all the time she was standing by the window looking down upon the swelling river she knew that he would come, though she started when he knocked.

"You can see the river from my window," she said.

"Do you really think it will come into the hotel?" he said.

"You mean Otel?"

"Those lights have been out on the H ever since I got here."

"How long have you been here?" she said.

"Two weeks."

"And when does your boat leave?"

"In a week."

"You'll make it," she said, and she was thinking that a week is only seven days, but that if they didn't sleep at all, it would be like fourteen and she knew she must stay even though the roads should be safe, even though she could get a telegram through to Rick.

"Is that west?" she asked.

"Yes," he said, "where the river is. That's where it's the worst."

"Yes," she said, "I know. But you're going East. You'll make it."

But all the time it was there, the question between them and there was nothing else, really, to talk about.

And it was good for her to be shaken so profoundly, as nothing had ever shaken her before, nothing. This was not friendly like meeting Rick, nor sorrowful like leaving Jennifer. This was like nothing that had ever happened to her before.

And she was glad, glad of it.

And they both of them knew it, but they were afraid of the daylight and of the proprietor's coming to ask what they wanted for lunch and of a sudden flood warning and they were waiting, waiting for the night now and it would be hours yet.

"What shall we do all day?" he said. "We can't go out." For he knew it was no good to touch her now, to start this thing without the night.

"Well, here," she said, and she handed him the boy's present, the model farm, and she was surprised to find no guilt in herself and chilled to know that she was capable of giving him the child as well.

He opened the box and the red cows and the sheep and the pieces of the farm buildings were all lying scrambled together.

"How wonderful you are," he said, "to be carrying things like this around with you."

"There are a hundred pieces," she said. "That ought to last us a long time."

They sat on the floor, piecing together the cylindrical silo and the windmill that really turned. They put the cows to pasture and had a sheep shearing and the horses would have none of their plow, but stood all day lolling at the water trough.

And John carved a man and a woman from the bar of soap in the bathroom and these they put in the hayloft in the big red barn.

And now there were a hundred and two pieces.

Towards evening they put all the cattle where they thought they ought to be for the night and they shut the barn door and the soap man and woman went into the house. Then Penny combed her hair and they went down to dinner.

But the lobby was a foot deep in water and all the food in the hotel had been taken in a boat to the flood refugees.

So there was no need to wait any more and they turned and ran up the stairs, the woman a little ahead, and as soon as they were inside her room they locked the door and, holding each other, they leaned against it, so glad now to have the day over with, the waiting done, and John lifted her into his arms and carried her over to the bed and she could hear the wind rising in the trees like a siren.

Awake in the night she sat up in bed smoking and it was like a spike through her chest to see his fragile knees with the bones so near the skin, so bare to the wind. And seeing them, she remembered El Greco's Pieta and she wondered how El Greco could have known how it is to long to hold a grown man across your legs, not cradling him, not loving him even, just holding him there with the knees spread apart, being heavy where he is light, protected where he is fragile. And she could remember in the picture that Mary was not only looking at Jesus, but out, out into a world where he was not any more. And she remembered, too, how Frieda Lawrence had held D. H.'s feet in her hands while he was dying and it did not seem silly to her any more the way it had when she had first read it.

In the morning they went first to the window and they said together *it is still raining* and they were glad, even though they knew that some people would be drowning now and their houses washed away and floating down the river and in other houses the mud and the ooze would be crawling into the kitchen stoves and into the drawers where the linens were.

And she did not even try to get a telegram through.

"Have you got another toy for today, Penny?"

"Yes," she said, "but you won't like it."

"Let me see." And so she got out Janie's sewing set and there were patterns for every kind of doll dress, with the underwear to match, and there were pieces of cloth: dimity and organdy, satin and crepe, thin and heavy, smooth and rough. There was everything there that a doll would need but shoes.

"Here," she said. "Here's the directions." He took them from her and began to read: *Lay the pattern on the cloth and pin it down so that it will not slip.* "God," he said, "how deadly dull," and he threw the directions across the room.

"I'll design you a wardrobe," he said, and he got a pencil and began to sketch the doll dresses on the hotel stationery.

"I want her to have a morning dress," Penny said, "to wear in the rose garden."

"All right," he said, "which cloth do you use for that?" And Penny began to sort through them until she found a thin white organdy with a tiny flower all through it. "This one," she said, and she lifted it from the pile and handed it to him.

"Penny," he said, "take off your ring. Please."

She took it from her finger then, easily, and started across the room with it, but there was no place in the room big enough to hold it (can you put a wedding ring in an eye cup?) and finally she took it in the closet and hung it on a hook and shut the door upon it.

And all day he would cut the cloth for her and she sat in the big chair sewing, hurriedly now, not even stopping to smoke, as though the doll would be dead if she didn't have her clothes by nightfall.

And at nightfall he took the needle from her fingers and took off the little thimble and they clung to each other and she was crying now. It seemed right to him that one of them should be crying and so he did not try to stop her.

This night they did not even go downstairs and so they did not know that the water was receding a little in the lobby.

The smell of the river had begun now to permeate everything in the room so that the sheets and the towels and even their skins were so full of it that there was nothing divorced from it, nothing now but what was heavy and floating and destructive. When the rain stopped in the night it woke them with its sudden demanding stillness.

Early in the morning the proprietor knocked on Penny's door and she answered it, not caring any more who should see them together.

Mrs. Curtess," the man said, "I think you can get a wire through now to the South."

"But East?" she said. "Can you go East now?"

"Yes," he said. "There's to be a train leave at noon. And we've got some food now. Would you like to have breakfast in your room?"

"Yes," she said.

And then she went back to John. "You can get your train at noon," she said, "and you'll be in time for the boat. You have to allow for its not getting through, you know."

And he did not say that he wouldn't go. They were thinking it, but they did not say it. They had not said any words. They had not called this thing any name, had not made it different from what it was, no better and no meaner, no wider and no deeper.

"Will you go with me to the station?" he said.

"Yes," she said, "but only to find out if the train is safe."

When he bathed she handed him Rick's soap with less compunction than she had given him the children's toys, for they had used most of their soap to make the man and the woman in the hay loft. But before she gave it to him she cut the cord off it because she could not bear to see him sitting there in the antiquated tub with the soap heart hanging around his neck.

And at the station they said the train would really leave at noon, but she did not believe it was safe and the agent kept trying to reassure her.

"But it's all right EAST," he said. "It's west of here where the real damage is."

"I know," she said, "but the bridges?"

And then when she knew he was really going, she left him.

"Where are you going?" he said.

"I'm going back to our room," she said. "I'm going to lay out the doll dresses in order with the panties to match and put all the animals out on the bed and leave them there, all hundred pieces."

"It's a hundred and two," he said.

"That's right," she said. "The man and the woman now."

And she turned and left him because it was not the kind of love that had to do with kissing in a railroad station. There had never, for a moment, been any comfort in it for them.

In the room, she laid out all the dresses in a row across the pillows according to the time of day they were to be worn, She laid them out with order. And on the bed she set up the stock farm and all the animals were out to pasture in small congenial groups, but she could not put the man and the woman back in the hay loft, now that it had stopped raining.

It was not a floating soap that they were made of, so it was easy to drown them in the horse trough because they were so small, to drown them in the water that was no longer safe for drinking.

And then she put on her coat and walked down the stairs and out of the hotel and she began walking slowly and with difficulty through the mud of the west road.

She was very alert, now, very attentive to the record of the flood. She saw the world lying at an angle, quiet from its outrage, saw the intimate still lives of domesticity exposed to the open air. She saw a live yellow hen sitting in doubt beside an horizontal can of baking powder and a douche bag full of mud. She was walking on the west road now and she knew it.

It was not that she was confused by what had happened to her or that she did not know what direction she was going. She knew that she was going away from the three of them. She knew that she was not going east after John and his yellow lions, the yellow lions lying in the fat sleek green vegetation.

She knew she was not going east, or north to Jennifer, or south to Rick.

But west, where, as they had all insisted on telling her, the worst of the wreckage lay.

The Father Stories

1. Father and Fatalism

Father said he was a fatalist. He said he was absolutely convinced that it was impossible for a man to die until it was his time to die, no matter what he did. He said that it was all settled and there was absolutely nothing you could do about it.

"And I'll tell you why I think so," he said. "Pa went clear through the Civil War. He had his whole knee cap shot out. He had one eye shot out and he had a sword stuck clear through one side. He had cholera in Andersonville prison and he lived through all of it. Then by God, he came home, had a tooth pulled and bled to death. That's what made me a fatalist. There is just no sense in worrying about whether a thing is going to kill you. And if it's time to kill you, it doesn't make any difference what you do, you're going to die."

It would have been much easier for me to believe that Indians are loquacious or that it will rain in Kansas in August, than that Father had resigned himself to anything. The sun never set on a day that Father wasn't worrying about something. Why, the reason we were Methodists was because that was the only Sunday School that we could get to without having to cross a railroad track. And if my mother was even ten minutes late in getting home from shopping she would find Father pacing up and down on the front porch. Whenever we were sick, even with the mildest of colds, we were quite likely to awaken from a nap to find Father sitting by the bed staring at us with fear that the breathing he had just heard was our last.

If one of us proposed to make a trip to the other side of town, especially one that necessitated a transfer from one streetcar to another, he would live in advance, and out loud, every dangerous step of the journey.

"Now look both ways before you walk out to the streetcar line," he'd say, "and then when you get off, watch out for Kellogg. There's a diagonal street comes in there and it's all your life's worth to cross it."

In his mind he would walk every step with you till you arrived at the door where you were going. He never missed a single dangerous possibility of the horrible things that might happen to you on your way there and then he would start in on your home trip, with all the dangers in reverse. There were all the things that could happen to you from other people's negligence, like being run over by an automobile, train, streetcar, bus, runaway horse, bicycle or grocer's cart, and all the things that might happen to you from your own carelessness like stumbling, slipping, falling, fainting, getting a cinder in your eye, stepping on a banana peel. Then there were all the hazards of the weather. A car might slip on a rainy street, you might slip on snow or sleet, the wind might blow your hat off. "Never chase a hat," Father said, "let it *go*."

If you still had enough courage to try to make it to the public library, there were yet to be considered vicious dogs, cats that had fits and old men who offered you poisoned candy.

Not that the home ground was safe. He was afraid for us to climb trees because we would fall out. He was afraid for us to go barefoot because we might step on a rusty nail and cucumbers were poison if they hadn't been soaked in salt water. It was a dangerous and thrilling life we led the way Father said it and all you had to do was drop a very small book on the floor to have him jump two feet straight into the air yelling, "Jesus Christ! Dja hurt yourself?"

That's why, when Father had the nerve to look me straight in the eye and tell me there was no sense in worrying about dying, I couldn't take it lying down. "How can you say that about fatalism," I said, "when every time I start across the street you tell me to be sure and look both ways and then run all the way across. Why, if what you say was true and you really believed in it, why can't I just close both eyes and *saunter* across the street?"

"Because," Father said, "it only applies to dying, fatalism does. It has nothing to do with getting all crippled up."

2. Father and the Goose Grease

Father came home with a goose and it was big enough to feed everybody in our block. He rarely bought the food for the house, but when he did he always over-bought. Not under any circumstances would it have been possible to put a list in Father's hand and send him to the store and on the rare occasions that he did come home with food, the purchases had no relation to the needs of the larder.

It would just be that on his way home from work he would be very hungry at the same time that he passed the bakery. The bakery would smell so good to Father that he would go in and buy whatever it was that he had just smelled and, being hungry, everything he saw would look so good that he was likely to arrive home with a German coffee cake, two dozen fresh cinnamon rolls, a loaf of salt rising bread, two loaves of fresh rye, one with and one without caraway seeds, a dozen cream puffs and two dozen chocolate eclairs, all on the same night. He worked all over the city and was always coming home by different routes so it was just as likely to be an arm load of assorted cheeses or smoked sausages. There was no way of forecasting what delectable smell or window display was going to coincide with one of his great hungers. The only thing you could tell ahead of time was that whatever it was it would be about ten times as much as we could eat.

That was the way it was with the goose. My mother could hardly get the oven door shut and within a short time after she began to cook it the goose began to give off an enormous quantity of grease. My mother would draw off the grease and put the goose back in the oven and in a little while there would be that much more again. By the time that the goose was done every pan we had in the kitchen and almost all the mixing bowls were full of grease.

"I never saw so much grease come out of one goose in my life," Mother said. "I don't see how it's possible. I don't know what in the world I'll do with it."

Father had no truck with the cooking and never took any interest in the kitchen except for the finished products that came out of it and so when he said in a strangely positive tone, "You must keep it; it's very good," Mother was so surprised that she didn't even argue the point.

"But what'll I keep it in?" she said. "I have to cook in these pans."

"Oh," Father said, still very positive, "you put it in Mason jars and store it away. My mother always kept it. It's very good. Very good to have around."

Mother was still so surprised to have him showing an interest in the housekeeping like this that she went right down into the basement and got out her Mason jars and filled them with the goose grease.

It was not until several weeks had gone by and Mother had found herself moving the goose grease jars for the third time in order to make space for her jelly, that she said to Father one night, "What did your mother use that goose grease for?"

"What goose grease?" Father said.

"That goose grease you told me to save," Mother said. "Those jars and jars of goose grease that I've been shifting all over the basement for the last three weeks. You told me to be sure and save it because your mother always did. What did she save it *for*? Every time I want to do the simplest thing down in the basement there are those jars of goose grease in the way. I'm tired of looking at them."

Father put his newspaper clear down flat on his knees and even took his pipe out of his mouth. He looked up at Mother in the most puzzled way. "You know," he said, "I can't remember."

"Well, that's great," Mother said.

It worried Father all evening long. He was preoccupied all through dinner and afterwards didn't even pick up his *Argosy* magazine. He sat with a frown on his face, letting his pipe get cold, while he rapped ta-da-da-*dum*, ta-da-da-*dum*, with his fingers on the arm of his rocking chair. He would shake his head suddenly and mutter, *I'll be damned*, and when I was sent to bed he was scratching his head violently and muttering, *You'd think I could remember*.

Mother had to shift the goose grease once again to make room for the pear honey, and again for the mincemeat and both times she threatened to throw it all out in the garbage but Father kept insisting that there was something very valuable you could do with it, if only he could remember what it was.

One night while he was sitting in the kitchen in his rocking chair, watching Mother do the dishes, he suddenly put *Flynn's Detective Magazine* face down on his knee, looked up with a bright and triumphant smile and said, "I just remembered what Ma used to do with the goose grease."

"Well, it's about time," Mother said.

"She used to rub it on our chests," Father said, "when we had a cold. Yes sir, I can remember how she would come into the bedroom at night with a pan of warm goose grease and an old soft rag and rub my chest."

"Oh," Mother said. "Would it help any?"

"Why, it's the best thing in the world for a cold," Father said. "Ma always said it was the best thing there was."

I don't know if my mother had actually been waiting for it or not, but it was only a few weeks later that my father came down with a terrible cold. Looking too sweet and gentle and maternal for words, my mother glided into the bedroom with a pan of warm goose grease and an old soft rag. She pulled back the covers and reached toward my father's chest.

"What're you doing?" he said. "What's that?"

"Why it's goose grease," Mother said. "You know, you said it was the best thing in the world for a cold I'm going to rub your chest with it."

Father jerked the covers up to his chin. "Go way," he said. "Take that stuff away."

Mother put her hand on the covers but she couldn't break Father's clutch. "Why, I've been saving it all this time," she said. "You *told* me to save it."

"But it stinks," Father said. "It smells terrible. Take it away."

Next day there was a great rattling of goose grease jars in the basement and Mother came struggling up triumphantly with a bushel basket full of them. She smiled all the way out to the alley where she dumped them. She walked a few steps back toward the house and then she turned and looked thoughtfully and sadly at the pile.

"You'd think it would be good for something," she said.

3. Father and the Burgundy Coat

Father could never understand anyone's being just naturally cheerful. In most people he really distrusted it but when it happened right in his own family, to one of his own children, he couldn't of course allow himself to be distrustful. He settled on being puzzled. How I could toddle around the house humming to myself and, upon being charged with it, say that I did not even know that I had been humming, he couldn't understand. If Father had felt good enough to hum he would have felt good enough to sing and if he felt good enough to sing, he felt good enough to sing *and dance.*

This actually did happen on rare occasions and he would stand on the square of bare floor space that separated the living and dining room carpets, leaning nonchalantly against one of the colonnades. He would give us a few program notes and then he would suddenly spring into a soft shoe dance or, spreading a handkerchief on the floor, he would show us how to do an intricate tap dance confined to the handkerchief's area. And to accompany himself he would sing:

> *Don't never marry an old man,*
> *For his chin is never dry.*

The night that I first tried on the burgundy coat, though, was definitely not one of Father's rare good nights. He was sitting behind his newspaper in his light oak rocking chair with the high-curved arms.

The burgundy coat had first belonged to my sister. She was fifteen that year and I was seven. It was not the same color that they call burgundy now; it was redder. My sister had fallen in love with the color and after about a week had fallen right out again. She was utterly miserable. My mother, who could remember very well what it was like to be fifteen because most of the time she still felt that way herself, understood perfectly well that my sister had not bought the coat to keep her warm.

"That's all right," she said to my sister. "You made a mistake, that's all. You can get another coat and it won't really be a waste because I can cut this one down and make it over for Rachel. She has to have a new coat this year anyhow."

That's how I got the burgundy coat. I loved it because it was red and mostly I loved it because it had been my sister's. Voltaire and his father didn't have a thing on me and the way I felt about my sister.

My mother had just finished the coat and was trying it on me to see if the buttons were placed right. I never wanted to take it off. I didn't care how hot it was in the house. I walked about the house wrapped in the enchantment of my sister's burgundy coat and I must have been humming again because my father stuck his pipe out from behind the newspaper and followed it with his face.

"How can you look so Goddamned cheerful in a second hand coat?" he said.

I stoked the lapels and gave him my most infuriating, dreamy smile. "Oh, but it's Erma's," I said, "it's Erma's coat."

"Well don't," Father said.

"Don't what?" I said.

"Don't look so cheerful," he yelled.

"Why not?" I said.

He bent the top of the newspaper over and smacked it with his fist. "It just isn't right," he said, "nobody ought to look cheerful in a second hand coat."

If I was a puzzle to Father, he was an enigma to me.

My sister played safe the next time. She got an ultra-conservative teal blue coat with a demure grey squirrel collar. I stuck to the burgundy. I loved burgundy with the love that passes all understanding, the love that endures.

The House in the Woods

When I used to go see Bruce in the hospital every day I never got anything else done at all. He was at Fort Belvoir in Virginia and I was staying with my sister in Bethesda, Maryland. Now if it ever were a clear day there, you could almost see Fort Belvoir from Bethesda, but to get there is the darnedest journey in the world. By the time that I made the round trip, I had been on ten buses, and in order to spend a few hours with Bruce each day I had to spend twelve hours away from the house. It was, need I add, June and July and part of August.

Well, at first it was horrible. Right in the middle of OCS Bruce had come out to see me one day, and my brother-in-law, who is a doctor, had said to him, "You better report to the hospital tomorrow. You are a funny color." It didn't show so much then, but in the hospital they wear purple bathrobes. He and several hundred others had the Army's jaundice and the purple bathrobes, being the complementary color, brought out the bright yellow (especially of the eyeballs) to an amazing degree. There was one Italian boy there with very dark hair and eyes who looked exactly like a Baltimore oriole.

It was all a mystery then. No one knew what caused it and, although they were not in pain, a couple of the men had died of it; so not knowing what was going to happen to them or how long (how long, oh Lord!) they would be kept in the hospital, they could only sit around and stare yellowly at one another. Then all the beds were moved closer together and another hundred men were brought in. Then a row was made down the middle and still another hundred came in.

There wasn't enough room to move around in; there was no quiet for sleeping. And there was no place to go except to the

Red Cross Waiting Room. So there we sat, wives and yellow husbands, two by two, packed in like sardines. The heat was simply awful. Now and then someone would say, "But, darling, I paid the insurance," or "Haven't we got *any* money in the savings account?" and then everybody would stop talking and get self-conscious.

Across from the hospital barracks there was a spacious, lovely, cool, green, wonderful woods.

But, verboten. Someone had discovered it first. Looking like Robin Hood's men in their purple robes, a group had gone into the woods and started a poker game. They had been found. From then on, the woods were forbidden. But we could not stand the crowded Red Cross Waiting Room any longer. We stood on one side of the road and looked longingly, longingly across at the forbidden woods.

"Do you see that tall tree standing by itself?" Bruce said. "Beside it is a path. Tomorrow when you come, go down that path until you are out of sight. I'll meet you there."

"But what about the rule?" I said.

"Yeah," he said. "What about it?"

Next day I snuck off the bus and ran to the big tree. Like an Indian, I padded down the path. There was Bruce. We were alone. It was wonderfully quiet and, for Virginia, it was cool. We walked down the path and suddenly we came to five pine trees in a circle making a lovely enclosure. It was a perfect room. The floor was all covered by pine needles. It was secret. It was quiet. It was private. It was ours.

At first, in our room made by the trees, I was too worried that someone would find us and it did not seem like home. Bruce brought out his blanket and we would sit on it in the quiet and, for a while we would really talk, but if a bird stirred or a twig snapped, I would jump. But I suppose if you began to steal and you stole something every day it would gradually come to be quite natural to you and so, as the days went by, I began to get calmer about being in the forbidden woods.

My sister's husband has been in the Navy for fifteen years and in this time my sister has planted fifteen gardens, one for every spring, but she has only seen two of these come up because her husband always got transferred. She has come to be very superstitious about morning-glories because it is always on the day when they blossom that the orders come. So I told Bruce that next time I would bring out morning-glory seeds and maybe then he would get to leave the hospital soon.

We had to clear a place at the base of each of the five trees because the pine needles were very deep and thick. We spent the whole afternoon digging in the dirt and putting the big seeds in; it was good we had them because Bruce had just found out that his blood tests showed he was still full of jaundice; he had next to the highest index in the whole group and he had begun to feel that it would never drop and that he would never get out of the hospital.

Next day I was late getting there and when I came to our room I found Bruce sitting in the midst of it, looking very tired and yellow and triumphant. He had outlined the boundaries indicated by the five trees with stones—beautiful, whitish, uniform stones about as big as the bottom of a glass coffee pot; they made the room ours, somehow, just as though they had been high walls. And this was the first day we laughed out loud.

Gradually the room came to be the *only* place where we were at ease. If we had to go into the great dining room to eat, we would hurry to get back to our own place, and we lived only for the hours that we spent together there. Now we were spoiled and if we had had to sit in the Red Cross Waiting Room as we had at first, it would have been intolerable. That was why I stared at the sky with such apprehension one day all the way out on the five buses because any fool could see that it was going to rain. In fact, as I ran down the path a fine, misty rain had already started. Not only was it going to rain but I had lost our room. I stood there in a panic, afraid I had taken the wrong path and that I was lost in the woods, when right close beside me I heard a voice saying, "What's the matter? Don't you know your own house?" and there was Bruce and *there* was *a house*, so wonderfully camouflaged I had never noticed it.

He, too, had seen the dark sky early in the morning and (how motivating is the dread of the Red Cross Waiting Room) he had been hard at work. Two sawhorses, stolen from the carpenter shop, were the framework. Over this, canvas. Over this, branches and little trees. You had to crawl in, but once in you could sit up, though you could not stand. It rained all around us. Well, to tell you the truth, that first day it rained in a little too, but later Bruce fixed it. Now we had a shelter. We had a secret hidden place with a *roof* on it.

A *roof* is a wonderful thing. As long as it was just a stone boundary around five trees, open to the sky, I simply accepted the room as a marvel. But as soon as the roof was on, I began to have ideas. I wanted a bookcase.

And one day, when I arrived in our secret house, there it was. It was quite a wonderful bookcase, made out of two boards supported by stones. And that evening before we went to dinner we walked further into the woods and we found a magnificent striped caterpillar, so we brought him home. He had not been eating when we found him, so we picked a few leaves and put him in a glass jar. And it was on that walk that we turned over all the big stones we found to see what was underneath, and for the first time I saw an ant colony. The eggs (well, later I found out they're not really eggs, but cocoons) would be directly under the stone all laid out in even rows. There would be hundreds of them, each about the size of the end of my little finger. Bruce transplanted a colony to a huge Army mayonnaise jar and this we put on the top of the bookcase. Sitting in our house we could watch for hours the huge red ants, just the color of the red earth of Virginia, running busily around doing their chores.

The morning-glories began to come up, the first pointed, folded leaves growing atop the white stems. So we fixed strings for them to climb on and we said we would never be there to see them, they would be climbing without us. But we were wrong. The morning-glory vines began to climb up the trees higher and higher and still Bruce was a bright yellow color and he thought he would become an old, old man there, would never get back to OCS, would never, never get out of those gray pajamas and that purple bathrobe. We had now an ash tray and a drinking mug and a jug for water. We had, too, some books. But, most important, we had a set of Faber water-color pencils and a sketchbook and Bruce was keeping a record for us of the caterpillar, the ants and of how the house was constructed.

One day I crawled into our house conscious of something sticking in my brain, like a song you cannot quite recall. So finally I poked my head out and crawled back onto the path where that fleeting question had first happened.

"What is it?" I thought. "What troubles me? Have I forgotten something? Is there something missing or. . . ."

There it was, a square corner in the woods. It was not right, somehow, not congruous, *and it had not been there yesterday.*

"What is that?" I said to Bruce. "Way up the path there? Something's funny about it."

So we crawled in our house and we lay on our bellies and stuck our heads out the door and we watched this strange thing, a straight line, a square-cornered plane, a thing that does not happen in the woods. After a while a man appeared, lugging a huge load of wild grapevines. He had discarded his purple bathrobe. He had discarded the top of his pajamas. In gray pajama pants and moccasins and rivers of sweat this man was building a house! So much had our house become mine, so much at home was I there, that I no longer thought of the Army at all and I was only delighted and flattered.

"Oh, Bruce," I said, "how nice. We have a neighbor."

"Oh, Lord," Bruce said. "*Now* they'll find us out for sure. We'll lose our house because of him. I could kill the guy!"

The man stood there, sweating and exhausted, but pretty soon he got rested and went off for another load. We knew where the wild grapevines were and we knew he would be gone for a long time, so went down to take a look.

"Oh, look," I said, "how neat it is. Oh, what a lovely house."

"The fool!" Bruce said. "The crazy fool. He's used tracer tape. They've blocked this out for some kind of practice. Now they'll go on a hunt for their tracer tape and when they find it, they'll find his house. Then they'll find ours. Then we'll be back in the Red Cross Waiting Room."

Yes, I had forgotten. This was the Army. The woods were forbidden. Our house was a transgression. Stealth was the essence of our home. But, oh, our neighbor had done a lovely job. For camouflage it was wrong. But for a *house*, it was fine.

Four trees, he had taken, and these were the corner posts. Higher than his head, he had built a closely woven lattice enclosing the four trees, except for the front door. But the lattice was made of stolen white Army tracer tape. In and out, in and out among the squares of the lattice he had woven and stuck and anchored twigs and leaves and branches and the wild grapevines. Everything neat, everything tidy, everything at right angles. Good for a house, but bad for stealth. And very dangerous for us, his neighbors.

We went back to our own house and I was still somehow thrilled with the discovery, this strong domestic urge cropping out so powerfully in a soldier, in a *sick* soldier, that he would heave the wild grapevines in the blistering sun, that he would sweat and suffer to make a house, a temporary house. They were all of them thin from the sickness. Bruce had lost twenty-five pounds and his ribs were heartbreaking to see or touch, so sharp they were.

But Bruce was not thrilled. He did not care what it proved about the soul of mankind. He was depressed and he hated our neighbor with a terrible hatred. And then we heard footsteps coming down the path. This had happened before, and we were not alarmed any more because our house (not neat, not tidy, not square-cornered) was so well camouflaged that several times when officers had stood holding conversations near by—so close we could have reached out and put our hands around their ankles—no one had ever noticed us. So we lay still, hugging the ground, hardly breathing, not looking at each other for fear I would giggle. The footsteps stopped. We saw the knees bend. A face came in our front door.

"Hello," it said.

"It's okay," Bruce told me. "It's only Private Farinucci."

"Come in," I said.

"Well," he hesitated. "No. I only wanted—Well, I have a house, too, you see."

"I know," I said. "We saw it."

"Would you come up?" he asked. "I want you should look at it and tell me."

So we crawled out and I looked at Bruce's face but, though he did not look very cordial, still he no longer looked very angry. Private Farinucci smiled. He stood there on the path and he was shy and he blushed and rubbed his hands together.

"I want you two should see it," he said, "because it was from you that I got the idea. I come out here one day alone and I stumbled on your house and—and so I owe it all to you that I thought of it at all."

I snuck a look at Bruce's face and he was softening a little. We walked along the path until we were at Private Farinucci's house and he paused there before the portico under the soft wild grape-vine leaves.

"You are a woman," he said to me. "I have watched you in the Red Cross Waiting Room. You can tell me if it is right—this house. If a woman would like it. If I should change it. My wife, you see. It is all a surprise. She does not know. Tomorrow she comes. Tomorrow is Sunday. I must have it done by then."

I looked at Bruce and I knew that he would never berate Private Farinucci about the stolen tracer tape. Now Farinucci was our neighbor. If he lost his house, we would lose ours with him. Even to keep from sitting in a crowded waiting room you cannot tell a man his house is no good.

"Oh, it is beautiful," I said. "She will love it. It is wonderful the work you have done on it. You can stand clear up in it. And the archway. It is lovely. She'll be pleased. What time is she coming?"

"Two o'clock," he said. "Sunday is her day off. She does not know. She thinks we will sit in the Red Cross Waiting Room like last Sunday. I will take her hand and lead her down the path and then . . . and then . . . we will stand here, by the door."

"And she will like it," I said. "She will like it fine."

"And there is nothing," he said, "nothing, as a woman, that you would change?"

"Nothing," I said. "It is fine. It is beautiful. There is nothing I would change."

We went back to our house and the tears were streaming down my face, that women can be loved so well and so profoundly and yet most of them do not know it.

"You like Farinucci's house," Bruce said. "You like it better than ours."

"Oh, no!" I said.

"You do," he said. "You like it because you can stand up straight in it, because it is square."

"But I'm not Mrs. Farinucci. I like the house you built."

"Those leaves will wilt," he said. "In two days they'll be all dry and withered."

"You're jealous," I said. "Oh, Bruce."

"You'll see," he said. "They'll wilt. So will the oak leaves. He'll have to replace them every two days."

I looked down at the blanket and the color is called olive drab.

Oh, drab, drab. Drab olive. That's the way I felt. Bruce began to laugh at me.

"Oh, I was only teasing you," he said. "We'll go and *call* on them tomorrow if you want to. Let's go eat." He gave me his handkerchief and I dried my eyes and blew my nose and we started down the path.

"But anyhow," Bruce said, "it isn't waterproof. You wait and see. One day it will rain and the Farinuccis will be sitting in the Red Cross Waiting Room, them and their square-cornered, tracer-tape house."

On Sunday, we left the Farinuccis to themselves but on Monday I just couldn't wait to hear what Mrs. Farinucci had said, so Bruce and I went calling. We walked down the path and there was Private Farinucci in his pajama pants and his rivers of sweat, carrying *boards*.

"Well?" I said. "Well? Did your wife like her house?"

"Oh," he said, "my wife, you know, she does not like the ants to crawl on her. So now" (he pointed in through the doorway), I am having to make a floor for her."

We looked inside and, sure enough, there was a real floor. New lumber, too, no doubt stolen from the carpenter shop. (How long, O Lord, could this go on? We had two sawhorses and a piece of canvas. Surely they would *notice* after a while.) It was all beautiful and even and raised off the *ground*. He had no tools. I have no idea how he did it.

"I don't know," he said. "Maybe I should make a chair for her to sit on. What do you think?"

Well, somehow I managed *not* to tell him what I thought. We started home.

"That woman!" I said. "Oh, how *dare* she be critical? All week he has sweated and worked, *a sick man*, to build that house and she does not like the ants. Oh, I could kill her. I could just kill her."

"But *he* doesn't mind," Bruce said. "Didn't you notice? She doesn't like the ants, so now he'll put in a floor. If she doesn't like the floor he'll make a chair."

"But of course he minds," I said. "No one who has worked as he has worked on a house could help minding having it criticized."

"No," Bruce said, "don't be so exercised. She isn't your wife. Don't you see, however your wife is, that's right. He knows her. He probably knew she would be critical. Maybe he would have been disappointed otherwise."

"No," I said. "I don't get it. I think she's horrible. I think she should be poisoned."

"If he's disappointed in anyone," Bruce said, "it would be in you because you have such low standards. To him it's this way:

You may be content to sit upon the
ground
With ants in your umbilicus,
But *his* wife,
His wife is fastidious."

I never will learn. There is no justice. There *is* no justice. Private Farinucci built the floor. Over the floor he spread clean newspapers, *all parallel*, all the edges even. In time, he enthroned that unfeeling wench upon a chair and he built it with the use of a huge stone (rivers and rivers of sweat) for though carpenters do not miss their horses, do not miss their canvas, do not miss their lumber, they always keep their hammers with them. On top of all this, Private Farinucci's index went down immediately and he got *out*. Bruce's index stayed forever high, high, high, and the morning-glories grew and grew—a bitter mockery. . . .

Every week we would have a fine day followed by a horrible day. The fine day was the day they took the index. Bruce would be sure that it would be low this time. In himself, he *felt* he had a low index. Sitting there in our house with his gaunt cheeks and his ribs hanging out like a xylophone, he would tell me how fine he felt and how tomorrow they would certainly let him go. Next day the reports would come out. Once Bruce's index slipped a few points, but he still had over a hundred to go and after it did drop this once it stayed right there.

Some did get out, though. Farinucci got out and lots of others. Bruce's class in OCS had long ago graduated and most of them had already gone overseas. One night we were walking down the endless wooden corridors to dinner and there, coming toward us, was a tall, handsome, *healthy*-looking lieutenant. Among all those purple bathrobes, his uniform shone like a strange and wondrous thing.

"Why, it's Taylor," Bruce said to me. "He's come back. And he must have graduated."

Now, after we had gained confidence about our house, in the morning hours before I got there or on the rare days when I could not go to the hospital, Bruce had begun to take a few of the patients out to our house, the ones he liked best or the ones who were suffering claustrophobia worst in the crowded wards. Taylor had been one of those who went with Bruce to our house. And now he was coming down the hall and when he saw Bruce his face lit up and it was quite obvious that it was Bruce he had come back to see.

"Where you been?" he said. "I been looking all over for you." Then he saw me and he said, "Oh, sure. I know where you were."

They exchanged news and records of Taylor's class and still Lieutenant Taylor seemed to have more to say. He stood on one foot and blushed and finally he said, "Gee, could I speak to you alone, Bruce?" So I went into the Red Cross ladies room and powdered my nose and shook the pine needles out of my hair. And finally outside the door I could see Bruce coming for me, and he was smiling.

"You know what he wanted?" he said. "He wants our house for tonight."

"Our house!"

And it seems that Taylor said to Bruce: "Gee, Bruce, I got a date with a nurse, a beautiful girl, and I'm crazy about her. In the time we've got there isn't a single beautiful place I could take her. All there is is bars with drunks hanging all over them or movies where you have to stand in line. Could I take her to your house where everything is so nice and quiet, where the morning-glories are?"

"You said yes?" I said.

"Of course I said yes," Bruce said. "Just imagine having something so fine that a *well* man wants to borrow it."

"Let's hurry and eat," I said, "and go home and clean house."

Bruce began to roar. "Oh," he said, "some day we'll be living in the middle of a wheat field and you'll say: 'Company's coming. I have to make all the blades face the same way.'"

"Yes, I know," I answered, "but you'll help me."

"Oh, sure," he said. "I'll help you."

So, as soon as we had finished eating, we ran back to our place. We shook the pine needles out of the blanket and smoothed it down. We dusted all the books and took the cigarette butts out and buried them and wiped the ash tray out with a paper napkin. We lined all our livestock up in a neat row. Then we gave the house our blessing and went quietly away. We never heard how they had fared, but I hoped that there in the quiet evening, among the morning-glories, with the bugle calls at intervals in the distance, the nurse felt as secure and happy as I always did.

One day when I went out, Bruce seemed unusually cheerful. He was restless and full of a kind of secret excitement and it was not the day before index day so I couldn't understand it. We laughed a lot that day and finally we decided to go over to the Red Cross and bring back some ginger ale. On the way we passed a pale, sandy, ineffectual-looking guy and Bruce greeted him with great courtesy and stopped to chat a while. Well, Bruce is always pleasant to people but you can't really say that he goes out of his way unless it is obvious that they are embarrassed or frightened, so I was puzzled.

"Who was that?" I asked when we got back to our house. "That man you spoke to so cordially?"

"Oh, him?" Bruce said. "Oh, that's So-and-so." (I have forgotten his name.)

"So-and-so?" I said. "But I thought he was the one you didn't like, the one who takes all the boys' money every pay day playing crooked poker."

"Well, I like him now," Bruce told me; "I'm in love with him now. Ah, there is a rare combination, my innocent wife. There is a man who does not want to get out of the hospital."

"What's good about that?" I asked. "All the guys you like are crazy to get out of the hospital."

"Yes, but this one," Bruce said, "*this* one has a low index. A man with a low index who does *not* want to get out. That's wonderful. That's rare."

"I don't get it," I answered. "Why should *you* be happy?"

"Baby," he said, "get ready to say goodby to your house. Baby, we're gonna be out of here. We're gonna be out of here soon."

"Oh, what are you going to do?" I said. "Oh, you'll never get away with it, Bruce. And even if you could, you shouldn't. If you're too sick to be out of the hospital, you're too sick to go back to OCS."

"Do you like to read books?" Bruce said. "I like to read books. Red books, green books, any color books. Also, I think it is a nice day. Do you think it is a nice day?"

"You idiot!" I said. "You can't forge records. You haven't any experience."

"Oh, that would be sinful. That would be *dishonest*," Bruce said. "I wouldn't forge a record."

"Well, what then?"

"Yellow books I like to read, too," Bruce said. "And books with pictures. Sometimes I like to lie on my back like this and read them, but sometimes I like to lie on my stomach like this and lean on my elbows."

A sick man and I hit him on the back of the head. Heaven help me, I hit him hard, I was that exasperated, and then. . . .

Paralyzed, we saw it coming.

A bulldozer!

It was headed straight for us. In its path little trees fell over and were crushed. Rocks were ground into the dust. We could see it right on us. We could see the driver's unconcerned face with its blank look (how could he *help* seeing us?).

There was no time to do anything. To crawl out the door was to be crushed that much sooner. The crashing of all the vegetation made so much noise he would never have heard us yell.

There was nothing to do.

We lay flat on the ground. I don't know if Bruce watched it or not but I was chewing the olive-drab blanket and a mouthful of ants with both eyes clamped shut and, it's funny, I didn't feel very scared about being crushed to death. I just thought: *Don't give the secret away. They mustn't know about our house. Stay hidden, stay hidden. Don't scream. You'll give it away.*

And then I felt Bruce's hand on my back. "He missed," he said. "It's okay. Hey, hey! Don't faint."

I rolled over on my back and I weighed a thousand pounds. I was covered with sweat and I was freezing to death.

"Praise heavens," Bruce said. "He never did see us. It just happened he didn't want to go that way. He turned."

Later we crawled halfway out the door and looked at the tracks. Just about ten inches from the door he had turned to the right, I have no idea why, and gone right by the corner of the house. We were exhausted. We slid back into the house and lay there looking up at the roof.

"It's good we're going to get out soon," Bruce said, "because this is just the beginning. About tomorrow they'll start to hunt for all the tracer tape that's supposed to be marking off the ground. Then they'll find Farinucci's house. And when they find his, they'll hunt for ours. They must be planning maneuvers here. It's time to get out."

I thought about So-and-so and his low index. And I was too tired to argue. I was just too tired.

Next day when I came to our house Bruce had a neatly tied package of our stuff ready for me to take home.

"You really think you're going to get out?" I asked.

"I know I'm going to get out," he said. "I have to. I'll rot here. My toes will fall off."

So every day when I left I would carry back our things to my sister's house: our drawing books and crayons, our games, even our livestock, fluttering and thumping, in all my pockets. As the days went by, our house got emptier and emptier.

Farinucci's house, left neglected, began to wither and the tracer tape showed through and Bruce kept telling me it was a no-good house. Ours stayed green as ever, though of course after the bulldozer, we never felt very safe in it.

Bruce was absolutely confident, now that our house was all cleaned out and looked bare. "Don't even come tomorrow," he said, "because I won't be here. I'll telephone you."

I knew that they had taken the blood samples again that day, and that tomorrow the index would be returned, but we had been through this so many times and each time the return had been a disappointment. I thought we would live in the woods of Fort Belvoir forever, to tell the truth.

"Well, *how* do you know, Bruce?" I demanded. "Why is it any different from the other times?"

"Well, I just know," he said. "Now *don't* come out tomorrow. I *won't* be here. You see," he said, "each man holds his own tube of blood until they come to collect them."

"Yes?" I said.

"Well," he answered. "Well, it's a wise blood that knows its own donor, that's all."

"So-and-so!" I said. "You're planning to trade tubes with So-and-so."

"The tense is wrong," Bruce told me, "but the idea is right. It's already done."

"Oh, but they'll notice!" I said. "Why, they'll notice that last week So-and-so had a low index and this week it's high then next week it will be low again if he doesn't have your blood."

"He cannot think that far," Bruce said, "and by that time I'll be out of here and, besides, he is a stinker anyway. On top of all that you made a mistake. You are going on the premise that the Army puts two and two together."

So maybe I was hearing the bugle calls for the last time from that angle. It is sad to say goodby to any house, even a hospital house, if you have done a lot of living there.

Across the dark Virginia woods the notes of Lights Out came clear and from a long way off, with the first coolness.

"Goodby house," I said "Goodby morning-glories. Goodby red dirt path." And so Bruce kissed me and he picked up old Olive Drab from the floor and then we crawled out on the path and walked away.

You Nominate Yours;
I'll Nominate Mine

I have read of the warm kindness shown to a young actress by Sarah Bernhardt and I have heard of how the Queen of England aided Elsa Maxwell when Elsa's curtsy went awry, but for sheer graciousness, I will match Lola Martin's Aunt Flossie against them any day.

Lola Martin and I were in the fifth grade together in Wichita, Kansas, at the time when the Harry Street School playground was suddenly transformed into a mass of hanging, suspended, flying figures, all imitating a woman who hung by her teeth from a wire stretched above Douglas Avenue. The act was part of the advance ballyhoo for the coming circus and anyone who had missed the actual performance had seen the pictures in the newspaper.

"You know that lady hangs by her teeth?" Lola asked me. "She's my aunt."

The doubt that someone I sat with in school every day could actually be related to such a creature must have shown on my face.

"She is," Lola said, "and she's coming to meet me after school. She's in our house right now."

"Where's she going to meet you, Lola? Will she be on the corner?"

"In the drugstore," Lola said.

"You mean the drugstore right there across the street?"

"Sure," Lola said. "She's gonna buy me a soda and she said I could bring somebody with me."

"And are you? Are you, Lola?"

"I'm gonna take you," Lola said.

Between afternoon recess and four o'clock I allowed myself to believe it and at 4:02 Lola and I entered the drugstore. There was no mistaking Lola's aunt who was already seated at a table. She wore make-up. She was altogether glamorous and, as we drew closer, she emanated perfume. It wasn't glycerin and rose water, either; it was real perfume.

"Sit down, kids," she said. "What'll you have?"

I said I'd have a strawberry soda and when it came I was very glad to give it my attention because I was having a terrible time *not* looking at Lola's aunt. I wanted to see her teeth. Everyone I knew wanted to see her teeth. Here I was with this golden opportunity and I was overcome with shyness. I knew it was impolite to stare and it was worse to make personal remarks about people's teeth, but it was unthinkable to do either to a lady who was standing treat.

I looked at the straw holder and at the Three Flowers face powder display and at the four-bladed fan on the ceiling, but somehow Aunt Flossie's face seemed to be everywhere. My soda went the wrong way in the straw and made a noise. I kept remembering Joe Brady had said during recess that her teeth had hooks grown on them and I realized that a button on my dress had got caught in the coils of the ice cream chair and that it would be necessary for me to lean backwards slightly in order to keep from ripping my dress.

Lola had produced the promised celebrity and the audience for it and apparently felt no further effort was required of her. Aunt Flossie didn't have anything to say, either. I supposed she had to rest her teeth and naturally couldn't be expected to talk. I certainly couldn't say anything because the effort to submit to the clamp of the ice cream chair on my dress button had set off a chain of events that required all my attention. The necessary shifting in position had caused the crotch of my white muslin combination to ride to a position which was putting a serious and familiar strain on the supporters which held up my long, cotton stockings. At any moment (a cough, a sneeze, even a deep breath could do it) one of the metal supporters would fly loose and hit the tile floor. Already I knew that when I had to bend over to retrieve it, if it should fly, I would either tear my dress or bring the chair down with me. There was a circle of water on the marble-topped table from the place where I had shifted my soda glass and I concentrated on this.

Lola's aunt reached over and touched my wrist lightly. "Kid," she said, "I know what you want. You want to see my teeth, don't you? Everybody does."

Now I had to do it. I had to lift my eyes from the puddle of water on the table top and let them climb slowly up the front of her dress, pausing at each button to think. If they did have hooks on them, what was the proper thing to say—what *nice* hooks, what *pretty* hooks? By the time I had reached her collar, I had decided on: what *interesting* hooks. Then I forced myself to lift my eyes right up the neck and over the chin and there was Aunt Flossie smiling at me with a mouthful of teeth just like anybody else's, only whiter.

"Why," I exhaled. "Why, they're *beautiful*."

Aunt Flossie laughed. Lola laughed. Even the three sisters on the Three Flowers display seemed to be laughing. Miraculously, my button came loose from the chair, my combination seemed to enlarge, my supporters held firm. Smoothly the soda traveled up the straw and bathed my parched mouth in cool sweetness. We had another all around. Then Lola said, "Go ahead, tell her, Aunt Floss. Tell her about that thing you hold in your mouth."

I think after this Aunt Flossie explained how she performed her aerial act, but I don't remember it. What I remember is sitting there with my clothes all loose, dying to be grown up, dying to have a chance to duplicate the performance that seemed more wonderful and difficult to me than hanging on a wire high above the Boston Store by my teeth.

I, too, would wear make-up and spike heels and my shining

black patent leather purse would likewise hold money for rounds and rounds of sodas. I would lean forward slightly, dishing out waves of ease and perfume. I would smile, showing my beautiful teeth, and lightly touch the wrist of some hot, sticky, squirming little girl with her crotch chafing, her buttons caught and her supporters threatening.

And I would say, "I know what you want, kid. . . ."

Final Clearance

"Hello. Oh, Evvie? Nice of you to call. Oh, I was just trying to get some of these sympathy notes acknowledged. You and Ed have been swell, but honestly, you don't need to worry about me. As a matter of fact, I'm going to turn in very soon. Yes, I have my sleeping pill and my glass of brandy and my book all laid out beside the bed. I'll call you tomorrow, Evvie.

"The notes? Well, I don't see how you could help, really. It isn't anything anyone else can do for you very well. Evvie, you'd be amazed. Do you know there are at least a dozen from people I never even heard of? There's one (I must show it to you) so very touching, in the most labored handwriting, from a man who owns a fruit store where Tom used to stop on his way home. Tom never even mentioned him and this Tony what's his name must have poured out all his troubles. . . .

"What? Yes, he was. The most wonderful. I can see him so clearly standing there chewing on an apple, giving this little man that vague smile he had and nodding his . . . nodding. . . . Evvie, I'm slopping over again. Sorry. Call you in the morning."

Madeline replaced the receiver carefully and pressed the back of her hand against her lips. This treacherous blubbering that sneaked upon her without warning served no purpose. It neither assuaged grief nor eased bitterness; it did nothing but choke up her mouth and bring on another spell of vomiting.

"I won't have it," she said aloud. She reached for a cigarette and finally got the match flame aligned with the end of it. Every handkerchief she owned was a small hard ball lying in the laundry hamper. Even all of Tom's were used up now. The thing was she had to wash tomorrow, absolutely. She got up from the desk and walked into the bathroom. Even the Kleenex was gone. This very afternoon she'd been in a drugstore and hadn't remembered. She blew her nose on a piece of toilet paper and missed the wastebasket when she tried to throw the paper into it. With a grotesque kind of patience she bent over slowly to pick up the toilet paper, holding on to the wash basin against her dizziness. When the phone rang again she straightened up slowly and limited herself to a deep sigh. Against the ringing she told herself to remember that somewhere she had left a cigarette burning.

"Hello? Hello? Oh, yes, Uncle George. Why, I'm all right. How are you?"

The cigarette, she saw, was safely here in the ash tray on the desk and she reached for it gratefully.

"That's very kind of you and Aunt Emily, but really I'd rather be here. I'm just more comfortable in my own place, you know. Oh *no.* Don't come. I mean, I wouldn't think of it. No, please. Why, you'd have to get the car out and everything and it's so late. Really, I'm all right. I'm fine. Certainly. I'm keeping busy, as you suggested."

That emergency frustrated, Madeline leaned back in her chair and discovered that, at a certain angle, it would produce a squeak. Now, by moving forward and back only a little, she could punctuate Uncle George's endless talk with little squeaks.

"Yes, I know you did, Uncle George *(squeak, squeak).* Tom was so fond of you both *(squeak).* Oh, you did? That's very kind of you. I'm so stupid about things like insurance *(squeak, squeak).* I know Tom would appreciate. . . ."

She sat through two more cigarettes saying yes, saying no, saying thank you and squeaking the chair. It sounded exactly like a pig and for a while she played with the picture of having turned the phone over to a small white pig. She could see Uncle George talk pompously on and on, Aunt Emily hovering nearby, while at the other end of the line the neat, white pig squeaked back appropriate responses.

Even this came to an end at last and now she sat at the desk, too worn out to tackle the notes of sympathy. The big thing was, did it really matter if she washed her teeth or not? If she just fell on the bed, for once, and didn't carry on, what would happen?

"What?" Tom had said after the Andersons' party. "You mean your pores aren't cleansed? You're going to leave them clogged up all night, choking, like it says in the ads?"

Suddenly a picture of her proper little mother came into Madeline's mind and filled her with such warmth and affection that she actually smiled. Relatives had swarmed over the house after her father's death so that her mother, in order to escape them for a moment, had walked into the bathroom while she was lying in a hot tub. Her mother had closed the door firmly and, with a sigh, had let her very proper widowhood slip from her. "If Cousin Norma asks me one more time what I'm going *to do now*, I'll spit in her eye," she said. The two of them had started giggling there in that house of death. Madeline had crawled out of the tub and put her arms around her little mother while they tried to stop the sound of their giggling lest they shock one of the relatives. She had started to shiver and they had seen then that her mother was all wet from the bath water.

Cutting as it did through so many years and such a distance the phone's ringing frightened her so that she knocked her elbow against the edge of the desk and, cradling the sharp pain of it, she let the phone ring twice again before she could answer. But that fright had been as nothing to the fear which, at the sound of the voice on the telephone, had her at once on her feet. She was electrified with fear and she put out one hand to hold onto the desk while, with the other, she carefully moved the receiver away from her ear and laid it upside down on the desk. Her knees simply fell away from her and she sank into the chair staring with horror at the receiver which went on calling her name: "Madeline, darling, are you there? Muffin, are you all right? Look, it's Tom. I was afraid to walk in on you without warning. Muffin, Muffin, please say something. . . ."

The first shock over, she quickly found a furious strength to pick up the receiver. "What kind of horrible joke is this?" she said. "Who would do such a thing? What kind of person. Who is it? I said. Tell me who it is."

The voice became quieter suddenly, almost a murmur, and Madeline closed her eyes and succumbed to it. Slowly the tears slid down her cheeks and at last she held the phone against her breast and bent over it in caress until it gave a clicking sound and then the dial tone began like some huge insect caught against a windowpane.

It would stop of course if she replaced it on the cradle and, what's more, her mouth was open and she was aware of it. That was a good sign if she was aware of it, surely? After all, it was perhaps a very common thing. Anybody might have such an experience in a state of shock. Perfectly understandable. Funny, she couldn't remember the doctor's number. Well, was that a crime?

She began to thumb through the pages of the address book. There it was. Now she must dial it carefully. Might as well get it right the first time. While she listened to the ringing, she tried to think what time it was and whether she couldn't wait until morning.

"Hello, hello," she said. "Is this the exchange? I'm trying to reach Doctor Morse. Sorry to disturb him but . . . but it's rather an emergency. What? Out? How long? Oh, I suppose so. Thirty minutes? All right. Yes, I'll give you the number."

It was printed right there before her. All she had to do was read it off.

But the footsteps. They couldn't be anyone else's. They couldn't.

She put down the phone and walked out of the room and down the hall and all the time she kept thinking: I'm not frightened at all, isn't that strange? And then, tentatively, as she heard the door open, she called, "Tom? Tom, is that you?"

At last he held her away from him and looked at her. "God, darling," he said, "you look awful. Did you really have a wretched time of it?"

"Well, naturally," she said. "What did you expect?"

"I don't know," he said. "I've been so busy filling out the questionnaires I guess I haven't thought."

"Questionnaires?"

"Yes. That reminds me, Muffin. What county was your mother born in?"

"Pasquotink. Why?"

"I couldn't remember," he said. "I've been beating my brains out trying to remember. How do you spell it?"

"Tom, stop. Wait a minute. What difference does it make how you spell Pasquotink?"

"Of course. You don't understand, do you, Muffin? Poor baby. Let's sit down. I've got quite a lot to explain."

It tore her heart the way he looked, as though somehow he had done something naughty, and she went to him and put her hand on his shoulder. "Darling," she said, "I . . . I don't mean to be indelicate or anything, but do the . . . I mean, can you still drink coffee . . . and all that?"

"Sure," he said. "You make some, huh?"

While she was in the kitchen she could hear him walking around the living room.

"Any fruit in the house?" he called out to her.

"On the coffee table," she said. "Your uncle George sent it."

"How is the reactionary old bastard? Giving you a bad time?"

She saw him reach for an apple and bite into it with great relish. This is silly, she thought. The dead don't eat apples.

"Your uncle is driving me mad," she said. "That insufferable bore calls me every morning and every night. He's disturbed about my being bitter."

"Are you bitter, Muffin?"

"Oh well, at first, you know. I guess I got pretty hysterical. He kept telling me about all the young men who had died of heart attacks and I blew a fuse and said you hadn't di——"

"Died, darling. You're not being indelicate. It's all right. You said I hadn't died of a heart attack. Yes?"

"I said you had been worried and tormented to death by their goddamned security system and . . . I don't know. I probably was going to blow up the State Department with a bomb, or something. I don't know what I said."

"Anyhow, it bothered Uncle George, I see. It's his government and the worst his government could be responsible for is an unfortunate misunderstanding, if it takes every last nephew he's got."

"You *are* the last nephew. He keeps telling me you're all *he* had."

"The water's boiling over, Muffin."

When she came back with the coffee and the cups on a tray, Tom was standing by the pile of sympathy notes.

"What's all this?" he said.

"Just letters, darling. You know. From people."

"About me?" He sat down and began to go through them in the most natural way. "Well, what do you know?" he said. "Old Tony."

"I haven't answered it yet. It's so touching. How does it happen you never mention him, Tom?"

"Tony? Didn't I ever tell you about Tony?"

"Tom, listen. I don't know if you ever told me about Tony or not. That's not what I want to hear about."

"Of course, Muffin. I'm sorry. It's just that I'm used to it already, you know, and . . . I keep forgetting."

"Tom," she said, *"please help me."*

Instantly he was beside her, holding her, stroking her hair.

"This doesn't happen to other people, does it, Tom? Why *us?*"

"It's because of the delay, Muffin."

"The delay?"

"The delay in my clearance. You know how poor my memory is. I couldn't remember where your mother was born and ———"

"Tom, are you telling me you have to be cleared for *death?*"

"Sure, Muffin. Look, let's sit down, huh? It's not really so hard to accept. Don't you remember when I was trying to get clearance before and every time I'd go to a new place to get a job we'd be so surprised that we had it to do all over again?"

"Yes, and I'd say, just the way I'm going to say right now: *but surely not here, too?*"

"That's right. We were always surprised. Well, it's just another step, you know. Just an extension of the same thing."

"Everything that comes in my mind to say, I've said before. I can remember not believing before. I can remember saying *but it's fantastic*, just like I want to say it now."

"I know exactly how you feel," he said. "That's exactly how it was with me."

"But, Tom. . . ."

"Yes, Muffin?"

"Tom, if you're not . . . well, if you aren't cleared for death, then you must be alive."

"Well, no, Muffin. Not exactly. You see, I'm in Uncertainty."

"You mean they've got a cold-storage room there, *too*?"

"Sort of. Yeah, come to think of it, it's quite a bit like that place in Connecticut. Remember? Guys sitting around waiting and beefing. Say, look here; it's almost light. I've got to get out of here. Write that name down for me, will you?"

"Why?"

"Why? So I won't forget it, that's why."

"I mean why do you have to get out? What does it matter if it's light or not?"

"Because I might be seen."

"Well, what if you were?"

"You don't understand. You get seen, you get questions started, and that puts you back to the beginning again, because it all goes in your file."

"What do you care?"

"Because I was already through the first six interviews before the IBM belched up that blank natal county, mother-in-law."

"Tom. *Listen to me.* What's the hurry? Why would you want to hurry it? It's death, isn't it, after all?"

He sat and looked at her for a long time. "I don't know, Muffin," he said. "I don't know why everybody there wants it, but they all seem to."

"All?" she said. "There are lots of them?"

"Sure. And they're all impatient. I don't know why. I never thought about it. They just want to get it over with, I guess. Some of them blow their tops and they get a phony notice all of a sudden. Man, they're so proud. They made it. They're really dead. Those sorry bastards. They give everybody the big handshake, see, and they go through this door and it just leads back to the beginning again. Pretty soon they show up at the first desk again, very quiet-type fellows all of a sudden."

She had never really been crafty before and she was surprised how easily it came to her. She began to chatter about Ed and Evvie and about the sympathy notes, and all the time she was moving about the room, pulling the cords on the venetian blinds, turning up the lights a little, silently flipping the night locks on the doors. Meanwhile, as she had hoped, Tom had got distracted by the sympathy notes.

"Hey," he said. "This one. Have you answered this one?"

"Which one, darling?"

"That sanctimonious hypocrite."

"Oh, him. No, I haven't."

"Good. This is one I want to answer myself. The opportunity of a ——"

She had known the phone would ring as soon as Uncle George had had breakfast. He was so firm about believing one should get up out of bed and get the day started. Keep busy, that was the way.

"Tom, dear," she said, "would you mind? I know that's Uncle George and I really can't."

"Sure, honey," he said absentmindedly. "I'll get it."

She stuffed a napkin in her mouth, knowing exactly how it would be.

"Hello? Uncle George? This is Tom. Hey, Uncle George? Are you there?"

She turned her head away and tried to control herself when Tom walked back in the room.

"Funny thing," he said. "Must have got cut off. Say, is the coffee still hot?"

"I'll make some fresh. Why, what happened?"

"There was a thud, sort of, and then—*My God, I forgot.*"

"Did you, dear?"

"This will cost me a thousand years in Uncertainty," he said.

"Well, was it worth it?" she asked.

He turned to her in anger and then it began to sneak out of him, that reluctant, devilish laugh that he had. Suddenly they were both of them howling like fools.

They had hold of something. Not that they knew what it was or understood it yet, but they were holding tight to it. They laughed until tears rolled down their cheeks and they fell down weakly on the couch and tumbled against one another like two rag dolls.

"God," Tom said. "I'm bushed. You know? I'm really beat."

"Of course you are, darling. Tell you what. Why don't you lie down right here for a little nap? I'll get a blanket for you."

When she came back he was lying on the couch and he mumbled sleepily while she took off his shoes. She put the blanket over him and hovered there a minute and then carefully tiptoed into the room where the telephone was. She had the tip of her tongue between her teeth while she eased the door shut so it would make no sound and then stealthily she dialed long distance.

"Mamma?" she said at last. "No, I'm all right. No I don't care what time it is in Connecticut. Listen, Mamma. Would you do something for me absolutely and no questions asked? Mamma, do you promise? Well, promise. All right. I knew I could count on you. No listen, Mamma. It's a matter of life and. . . . It's important, Mamma. Now listen. No matter who asks you, you understand. No matter how many times. You were *not* born in Pasquotink County. Have you got it straight?"

The Marbles

Though the boy was big for his age he somehow never managed to give an impression of strength. Though his head was large it was not powerful and though his hands were big they had a kind of softness about them. There was something soft and gentle about all of him and perhaps this was because of the roundness. His head was round and his large eyes were round and while he talked in his too gentle and apologetic voice, he constantly made in the air little circular gestures. It was easy to see under his hand the arched back of an imaginary cat, the furred, curved haunch of a rabbit.

We are accustomed to thinking of strength as being longer than it is wide, of being attenuated and pointed, having a beginning and a direction. We never think of strength as being round. We never say that power is spherical.

Perhaps it is because he was like this that he was so happy when they gave him the marbles on his ninth birthday. A marble is perfectly round. Even when it moves, it rolls. And the best one, the most perfect one, was all milky white as though in its great perfection and completeness it could not bear to limit itself to one color only but must embody them all the way that it embodies all directions, since it had none, the way that it could be everywhere since it had no beginning and no end place and no corners.

His father gave him the marbles. He brought them home when he came from work Saturday noon. His father did not have to work on Saturday afternoon and he and the boy played with the marbles on the living room rug, using the big center circle of red roses for the ring.

His mother came in the room, though, after a little while and asked his father to take her to the grocery store in the car and so he was left alone. He picked up all the marbles except the white one and put them back in their chamois bag. The white one he held in his hand. He could feel it evenly on the finger side and the palm side. He put the chamois bag in his pocket and went out of the house by the back door and through the yard to the alley and down the alley to the vacant lot.

Skinny and Mort were there playing marbles the way he knew they would be. He had always stood and watched them before, not having any marbles of his own and not really liking to touch other people's things. He put the perfect white marble in his left pocket and from his right he drew the chamois bag.

What ya got? Skinny said.

Marbles, he said.

Want to play? Skinny said.

Sure.

Hey, look, Mort said. Look at them moons. Where did you get em?

My dad gave em to me, he said. It's my birthday.

Well, come on, Mort said. Put in.

The boy shook the marbles out of the chamois bag into the circle in a kind of feverish haste because these were the boys they all talked about in school. These were the ones who played for keeps. Mort, especially, they all talked about. Mort did lots of other dangerous things, too. He went in the back room of the chili parlor, the room that the W.C.T.U. had sent the police to. Mort had a pair of pink girl's garters in his gym locker, too. The garters had a round circle of blue flower petals on them and in the center of the flower petals were little yellow stiff dots.

But he was not afraid of Mort today. He felt very confident because it was his birthday. How could anything happen to you on your birthday? He would get another chamois bag to hold the marbles he would win, but he would always keep them separate, the ones that were his and the ones he won.

Come on, Mort said. We ain't got all day. What you going to use for taw?

The others were standing there waiting on him the way people almost always had to wait on him but it did not bother him today. He drew a big circle in the air with his hand and smiled at them with a round smile. And then it came to him. He would, of course, use the white one. If he used any other one it would be an insult to the white one, as though he did not have faith in it, as though he did not believe in it.

He was lying on his own bed, on his back, with his hands behind his head, looking up at the ceiling when he heard his mother and father come in the house. His mother said, Now hang up your coat. Don't just throw it down.

And then he could hear his father going toward the hall closet. He knew that his father would be able to see into his room from the closet, but he did not have time to get outdoors and so he just lay there, staring up at the ceiling.

What's the matter? his father said. Don't you feel good?

I feel all right, he said.

Where's your marbles? his father said. Come on and I'll play you some more.

I lost em, he said.

Where?

I just lost em, he said.

Oh, you mean you lost em to some kid.

Yeah, he said. Mort won em.

All of em? Did you even lose your taw?

The boy opened his fist. The white marble rolled out of his hand onto the bed. His father picked it up.

Well, come on, his father said. That ain't nothing to feel bad about. We'll go get em back.

How? he said.

I'll get em back for you, his father said. I ain't so old but what I ought to be able to beat a ten year old kid playing marbles.

As they went down the back steps, his mother called, Where are you going? but his father didn't answer her and began to walk so fast that it was hard for the boy to keep up. His father was very excited and he kept telling him how easy it was going to be, but the boy could not work up any enthusiasm and he wished he could go back in his own room and lie on the bed. His father kept laughing and walking fast and saying, Why, hell. Why, hell.

The boy hoped that Skinny and Mort would be gone when they got to the lot but they weren't. He thought that maybe they would refuse to let his father play with them but Mort seemed to like his father right off. He couldn't understand it.

His father traded Mort an agate and five glassies for the white one. When his father had won the white one back the boy wanted him to stop, because if he could just have the white one, he wouldn't really mind about the others, but his father wouldn't stop.

This is more fun than I had in fifteen years, his father said.

Well, just give me the white one, then, he said, and you can go on playing with the others.

Hell, I can't give you that one, his father said, laughing and spinning it up in the air. That's my lucky one.

The boy stepped back a little then and relinquished the outcome to Fate. He quit holding on. When his father had won all his marbles he could hardly believe it and he turned around and started for home.

Where are you going? his father said.

Home, he said.

I can't leave now, his father said. I'm gonna clean these guys out. He hit Mort on the shoulder and Mort laughed and hit his father back. Mort hit his father and his father just laughed. He couldn't understand it.

Why, when I leave here, his father said, I'm gonna be bulging with marbles. I'm gonna have my hat full of marbles.

He knew how it would be then and he didn't want to see it. I got to go, he said. I got to go to the toilet.

A whole vacant lot, Mort said to his father, and he's got to go home to go to the can. Skinny and Mort and his father all laughed but he was started now. All he had to do was keep on going.

It was almost dusk before he heard his father's step coming up the alley, slow, the way he knew it would be, kicking the cinders out in front. He just barely had time to get out of the house and into the front yard. Standing by the hedge he could see his father at the garage door. His father reached down and brushed the dust off his trousers. He brushed hard and thoroughly and then he began slowly to walk toward the boy. The boy moved slowly over to the lilac bush. He pulled off some leaves and rubbed them between his hands and out of the corner of his eye he could see that his father was even with the maple tree. Then for a long time it was not as though they walked at all; it was as though they were two opposite spokes of a great wheel encompassing the whole yard.

It is a good thing that a wagon wheel is really dead. It is a good thing to know for sure, like they tell you, that there is nothing alive about a wagon wheel because suppose every time you saw one you had to stop and wonder if the spokes really wanted to catch up with one another. If one of them, say, had something to tell another one, how terrible it would be for you to know that and have to watch them following, pursuing, chasing with the distance between them always the same, no matter how the speed of the revolution changed.

That was the way it was with the boy and the man. The boy would be at the garage toying with the padlock on the door while his father was pressing the flat of his hand again and again into the even top of the hedge, saying: If it hadn't got dusk. If it hadn't got dusk. The boy would be leaning against the maple tree, kicking the toe of his shoe into the root when his father had got to the lilac bush. The hedge and the garage, the lilac bush and the maple tree, the hedge and the garage. And then his father stamped into the house and came out almost immediately with his hat on. He went walking toward town very fast. His mother came to the door and yelled: Where are you going? but his father did not answer and the boy went in and lay down on his bed again.

It was completely dark when his mother came in and clicked on the light and told him to come eat his dinner. His father was not home yet and he and his mother ate alone. His mother did not say much and when she brought in his cake she said he probably didn't want any candles on it because they ran down and got all over the icing and she left the electric lights on. But he knew she had the candles because he had seen them on the kitchen cabinet yesterday. They were small and pink and came out of a green flower and under the flower was a long sharp metal pin.

He asked his mother if she wanted him to help her do the dishes but she said no, it was his birthday. So he told her he was tired and he went back to bed. He thought that she would make him take a bath, but she didn't say anything about it and he thought probably that, too, was because it was his birthday.

In the night his father came into his room and fell down on the bed beside him. He kept moving over but his father kept taking more room and so, finally, he slipped out the other side and lay down on the floor. He reached under the bed and found his father's topcoat on the floor and this he pulled over to him for a pillow. His father had come into his room and fallen down on his bed several nights. In fact, that was almost the first thing he could remember about his father and it had only been the first time that it had frightened him.

He was only afraid of things when he did not know what was coming next and he could tell you exactly what would be coming next for twenty-four hours after his father fell on his bed.

In the morning very early his mother would get up and start the vacuum cleaner. After that he would get up and she would give him his breakfast and make him wash his hands twice and jerk at all his clothes and send him to Sunday School. When he came home the radio would be going and his father would be in the bathroom and they would have cornbread for dinner.

His mother was always real sweet at dinner. It was not sweet the way she was the time he had pneumonia or the time when his kitten died or the time when she spilled the hot water on his foot. It was sweet the way his teacher was when parents came to visit class and the way the girl was when the sixth grade gave their dramatic play. That's the way it was; it was just like his mother was giving a play.

Goddamn it, his father said at the table, we're not so poor we can't afford bread. Get me some bread. You know I hate cornbread.

Why, that's not cornbread, his mother said in her play sweet voice. That's cake. That's *marble* cake.

It was really like a lot of other days, but it stuck in his mind more than the others. It was a sharp place, a place with corners. And he could always remember it as he got older, the way his father looked and the sound of his mother's voice and the yellow cornbread against the white table cloth and the spring sunshine coming through the square holes of the window screen.

There were other things, too, to help him remember that day always. After that day he never liked cornbread. He always felt as though if he put a piece in his mouth it would turn out to be full of round glassy marbles, sliding off the sharp edges of his teeth, sliding before he knew it down into his throat. Nobody would know that it was marbles choking him and with the marbles in his throat he could not tell them and so they would not know in time to hold him up by his heels. And that was the day, too, that he didn't like his mother any more. And no matter how old he got, he always said that that was the worst birthday he ever had.

They're Laughing

Whenever I happen to be in a big city at Christmas time and see the department store windows, I always get to thinking of Mr. Wexler. I stand there among the Christmas shoppers marveling at the wonderfully animated displays—the sugar-plum fairies that really dance, the reindeer that really leap, the dwarfs that lift hammers in the air—and I think of Mr. Wexler and shake my head. Even after all these years I still haven't found any appropriate reaction. Torn between the memory of angry surprise and later laughter, I am still puzzled and I still wonder. He was so exasperating, Mr. Wexler was, and yet, as the living symbol of the fix we were all in, he was so pathetically ridiculous.

Mr. Wexler owned and ran the Wexler Janitor Supply and Equipment Company which was next door to the paint and decorating store where I worked with Toby and Grace during the depression in Kansas City. There were also an upholstering shop, a garage, a dancing school, Smitty's Restaurant and Louie's Fruit Market in the same block, along with several run-down rooming houses. Across the street there was a school and, since it had a janitor, perhaps this explains how Mr. Wexler was able to keep up some signs of having acquaintance with cash. I'm sure *he* didn't explain it this way. It was very clear from Mr. Wexler's manner that he attributed his differences to his own efforts and in many ways he hinted to the rest of us that if only we would walk briskly and wear white collars and make out invoices in triplicate and not call one another by our first names, the depression would simply go away. It was very clear from his manner when, at eight o'clock promptly each morning, he swept the sidewalk in front of his store right up to the property line on each side, that it was slovenliness that made the depression and that if people would only act as if business were good, it would *be* good. We felt pretty confident that the reason no one was buying paint was because they didn't have the money to pay for it and not because our sidewalk was dirty. All the other men in the block wore work clothes and saved their one good suit in case they had to go to a funeral. They were neat enough and combed their hair, but only Mr. Wexler parted his exactly in the middle.

There were many other things that were different about Mr. Wexler. He did not live in the back of his shop as all the others on the block did. There was, somewhere in the city, a Mrs. Wexler and a Wexler, Jr., and their well-fed, smiling countenances were on his desk in a silver frame, just as an executive's family should be. Mr. Wexler did not eat at Smitty's and never joined the neighborhood coffee klatch. He carried a briefcase and he never borrowed or loaned cigarettes. His conversation concerned business only and he said *my inventory* instead of *the stock* and *my invoices* and, also, *my secretary*. No one else had a secretary and all the rest of us just referred to one another by our first names. What little clerical work that any of us had to do was done by anyone who could operate a typewriter when the machine was not in hock. About the only retail business we did in the paint store was with desperate landladies who thought if they "brightened up" the bedroom they might be able to rent it and they usually planned to invest seventy-five cents in brightening-up material and do the labor themselves. We usually just handed the can of enamel or the three rolls of wallpaper to them and didn't burden them with a carbon copy of the history of this transaction unless they asked for it. If they paid for it with a dollar bill, there would often be a short delay while one of us went to the upholstering shop to borrow the quarter change. Then after the customer was gone, we would burst into a few lines of song and dance, get the dollar changed at Smitty's, repay the upholstering shop and split the seventy-five cents three ways.

The song and dance was an ever-growing musical comedy composed in parts on the spur of the moment and having, I remember, for its best number, a song called *Just Give Me Fish In The Bathroom*. For some reason there was no landlady who came to buy wallpaper for a solid year who did not pause over the wallpaper samples and say, as though she had just brilliantly created the idea, that she thought it would be very original to have fish in the bathroom. This was hell on whoever waited on her, of course, because the other two would begin to hum the musical melody in the background with special emphasis on the saltier lines. We had a song and dance for practically every line that a retail customer can say about wallpaper and some of them made very good rhymes. Before I left, I think the thing had grown to a hundred verses or so, but all I can remember now besides *Just Give Me Fish In The Bathroom*, are *You Don't Think It's Too Gaudy?*, *Dirty Colors Don't Show Dirt* and *Ivory Goes with Everything*. Of course we didn't do the dances except after hours, but there is a certain posture that all middle-aged retail customers have when trying to imagine how this would look on *their* walls that does lend itself well to the comic ballet.

Mr. Wexler would have been terribly shocked and probably also would My Secretary, although no one ever knew for sure what she would have been or even what she would have had for a name if we could have found it out. My Secretary wore a suit and a blouse with a white lace collar. Her hair was rigidly waved and her earrings and necklaces (very small and discreet ones) always matched. She arrived from some other part of the city on a street car, carried her lunch, and left promptly at five o'clock.

Mr. Wexler sold trisodium phosphate in bulk and we bought it from him, repackaged it and sold it under the name of Blotzo. It was over these transactions that we had our small contact with My Secretary. She made out our sales slip in triplicate and later sent us a statement of what we had bought and, later still, sent us a regular bill for what we owed. However, no money ever exchanged hands. Mr. Wexler seemed not to trust us with over five dollars and, whenever we reached this amount, he would send over My Secretary to buy five dollars' worth of paint solvent and lacquer thinner. She was always so nervous about being away from "the office" or fearing the telephone might ring in her absence that we never detained her.

Most business was done in this barter form in all the little neighborhood shops and, now that I look back on it from more prosperous days, I am amazed at how much business everybody did without ever any money changing hands. We ate at Smitty's because we were eating up (at twenty-five cents a meal) the $150 paint job we had done on the restaurant. And what made *this* possible was that the paint stock was on concession from the paint factory. I suppose the upholsterer's stock was on concession too, though before the day of reckoning ever came I was gone from there.

Anyhow, as Christmas came nearer that year, Toby and Grace and I began to hanker for a real Christmas dinner served on a white cloth. Somehow the thought of sitting on a stool at Smitty's counter for Christmas Day was not appealing, even though you got a doughnut free with every five-cent cup of coffee. We wanted a bird of some kind, not just a serving, but the whole bird intact on a plate to look at. Turkey, goose, duck or chicken, we didn't much care, but there was not a poultryman we knew who needed any paint or wallpaper or even any Blotzo in exchange. It looked as though we would have to have a little cash, at least five dollars cash, and Toby said he thought maybe painted Christmas trees might sell if he could work out a deal with Louie to sell Christmas trees at the fruit market. But it was just a little too early and everybody was afraid to buy a tree yet for fear the needles would all fall off before Christmas.

And then one day, when I arrived at the paint shop, Toby said, "Hey, get going. Get ideas. Wexler was in and he wants his window decorated for Christmas. I told him you'd do it. I told him you had a lot of experience."

"You do me another favor like that," I said, "I might break your neck. What's the matter he can't decorate his own window like everybody else?"

"No, no, you don't understand," Toby said. "He wants to *pay* to have it decorated."

"Cash?" I said.

"Five dollars cash," Toby said, "and we're even with him on the books so he can't just give us credit for it on the bill."

"Well," I said, "why didn't you say so?"

"He's going to be away all day," Toby said. "We'll have it done by the time he gets back and surprise him. Figure out what you want and I'll help you."

"If we get a duck," Grace said, "we'd have enough for chestnuts and maybe even a bottle of wine."

We left her drooling and went next door. My Secretary was very nervous because Mr. Wexler hadn't said what he wanted or if it would be all right to use his extension cord for window lights or if Mr. Wexler would like to have those bricks in his window for a fireplace, or if. . . .

"And then," I said to Toby, "we could use all his own stuff, you see. Make all the decorations out of his janitor supplies."

"Yeah," Toby said, "the old bastard would like that. Business. He's crazy about business. . . ." And then suddenly he remembered My Secretary was there in the background.

Grace shut up our shop and came over to help and we borrowed the sewing machine from the upholsterer to make the clothes. We were singing *Just Give Me Fish in the Bathroom* and having new ideas for the window every minute and we could practically taste the roast duck already. Well, really, we thought it was pretty ingenious. There was a big family dinner scene and around the table there were a big, black papa brush and a medium-sized, natural bristle mama brush and two small brush children. In a little rocker in a corner by the fireplace there was an old grandmother with a lovely, soft, white mophead and lavatory-stopper eyes. On the hearth, on a chamois-skin rug, there was a hound dog cut out of a rubber sponge and, beside him, a fuzzy, yellow sponge cat with green rubber-washer eyes.

By the time we had clothes made for all the mops and brushes and a white cloth on the table, Toby had a fan and a red light rigged up to make the red paper flames in the fireplace move. Then all we needed was a small-scale Christmas tree, so Grace went into the back room of her place to see if she didn't have some decorations left from the year before and Toby and I went down to Louie's Christmas tree lot to see if a branch had fallen off a big Christmas tree anywhere, which it just happened it had. Louie was so flabbergasted to hear that Wexler was willing to pay to have his window decorated that he let us have the big branch for nothing.

We got the window all done before Wexler got back and then we went out in the street to admire it. Toby went back in to put a bigger bulb in one of the lights and I began to have my doubts about the window.

"I don't know, Toby," I said, when he rejoined me on the sidewalk. "Maybe we got carried away."

"What you mean, carried away?" he said. "It looks swell."

"Well, a streetcar just stopped," I said, "and I noticed nobody was busting to get through the windows to see it better."

"Well, hell," he said, "to reach clear across the street, you'd have to have big stuff, moving."

"I know," I said. "I just got carried away. In the window, all those little details like the cat's eyes show up, but out here they're sort of lost."

"Listen," Toby said, "quit worrying. It's fine. You can't build a phosphorescent merry-go-round for five dollars. Besides, now I'm going to tell Wexler it's worth ten."

"I don't know," I said. "Probably just one big lighted Christmas tree would have looked better."

"It's a small window," he said. "Wexler'll be crazy about it. You'll see."

"Wexler crazy about anything I can't imagine," I said.

"Well, let's go in and figure out something for our window," Toby said.

So we took the sewing machine back to the upholstering shop, picked up Grace, and we all went into Smitty's for coffee and doughnuts. While we were in there, school let out and when we came out, the sidewalk was so full of kids we could hardly get by. They were all looking at Wexler's window and squealing and jumping up and down.

"Look, it's a toilet brush," one kid yelled, "the Papa."

Well, it was. I hadn't thought of it. It was just that it had black, stiff bristles and gave the papa kind of a dish-faced, pompous look and made his white collar seem so correct.

We ducked in our place and turned out the lights so we could watch the kids' faces. Some of them went home and got their parents and the crowd began to get bigger with people standing on tiptoe and jostling one another to get a better look. There were an awful lot of people in those days who had nothing better to do.

"How you feel now?" Toby said. "Better?"

"Maybe it's not as bad as I thought," I said, wondering if Wexler, seeing that crowd, really might not pay ten after all.

"Which you vote for," Grace said, "duck or goose?"

I was about to say duck when I saw Wexler pushing at the edge of the crowd, trying to get in his own front door. It couldn't have been better timed.

"Wexler's back," I said.

We watched while Wexler got pushed in the stomach by a kid and spoken to familiarly by a laughing parent. And still he hadn't seen the window.

"Quit sweating," Toby said. "He'll see it. The cash is practically in our hands. We'll give him time to get a good look."

"We ought to put on the lights and get busy," Grace said. "He'll walk in to pay us and catch us peeking."

So we got away from the window and turned on our lights and tried to act as though we made five dollars cash every day. After a while there was Wexler beating on our door because he was so flustered he couldn't maneuver the latch.

The part in his hair was gone. His necktie was over one shoulder. A button was off his vest. Never had anybody seen Mr. Wexler in such a state. His face was scarlet and he was out of breath.

"Get your stuff out of my window," he yelled. "Right now."

"Get it *out*"? Toby said. "Why, Mr. Wexler, what do you mean?"

"I mean just what I said. Out. Out. I want it all out before the store is closed. And I want those ragamuffins away from my business."

Now we could see he was in a real rage. I don't know that I have ever seen anyone so angry. "Why, Mr. Wexler," I said, "what's the matter? It's a fine advertisement. You don't have that many people notice your store in a whole year. What's the matter with the window?"

"What's the matter?" he yelled. "What's the *matter?*"

I thought he might explode. His eyes were glazed over with a strange shine and the vein at this temple began jumping out at me. Suddenly his lower lip trembled. "They're laughing," he said. He turned and pointed to the crowd outside. "Look at them. Laughing."

And then some of the glaze over his eyes turned to water and threatened to spill and sizzle on his hot, red cheeks. "They're laughing at my brushes."

"Well, I'll be a. . . ." Toby said. "What do you want people to do at Christmas time—cry?"

Mr. Wexler turned and walked to the door and fumbled with the latch. He braced himself for the crowd and turned back to Toby. "I want that window cleaned out," he said, "in thirty minutes. Nobody can make a laughing stock of my business."

"Clean it out yourself, you old. . . ." Toby yelled after him, but the door slammed and we could hear Mr. Wexler angrily ordering the crowd to "Go away! Go home! Go away!"

"Grace," Toby said, "be sure to send Wexler a bill for the decorating in the mail, first thing in the morning." Toby walked the length of the store. "The first time he leaves his place I'm going in and get five dollars' worth of TSP and, so help me, I'll keep five dollars ahead of him if I have to sell Blotzo from door to door."

"But you can't roast Blotzo for Christmas dinner, Toby," I said.

"Oh, don't feel bad, Kid," Toby said. "Maybe the painted Christmas trees'll go good this year. We'll think of something."

That Wexler. What can you do about a guy like that? In fifteen years I haven't been able to do anything but shake my head whenever I think of him. Sometimes I wonder if he tried to make the war go away, too, the way he tried to ignore the depression.

Oh, well, Merry Christmas, Mr. Wexler, wherever you are.

Mother of a Child

"You ought not to buy her a doll carriage, Tom," her mother said to her father. "You know she's too old now to play with dolls. None of the rest of the children in her grade at school do. She'll be over it all of a sudden one of these days. That's the way they do, you know. Seems like one day they wake up and they're tired of their dolls. You ought not to encourage her. She's played with them longer than most children now and the other children'll be making fun of her."

But her father had seen her face suffused with the rapture of anticipated possession and he knew what it was like to long for a thing so much and imagine yourself owning it until you couldn't believe that it wouldn't be the very end of every possible desire you could ever have.

It was a particular kind of doll cart she wanted, the kind with a long straight wooden tongue coming out from a single seat, so that the doll rode backward and faced you. As soon as she had got the idea of wanting one, a regular doll buggy seemed to have all kinds of disadvantages. In a doll buggy the child was lying down, for one thing, and therefore sleeping and if you wanted to look at it you had to stop wheeling and go around and peek under the hood. Oh, a carriage was much better, with the child sitting up laughing and looking right at you and you holding your arm straight out in front of you, tipping your wrist up and tipping it down to maneuver the curbings, and you talking to the child in the carriage about the things it would do when it grew up and how you would make it some new clothes.

This was the way she imagined it would be when she was standing alone in the back yard, cold in the early December dusk. She held her right arm straight in front of her and clasped the imaginary handle with her fingers and, holding her head high, she walked along with small steps, wriggling her hips slightly in what she thought was the manner of adults.

Her father, looking out the kitchen window, had seen her do this and, having seen, it was impossible for him not to get it for her. Besides, but this he did not tell her mother for it would have made her sad, this was his last child and, since she was thirteen now, this would surely be the last doll carriage of any design that he would ever buy. He was a man who felt that it was sad to do anything, even something you did not like doing, for the last time.

She had been sure that she would get the doll carriage all right, but it was a shock to her when she tried it out and found that it was really too small. The handle was so short that she had to stoop. She was terribly afraid that her father would notice that she had to lean over and she did not want to embarrass him. He had got the biggest one in the toy department, but, of course, he should not have gone to a toy department at all. All the time she had imagined having it she had been thinking about a real baby carriage and somehow it had not occurred to her before but that her father would have been thinking all the time about a real one, too.

She dressed the Teddy bear, the oldest of her two children, in a clean suit and took him out for a ride in the new carriage because, even if it was too small for her, it was still nearer to her dream than anything else she had.

But she didn't stay out very long because she had come to be ashamed for the first time that she still "played dolls." It was impossible to go out of doors and walk a block without meeting at least three other children, and, while they had been tolerant of her abnormal passion for maternity and her hanging onto her old things, the idea that she would ask for a *new* thing at her age with which to play dolls—that was legitimate excuse at last for their ridicule.

She felt quite miserable when she came home and put the new carriage in her room. Still, though, out of habit, she lifted the Teddy bear out carefully; not by his hands as other children lifted dolls who were not really children to them, pulling their poor shoulders out of joint, but with her right hand spread fanwise over his bottom and her left hand at his neck with the first two fingers behind his head.

She gave him his dinner of air and encouragement, changed his perfectly clean diaper, rocked him to sleep and put him to bed. With habitual care she saw that his arms were under the cover, but that his nose was not.

Then her mother called her and, with a quiet and resigned air, she went out and got the empty milk bottle off the back porch, dropped eleven cents in it for safe keeping and started to the dairy. It was quite dark now and, as she walked over the hard cold ground and listened to the tinkle of the eleven cents against the sides of the bottle, she quite suddenly had her idea.

"After today," she said, "I really can't carry my dolls around any more in front of anybody. Nobody else does it. Besides, today, for the first time, I know they're dolls. I tried to fool myself when I put Teddy to bed, but all the time I knew he wasn't really warm."

"Oh," she said, "if only I could have a real warm soft baby whose face would change sometimes, whose nose would really run, whose number of teeth would vary!"

She handed her bottle to the dairy man and answered his questions out of habit, but not for a second did she stop thinking about her problem. And then, on the way home, she hit upon the perfect compromise.

"I don't have to give it up at all," she said, "because I can imagine that I'm having a real baby. I know all about it and I can think it's growing inside of me because nobody else will be able to see it. And not to anybody will I tell a single thing about it."

She was marvelously happy and she decided that she would start having it that very night. When she was almost home she stopped and said, "Well, of course, it will have to have a father. It wouldn't be true if it didn't have a father. I'll just have to pick out somebody to imagine about." As soon as she had got the idea of having a father for it, she realized there was simply no choice. Nobody but Truman would do. Truman was the only boy in her class who was handsome as a man is handsome and not as a boy. He was a good foot taller than anybody else in the school and he was certainly the only boy there who would understand about such things. And, besides, he had black hair.

That was all there was to it. Without mentioning a word to anybody she had decided Truman was to be the imaginary father and so she started in right then to believe the baby.

She knew that it took nine months to have one, and that first night she counted it up and she thought that it was wonderful that it would be born the last of September when there would be soft fog in the air and bright colored leaves—and Christmas coming so soon after.

Not for one day of the nine months did she forget to think about it and it was wonderful to be walking down the street and knowing the secret and knowing that to other people she didn't look any different. It was wonderful, too, to know that September was only the beginning and that after she had had it it would really be hers. For years she could go on playing with it. Since nobody else would be able to see it, no one would laugh at her. She had never cared for variety much and most games she didn't like because they were so soon over and could so easily be interrupted—but this—this imaginary baby could go on forever. It need never stop at all or be put away.

She learned to walk softly by a trick of putting her feet down a little at a time, so that she could move along the street with no sound at all, letting her eyes get bigger and bigger. At school she refused to play any running games for fear she might fall and she learned to skirt puddles on the sidewalk so as not to get her feet wet—she, who had always willfully splashed through puddles for the joy of feeling the water flow over her toes. In crowds she held her arm bent in front of her belly to protect the child and sometimes in school she would look at the back of Truman's head and smile tenderly at what she was thinking, but she never told him. She never spoke to him at all.

Then, when she had come to walk quite slowly and to lower her eyelids when she smiled, it was September and her time had come.

She went to bed quite early, closing the door softly and lying big-eyed in the dark waiting for the pains. She knew that you had pains and that you were supposed to moan, because when she had been in the hospital having her tonsils out three years before she had heard all through the night the cries of the women in the maternity ward, but at the same time she knew that if she moaned her mother would come into her room and ask her what was the matter. The only alternative, then, was to be courageous even if it weren't quite correct.

There were several inaccuracies in the delivery, but she had the general idea. She had the pains spaced pretty well, with decreasing intervals between and she had them so bad that they drew up her knees, but she had them all in front. It did not occur to her to have any of them in back. Her baby was born perfectly clean and smiling, smelling of talcum powder.

This, then, this was to be the great moment she had waited nine months for. The nurse was to put the baby in her arms and she, so weary and heavy-eyed and gentle, was to look at it for a moment, smile a relaxed smile and go to sleep, knowing that tomorrow and every day after the baby was her secret to care for, to think about, to possess.

In the dark she saw the imaginary nurse very clearly, saw the boy baby. She held out her arms to the nurse to take the baby and. . . .

CRASH! Her skull split into a thousand pieces and all the atoms in the air bombarded each other with a terrible anger and she was left all alone floating above a crumbling world, because she knew with a cold, clear, dull certainty that her arms were empty and that you cannot will to imagine.

Toward morning she slept a little and when they called her she got right up and went to breakfast with her mother and her big sister just as though there hadn't been the difference of two worlds between yesterday and today. She looked at her mother and then at her big sister and thought, "From today on it will always be with me just as it is with them. I'll know every minute that there is a difference between a real thing and something you pretend."

She put her milk aside and asked for coffee and, although she had never had any before, there was something so casually factual in the way she asked for it that her sister poured her a cup without a word. She didn't much like it, but she drank it all anyway, and, getting up from the table, she carried her own dishes to the sink just as her sister and her mother did, because she was no longer a child to be picked up after.

She took her books and started to school and she realized that while, nine months before she could have carried a doll to school without any embarrassment, today she was apologetic about being seen with school books.

She was earlier than usual because she had got out of bed the first time they called her and so she did not meet the customary children on the way. Thus she was free to think about the night and draw conclusions.

"I'll bet," she said, "that as you get older it's often like that— that you wait for what you think is going to be the beginning of something and find out that the beginning is all there is."

In school she looked at Truman—looked at him hard—and all at once she saw why he was handsomer and taller than all the other boys. It was simply because he was older and he was older because he was stupid and had failed so many times.

Every once in a while during the day she would look at Truman's head and once she thought, "If you knew what you went through in my brain last night, you'd be tired today." It made her almost laugh out loud in school to think that Truman had been being an imaginary father every day for nine months and didn't even know it. But even as she laughed she marveled at her wisdom in not having told anybody, almost as though she had known in advance that it was a childish idea.

Going home from school she knew she had just one more thing to do and then it would all be finished and behind her.

All this time she had left her dolls and the new doll carriage conspicuously in her room and once in a while she had wheeled the carriage around in the house for her father's benefit because she didn't want him to feel that he had made a mistake in getting it for her.

When she got home, she spoke to her mother, put her books down on the table and went into her room. There she dressed the Teddy bear and the doll in clean clothes (the first they had had in months), set them together in the cart and carried them to the attic. She placed a newspaper like a tent over their heads to keep out the dust as long as possible and as she turned her back on them the stillness of all finished things descended upon her and upon her world.

She knew that she would never think again that they were real children and that, even if she held them, her arms would be as empty as they had been last night holding the imaginary baby that had somehow disappeared into the air, but still she left their heads uncovered so that they would not choke there alone in the dark night and she turned both their faces toward the center, so that at least they would have each other.

Guaranteed

The distance from Trenton to Lebanon is only two hundred and fifty miles, but it's a twelve hour journey by a slow train which closes in on Lebanon in gradually decreasing circles. I was going to meet my husband who had a day's leave from camp and he had chosen Lebanon because there weren't any soldiers there or any crowds or any noise. I think the way it was in his mind, there wouldn't be anything in Lebanon but us. Of course he had had two months to plan this day but, as you can imagine, he was not thinking of train schedules.

The bus was a little better than a train. By bus it is only six hours. First you take a big bus to the junction and from the junction a middle sized bus to Sedalia and from Sedalia a very small bus. Then for the last ten miles or so you connect up with the Super DeLuxe Special just for a kind of final send off.

The first bus let us off at the junction and I did not have to wait long for the middle-sized bus. The company had tried hard with this one. Somebody had told them, no doubt, that blue is a receding color and makes things look larger than they are, does in fact create space. But they had forgotten to tell them it is only light blue that does this. All blues do not. The one they picked did not. It was a bright, strong blue and they had painted everything with it: the ceiling, the walls, the floors. The result was that the ceiling was on your shoulders, the floor was up around your knees and the sides were smack against your ribs all the time.

But it was clean. Everybody realized the company had been trying. They realized it much better when we got to Sedalia and changed to the little bus which was no color at all and was not even clean.

I was sitting in the back seat, the one that goes clear across. On one side of me was a little German man in a blue denim shirt. He was very hot and red faced and friendly. He had all his lower teeth, but only two upper teeth and these two not together. It was very puzzling. I wondered how he had kept the lower teeth from knowing what the upper teeth were doing. These two upper teeth were exactly square. Well, it was not so much that they were squares as that they were cubes. These two cubes, sitting asymmetrically in that upper gum, moved up and down, up and down, as he talked. It was fascinating.

He was talking across me to the man on my other side. This man also wore a blue shirt. He carried a coat with him folded neatly, inside out, across his lap. Folded on top of this coat were his hands. He was much taller and thinner than the little German and I had to look up to see his face. When I did, I saw his eyes. They were the same russet color as the freckles. They were big and wide and open and very, very kind.

"I am sure glad to sed down," the little German said, "I can tell you."

"How long did you have to wait?" said the man with the russet eyes.

"Four hours. That is some wait."

"I had to wait four hours, too," said the other. "Where did you go?"

"Well, I tell you someding very funny," he said, laughing all over. "Such a silly ding. I thod to myself I would just see how beeg is this Sedalia, so I walk up town and . . . ," he began to chuckle, "and I god lost! I had to find a poleesman and ask him how to ged back to the station."

If you know Sedalia you know how funny this is. To Russet Eyes it was very funny indeed. "You did not take a good enough bead on the station," he said, "before you started out."

"I did not take ony," the little German said. "I never thod of getting lost in Sedalia."

"Well, now, I don't think I would get lost in Sedalia," said Russet Eyes, a little proudly. "Of course in St. Louis I might get lost, but not in Sedalia." Russet Eyes was a man who knew his manners and now he thought they had talked across me long enough. He looked at me. "You ever been to St. Louis?" he asked.

"Yes," I said.

"Well, I been to see my two daughters up there. One of them works in a cap factory. She makes twenty-seven dollars a week; the other works in a curtain factory. She only makes sixteen dollars a week." He paused at this and added, profoundly, "Curtains are not as good as caps."

"No," I said.

"I sure am tired," said Cube Teeth. He did not like us to be talking so much about St. Louis. He wanted to bring us back on his own ground.

"I am, too," said Russet Eyes. "I have been staying up late running around to shows." He laughed at this. He knew that anybody looking at him could tell how unusual it was for him to be staying up late running around to shows.

"What did you see?" I said.

"I went to the Wild West," he said. "It was sure good. It was about Wild Bill Hickock. I tell you it had everything in it."

"Did it have the time where he shoots a man by looking in the mirror?" I asked.

"Yes," he said. "That was there. It just had everything in it. They sure do have some good shows in St. Louis."

"Was the circus in St. Louis when you were there?" I said.

"I don't know, but I went to the zoo and that was as good. Why they had a man there got right in a cage with four lions, got right down on the floor and fed em raw meat. I tell you I'm just glad that's his job and not mine, that's all."

"Ya, I wouldn't like THAT," said the little German, "neither."

"Why," said Russet Eyes, "there was a lot of monkeys there, riding on ponies. The man would try to get them to turn somersaults. They wouldn't do it till he made the ponies go faster. When they were going just right, then the monkeys would do it (he made a quick circling motion with one freckled, gnarled hand) like that and land on the pony behind. It was wonderful how they did it."

"Ya," from the little German. He was trying very hard to get in the conversation, to get it steered back close to home. He did not much enjoy all this talk about St. Louis.

Russet Eyes leaned back against the seat. He looked straight ahead. "Why, you know," he said, "it would be pretty hard to teach humans to do that. And when you think those monkeys do it right every time. . . ."

Here I was just picking up knowledge right and left. Curtains are not as good as caps. It is harder to teach humans than monkeys. I was beginning to have a great fondness for Russet Eyes, for the way he would not let a piece of conversation go until he had seized the truth out of it and got it stated.

This was the pause that Cube Teeth had been waiting for. "You live at Neosho?" he asked me.

"No, I live in Trenton," I said.

Well, Trenton was as bad as St. Louis. He was going to get it on the home ground if it killed him. "But you're GOING to Neosho," he said. Well, we all knew now that *he* was going to Neosho. Russet Eyes, with a very deft hand, now took care of the little man. "*You're* going to Neosho," he said to him.

The little German beamed all over. The conversation was his now and it was almost with gratitude that he looked at Russet Eyes. "Yes," he said, "I live five miles from Neosho. I got *gut* neighbors. Why, while I was away I had a letter from my wife. She tell me how it was the boy's birthday. The neighbors come and bring in cakes and liddle presents. And I had some hay should be pitched. The neighbors they came in and pitched my hay for me." He looked out the window, "I got *gut* neighbors," he said.

Russet Eyes had given the little German his chance and now he was shedding his gentle politeness on me. "And where are you going?" he asked.

"To Lebanon," I said. "I'm going to meet my husband. He has a day's leave."

"Oh, he's in camp? I've got a boy in camp. He used to make five dollars a day before they took him. Last week I had a letter from Charlie. He said the lootenant asked him: Charlie, what would you think if you saw a battle ship right out there? Well, Charlie says this feller was pointing right out in the middle of a medder. Why, Charlie says, I'd think the ocean had gone dry. They ask me foolish questions, Charlie says, I can give foolish answers. That's Charlie for you. Cappin, lootenant, major—it's all the same to Charlie."

The little German was out of it again. He could not find any way to get back in that was at all relevant. "Say," he said to Russet Eyes, "I'll tell your wife you been sitting by a pretty girl." He began to chuckle again at the way he had got us both in this time with only one sentence.

"That you won't," said Russet Eyes, "for she's been dead twenty years."

"Oh," said the little German. "I am so sorry." He was overcome with sorrow that he had tried to joke in a friendly way about this serious thing. "That's too batt," he said. "Too batt."

"I am sorry, too," I said.

"It's all right," said Russet Eyes, absolving us both from any blame. "It's been twenty years."

"Well, I got a wife," said the little German, "but she's my second wife. You wouldn't think an old feller like me. . . . She's fifteen years younger than me."

Russet Eyes did not like this subject of wives much and so he turned back to me. "Well, now," he said, "I don't think these boys are ever going to have to fight."

"Don't you?" I asked.

"No," he said. "I think Hitler has bit off something this time. Roosia is big country. Roosia is different from what he's used to having. I think he's just about going to choke on Roosia."

"I hope you're right," I said.

He put one of his big freckled bumpy hands on mine and patted it. "Now don't you worry none," he said. "Don't you worry." He thought a while and took his hand back. "Why," he said, very profoundly, "Hitler. I never knowed him to tell the truth." He liked this; he said it over again. "No sir," he said, "I *never* knowed him to tell the truth." Just like my old friend Hitler, I never knew him to use a toothbrush. I never knew him to put sugar in his coffee. It was that intimate, that authoritative. But he did not think I was convinced. "You read," he said, "how one day they've taken a town. Then the next day you read how they're just ABOUT to take this same town. Why, he don't tell the truth."

Caps are better than curtains. Humans are harder to teach than monkeys. He never knew Hitler to tell the truth. The world was clear to Russet Eyes, simple and clear. I wished it were so to me. I took out a cigarette. I offered one to Russet Eyes. He took it very graciously, with dignity. I offered the package to the little German. He took one, too, but apologetically, as though he should have had cigarettes of his own. He was more apologetic than ever when he discovered he had no matches. Russet Eyes was a man of good manners. He did not smoke or eat or enjoy anything in front of others who were not smoking or eating or enjoying and so he took the package from my hand and offered it to the woman on his left, who had had no part in our conversation. The woman said "I don't smoke" and laughed. She was laughing because she thought Russet Eyes should have been able to tell from looking at her that she was not the sort of woman who smoked or who talked to strangers on buses. Russet Eyes was very sensitive to her laughter and he felt that it was in some way directed against me, who had given him a present. He wanted to make it up to me.

He lit his cigarette and inhaled deeply and appreciatively. Then he looked at the woman and said in a loud voice: "This is a VERY good cigarette." Then he looked at me kindly. "You know, I think this is the only thing a person should smoke."

"Do you?" I said.

"Yes," he said, and he looked at the woman again, "it is MUCH better for you than a pipe." He took another long drag. "Much better," he said.

Caps are better than curtains. It is harder to teach humans than monkeys. He never knew Hitler to tell the truth and cigarettes are better for you than a pipe. I was learning fast.

The little bus stopped then and we all piled out and waited at the side of the road in the heat for the Super DeLuxe Special. The little German sat up by the driver because he had to make still another change to get to Neosho and, after his experience in Sedalia, he was nervous about it. Russet Eyes folded his coat neatly and put it upon the luggage carrier. He sat by me. The Super DeLuxe Special was air conditioned and after the heat of the little bus it was a great change. I began to shiver.

"Are you cold?" asked Russet Eyes.

"I'm freezing to death," I said.

"I will get you my coat," he said and he stood up to reach into the luggage carrier for his coat. It was all very simple and natural. Young girls get cold. When they get cold you cover them up. Everybody knows that. But when he started to hand me the coat I saw the inside pocket. There was his billfold and his letter from Charlie and his eversharp pencil and it was all going through my mind how he was trusting me with those and he felt this and our naturalness was all gone.

He stood there in a little moment of hesitancy and you could tell how he was suddenly aware of all the other people on the Super DeLuxe and of how it was against the rules to stand up while the bus was moving. It was one of those moments when you are so aware of what you think is going through somebody else's mind that nothing will go through your own. He handed the coat to me, tentatively.

"And I guarantee *to you*," he said, "that it is not lousy."

"No, of course not," I said, and I took it and put it on. "It feels very good," I said. "Thank you." It was warm and of surprisingly good wool, very soft, much better than my own coat which I had forgotten at home. I should have known he was not the kind of man to buy a poor "piece of goods."

He had guaranteed it *to me*. I had had lots of things guaranteed before, but never so personally, never *to me*. It was very sweet and I was getting warm and had stopped shivering and very soon now I would be in Lebanon, meeting my husband. I looked out the window.

Russet Eyes jogged my elbow and pointed up at the little German sitting nervously on the edge of his seat. "You know," he said "I bet he's a GOOD old man." I looked out the window again and thought if the bus doesn't get there in two minutes I will bust a gut laughing because I guarantee TO YOU that if there was a week's difference in their ages, it was Russet Eyes who had the edge, but then I knew I was wrong, for it was not from laughing this gut was going to bust. It was from crying.

He sat there in his gentle russet eyed, good mannered dignity, more fortunate than all other men. He knew himself to be younger than all old men and warmer than all young girls. The shows he saw in St. Louis were more glamorous than the shows anybody else saw and I do not doubt but what the two daughters, the one of the caps and the one of the curtains, were more beautiful than other men's daughters. He was a man who could wait four hours for a bus without complaining and who could endure loneliness for twenty years without having to take a second wife. He was a man who told the truth where other men lied and he was less likely to get lost in St. Louis than other men were in Sedalia.

He knew a fundamental fact about everything, a fact he had discovered for himself. He knew that caps were better than curtains and humans were harder to teach than monkeys and Hitler did not tell the truth and a cigarette is better for you than a pipe and a young girl who is cold should be given a coat. And he knew a good man when he saw one.

He was sitting there so calmly in his wonderful sure knowledge and I did not think the bus could possibly get there soon enough, even if I looked out the window and thought about my husband, because I knew if I had asked him to he would have guaranteed *to me*, that the world is not lousy and time is not lousy and waiting is not lousy and death is not lousy. He would have guaranteed it to me and to all the other people on the bus, even to the not smoking woman, and he would have accepted the full responsibility for all of us, right up to the very last minute.

Groly Hale

Groly Hale was walking down the road, wearing a yellow shirt and a pair of blue pants that came half way between his knees and his ankles. His feet were bare and his ten toes were pointed straight in the air and all of them singing.

He laughed to see such sunlight ringing through the trees, and kicked a stream of dust up in the light. It went up brown and sifted down blue.

"If I'm ever going to be there, I'm there," said Groly Hale, and he looked on the other side of every tree.

"Peaches," he said. "I gotta have a peach. That's the first thing she said to me, the very first thing she said. There I was sittin' on the side of the bed, lookin' at the light slide over her face, and she opened her eyes and looked at me and said, Groly, I gotta have me a ripe peach."

"So far," he said. "So far I got this morning all to myself except for that turtle there."

And Groly began to sing.

"Oh, the turtle cannot get the peach,
The peaches are ahead.
The turtle's going back that way
Where my woman lies in bed
Waiting for a fine ripe peach
To put between her teeth
And feel the juice roll down
And dance within her throat."

Just as he began to sing he put his toes down first and then his heels, and he did his walking in the secret motions of a private dance.

He was proud of his feet, Groly was, the dancingest feet in Grundy County, and he took good care of them, too. Fine days he let them dangle and sweeten in the clear cold stream of Kennesaw Creek, and rainy days they rested (higher than his head) while he lay on his back in a redbank cave. But just before the harvest dance he polished them with fine white sand and muskrat oil.

His feet went rolling on and he followed his feet. His feet went straight and free. They'd never been in shoes.

Then he beat his fist on the gray unpainted door of the grocery store and rattled the knob with fury.

"Get up, old man, get up," he yelled. "I got to buy a peach, the biggest peach, the fattest peach, the one on the top of the pile."

The voice of Ferd, the grocery man, came over his head.

"God damn, my Christ, Groly Hale, leave me my door."

"Open it up then."

"Leave me dress, Groly, leave me dress."

"Hell, you can sell me a peach in your underwear."

Groly heard footsteps on the outside stairs and Ferd came down.

"Wake up," said Groly.

"Did you think I been asleep?"

Ferd unlocked the store with a long bright key and they went in to see the apples and the red berries and the peaches there in rising piles.

"You're up early, ain't you, Groly, for this day?"

"This day, the first day, the only day, I ain't been asleep, man, I ain't been asleep."

"Don't tell me," Ferd said, bending over and wheezing with laughter, "don't tell me the two of you been sittin' up all night waitin' for peaches and cream."

"We got cream," said Groly, and his face took light from the yellow mound. He was ready to lift a peach and run.

"Come on, old man, come on," said Groly Hale. He had his eye on one sitting in the morning sun.

Ferd pulled up his apron and smoothed his hands.

"Now how many might you need?"

"Just one, that's all. That's what she says to me. She says, Groly, I got to have me a ripe peach."

"A time like this," Ferd said, "you could have the store. Christ, man, when I hear you yellin' I thought she'd left you already."

"She ain't never gonna leave me now," Groly said. And he could see how she was when he left her, like the blade of a knife in a velvet box. "Not now. Not after I waited all them years."

"I thought for fair you was reachin' for a gold apple with the back of your hand, Groly. How come that special woman ever made up her mind to marry a willow pole fisherman like you?"

"It was my dancin' done it," Groly said, and smiled. "I coulda had her long ago, if she'd ever seen me dance."

Under the counter was a stack of sacks. Ferd reached down for a brown sack in which to roll a single peach. But Groly took the peach there waiting and backed out on his toes. And as he turned his hand went light and a dime leaped spinning in the air.

The dime went ringing on the counter and Groly's feet kept time.

Groly made no sound, though, going back. Now he didn't whistle nor jump nor shout.

He carried the peach.

He carried the peach in his two hands before him and he thought if he went quietly, if his feet were patient on the dust, that would keep her lying just the way she was.

There on the soft gray road Groly Hale made a dance, a dance of going home. And while the dew was still upon the maples and the ferns were matted down, he held the silk furred peach against his cheek and heard the solemn, proud thanksgiving of his heart.

My Mexican Wife

When Margaret and I first came to the desert to work in the date sheds, the only Spanish we knew we had learned in Los Angeles listening to the radio advertisements for Doctor Beauchamp's dentistry. In the early morning hours the ad was for the English speaking people and Mamma said, "Pass the candy to Madge, Harry," and Madge said, "No, thank you, Mother." "What?" Mother said, "on a diet again, Dear?" "No," Madge said, "I have a sensitive tooth." "Why, Madge!" Mamma said, "you didn't tell me. *Tomorrow*, you're going to Dr. Beauchamp." But after three o'clock in the afternoons the ad changed. Two men speaking in nasal voices, very tired nasal voices, came on. The tired nasal voices were to make you think they were Mexicans, though why I don't know for we never did hear any of them in the date sheds speak in nasal voices and it seemed to us that what they had to say they shot out like Cheerioats from a pop gun. Anyhow, this was the radio in Los Angeles and one of the men whined to the other: "Whadda matta, Ameego, don you *feel good?*" And the other one would whine back: "No, I god de *tood ache.*" Then his friend said he would certainly take him right down to the office of Dr. Beauchamp.

As I say, this was all the Spanish we knew when we came to work in the date sheds and in the evenings we would sit in the Desert Cafe wearing our jeans and old shirts and, the mark of all female date workers, our hair nets. Green with envy, we would listen to the Mexicans talking until we could hardly stand it any more and then I would say to Margaret: *Whaddy matta, Amigo, don you feel good?* And she would say: *No, I god de tood ache.* And then we would roar, this being at the time, the only joke we had.

While we were roaring, a quart of beer appeared on the table.

Each of us thought the other one had ordered it and that it was a very fine idea. As it got near to being empty, another appeared. Each of us felt guilty that the other had had the expense of two in a row and it was in this manner that we discovered, so far as we were concerned, it was coming out of the air.

"Say," I said to the waitress, "Where did this beer come from?"

She jerked her thumb over her shoulder. There in the corner stood a short Mexican man, older than most of the boys who worked at the plant, also more dapper in his dress than most. He wore a woolen waistcoat and an American felt hat. Well there he stood in the corner, holding (as, no doubt he had been holding it all through the two quarts) a glass of old flat beer in his hand. As soon as we looked he bowed, raised the glass in the air.

"Salud!" he said.

"Salud!" we said.

I then arose to invest a nickel in the juke box for number eighteen. I have forgotten the real name of number eighteen because later all the Mexicans came to call it (and we did, too) *Diez y Ocho*. No matter where they sang it, on the street or any place, they came for a joke to call it *Diez y Ocho*. It is a song they sing at work on the packing tables. They whistle it, too. It is all just like the first act of Carmen only dates come out instead of cigarettes.

So I put in my nickel for *Diez y Ocho* and when it was done, my friend of the Salud! advanced to the juke box. He invested a quarter, all . . . all for *Diez y Ocho*. In this he and I agree, one cannot have too much of a good thing. Each time that *Diez y Ocho* would begin again, I would smile at my friend and say, *Gracias, Señor*. It was hardly a surprise to anybody that soon another quart of beer appeared upon the table. I looked in the corner.

"Salud!"

"Salud, Amigo."

And it was time for *Diez y Ocho* again. Some time these lovely circles must stop if one arises at six in the morning. Also, the cafe closed.

Several days went by during which time Margaret and I were put on different shifts. I had learned to say *Ya me voy a la casa* and *Me duelen los pies* and *Yo estoy cansada* and *Yo estoy muy cansada*. Margaret had learned to say *Por favor no escupir en mi zapatos*. We had also learned to say *cerveza* and *más cerveza* and, when necessary, *no más cerveza*.

Sure enough, every evening I would sit down in the cafe and soon a quart of beer would appear on the table. I would look around in the corners of the room and either behind the slot machine or behind the ice box or behind the coat rack would be the same little man holding an old stale beer in his hand, ready to lift it.

"Salud!"

"Salud, Amigo!"

And then he would advance on the juke box and soon I would be hearing *Diez y Ocho* again.

"Gracias, Amigo."

"Sí, Señorita."

If any other Mexican started for the juke box, my friend would yell out in a fierce voice: *Diez y Ocho*!

This would go on every night and by now we had learned to say *Por favor siéntese*, so that José who had lived in El Paso for a while and Gilberto, who worked in the kitchen, and many of the younger boys would sit near us, but Salud! was always in the corner by the juke box or the slot machine or the coat rack, protecting *Diez y Ocho* and supplying the cerveza. One night it was too much. He advanced with determination upon the table, his fists doubled up in his intense concentration. He parted a couple of the lads who sat around the table, leaned in from the waist up and made me this speech. "Mees," he said. "You leeve all the time . . . en mi corazón . . . like a beautiful flower . . . (deep breath). I have . . . for you . . . in Mexico . . . una casa . . . if you . . . will have me for . . . for your wife."

"A good wife is just what I always wanted," I said to him. I am always saying this because the buttons are always off my shirts, and in any case, it didn't make any difference what I said since none of my memorized phrases were applicable.

My wife held one arm crooked at the elbow. "Vamoose?" he said. "Now?"

"No," I said. "Oh, no." Alas, he understood no English. What is more, the other boys could not understand his Spanish. He drew a map and showed me my house (if I would have him for my wife). It was almost to Guatemala. Damn, I thought, if I haven't drawn one with a southern accent. Just then another quart of beer appeared on the table.

"No más," I said.

"Sí," he said, "más."

"No más cerveza," I said, emphatically. "I'll be borracho."

"Muy bien," he said, nodding his head. "Si." Why not indeed?

"I'll bust," I said.

"No entiendo," he said.

Next day I had lunch in the cafe. Beside my lunch appeared a quart of cerveza. I looked around. Sure enough, there was my wife hiding behind the slot machine.

"No! No!" I said, "too early."

He came over to me and held out his arm. "Vamoose?" he said. "Now?" I guess he could have just walked out at any time. That was the most wonderful thing about them all, that they seemed never to have to get ready.

"No," I said.

Next morning I went to the cafe for breakfast. It was dark outside. I was having a short stack with bacon on the side. Beside the pancakes showed up a quart of beer. I looked in the corner. There stood my wife.

"No!" I yelled. "TOO EARLY."

That night he must have decided that I did not correctly understand his English for he came to the cafe with an interpreter. The beer again. Salud! again. *Diez y Ocho* on the juke box again. He and the interpreter came over to the table.

"Siéntese, por favor, my wife," I said.

He and the interpreter sat down. He made a speech to the interpreter. The interpreter said to me: "He says that you live all the time in his heart like a beautiful flower. He has for you a house in Mexico if you will be his wife."

I looked at my wife. "Mi esposo," I said, pointing to my wedding ring. Then I made a rattling noise and drew my hand across my throat and, in case it was not clear, I said to the interpreter: "Tell him my husband will slit his throat."

The interpreter did. My wife began to speak violently in explanation to the interpreter.

"He says," said the interpreter, "that that is all right. It would be worth it."

"Ah, but," I said, "mi esposo will slit MY throat. Achhh."

Again my wife spoke to the interpreter.

"He says," said the interpreter, "in that case, it would *not* be worth it."

He looked at me very intently, my wife did. He accepted it. I was not to live in the little house in Mexico that he had for me. It was decided. I was not to have him for my wife then. It would not be worth it. He smiled. He lifted his glass. He looked on me so tenderly.

"How you say," he asked, "how you say *Salud!* en inglés?"

"Mud in your eye," I said.

"No entiendo," he said.

The nearest I could get to mud was dirty. "Sucio en su ojo," I said.

"En inglés?" he said.

"Mud," I said.

"Mood," he said.

"In," I said.

"En," he said.

"Your," I said.

"Yoor," he said.

"Eye," I said.

"Eye?"

"Mud in your eye," I said and lifted my glass.

"Mud . . . ," he said, "in . . . your . . . eye?" He shrugged his shoulders and we drank to one another.

Next day he was in the grocery store. I think that he had decided to learn English rather than wait for me to learn Spanish and that he would buy whatever I bought and we could converse about it. I got a basket; he got a basket. I bought some dog food. He bought some dog food. I bought some grapefruit. He picked up a grapefruit.

"Drunka?" he said to me, I thought.

"No!" I said. "Too early."

He held the grapefruit up in his hand. "Drunka?" he insisted.

My God, I thought, if I won't drink a beer with him he's going to crown me with that grapefruit. This had really gone far enough. I stood there in the grocery store yelling at the top of my voice: "I don't care! It's TOO EARLY!"

I paid for my stuff and I left. Half way home I met the interpreter. It suddenly occurred to me. "Say," I said to him, "what's the word for grapefruit?"

"Toronja," he said.

Oh, my poor wife. I had treated him so badly. Even his friends no longer called him by name any more. Half of them called him "My Wife" and the other half call him "Diez y Ocho."

Surely now that I had been so stupid in the grocery store, he would never forgive me. With a heavy heart I went into the cafe that night. As I shut the door behind me, *Diez y Ocho* started on the juke box. My wife sat down by me. We had a lot to say to one another, but alas, no words to say it with. We finished the quart. Another appeared.

"No más cerveza," I said. "I will be grapefruit."

My wife sighed. He took a deep breath. "Mees," he said, "you leeve. . . ." Well, I knew it by heart now, too, so I joined him and we said in a duet, "Mees, you leeve all the time in my heart like a beautiful flower. I have for you a house in Mexico if you will have me for your wife." Then we said, "Mi esposo," and we made out we were slitting our throats. Then we lifted our glasses and said solemnly, "Mud . . . in . . . your . . . eye?"

It was, after all, the only communication that we could share.

We Are Each Other's Children

"And is that all?" the cashier asked. The young man stared at her, forgetting his new-bought package of cigarettes, his folder of matches, his change. Just for a second he had a glimpse in his mind of those railroad tracks you see in pictures and this time the two tracks met just before they dropped over the horizon. When they met they rang a bell and the bell brought him back to the cashier, the counter, the cigarettes, the matches and the change.

"Yes," he said, and he almost laughed. "Yes, that's all." He pulled up the collar of his coat and pulled down the brim of his hat and walked out into the rainy night.

"And is that all," he said to himself. "Baby, you've got my theme song. With every fifteen-cent package of cigarettes we give, absolutely free, the theme song of Thomas Andrieson."

And . . . is . . . that . . . all . . . and . . . is . . . that . . . all said his feet in their certain methodical tread upon the rain-wet street.

It seemed very strange to him and quite ironic that a cashier in a drugstore could give you back as a little piece of habit that was hers the thing you thought was your philosophy.

He had not always worded it so. When he was a little boy, this Thomas, standing on the curb watching a parade, he had said it differently. From the moment the first elephant appeared until the sound of the calliope began to diminish he had waited and waited and suddenly his aunt had touched his shoulder and said, "It's over now, Thomas."

"Oh, no!" he had said then (he was very small), "there's more." But of course there wasn't more because everybody knows that the calliope is the last thing, the very last, in a street parade.

When he was a little older (his aunt called it the difficult age) he changed the wording some. There was a new boy in his school named Alfred and one day Alfred said to him, "We'll be friends, huh, Tom?" and Thomas shook Alfred's hand and he was very happy. All that night he waited and waited and the next morning Alfred's voice was just the same as it had always been and his face was just the same and he didn't shake hands with Thomas again for he had his hands in his pockets just as he always did. This was when Thomas began to say about things "That can't be ALL." But, of course, everybody knows it can be all and Thomas in a few years was convinced of it, too.

But when he was older yet and quite past the "difficult age" (oh, quite, his aunt said) he got a job. He wanted very much to have a job and when he got it he did it very well. At eight o'clock in the morning he was told how much to do and just exactly that much he always had done by five o'clock. At six o'clock he ate dinner and at seven o'clock he went to a movie or saw a girl or read a book. At twelve o'clock he went to bed except, some nights, he got drunk. These nights he went to bed later, for it was mostly the nights he got drunk that he would think about eight o'clock, five o'clock, six o'clock, seven o'clock, twelve o'clock and that always made him say to himself in real amazement, "And is that all you get?"

He would think and think and that would keep him up quite late, but, really, it made no difference at all because the next morning he would begin work at eight o'clock and that *was* all he got, though there were lots of people unemployed who thought him very lucky because he kept right on getting it.

So it is possible to follow the development of Thomas Andrieson quite neatly and clearly by these little phrases of his up to the time when he had come to take "and is that all?" for his own motif and, being surprised to hear it given back to him from the cashier's lips, he had gone out into the rain and walked along the streets until he came to a smoky quiet bar with steam upon its windows. He went in and sat down and had a drink and then he had another and another and then he looked up into the mirror where there was a girl's face.

Thomas could not stop looking at the image of the girl's face because it had the answer written right on it—but written quietly, almost peacefully, in its certainty.

The drinks he had had crawled into his brain and, with a clear selectivity, dissolved out the old questions and crystallized them again in their order.

> *Oh, NO! There's more.*
> *That can't be all.*
> *And is that all you get?*
> *And is that all?*

There in the girl's face the answer was, but quietly, remember, almost peaceful in its certainty: *yes, that is all.*

Thomas Andrieson, held by the girl's face, Thomas, who had got through the difficult age—through several difficult ages—quite to everybody's satisfaction, Thomas knew there was no denying the answer in the face. This was the first time he had known it for sure and the knowledge filled him with a cold accumulative fury so that he stood up and, in a measured tread, walked behind the bar, knocked the bartender neatly upon the floor and, lifting the bottles one at a time, smashed them, in three-quarter rhythm, upon the solid surfaces within his range.

Everybody left in a hurry except, of course, the bartender who was out on the floor, neatly, and the girl who had for some time had an interest in violence.

Thomas, who was used to thinking of eight o'clock, five o'clock, six o'clock, was a very orderly person and so he smashed all the whiskey bottles first and then all the gin bottles one after the other and then he started in on the wine.

The girl with the quiet face joined Thomas behind the bar

after a while and said to him, "If you'll give me one of those bottles I'll help you."

"Well, hell," he said, and this was very unusual, for Thomas had never been a swearing man, "if I have somebody to help me I don't need to throw bottles."

"Can you run?" the girl asked.

They ran. They ran for blocks and blocks and fortunately because of the rain it was very dark and the few people who were out naturally thought they were running for shelter.

When they were quite out of breath they stopped and sat on a church step which, being the top one and sheltered, was relatively dry.

"To me," said Thomas, "your name will always be Ursula. I always wanted to know a girl named Ursula, so don't tell me any different."

Well, of course, that was not really her name, but this did not happen to be one of the few things the girl thought important so she shook the water out of her hair and dried her hands on her skirt and watched the rain under the street lamp.

The next night Thomas stood on the same church steps where Ursula had promised to meet him, but she didn't come. He waited an hour before he gave it up and all the way home he kept saying that, really, he wasn't surprised and that he hadn't thought she'd come, not really, but the next night he couldn't help just walking by the place. It wasn't much more than a block out of his way, anyhow, and a little exercise didn't do anybody any harm.

She was there sitting on the church step with her arms clasped around her knees.

"Well," said Thomas, standing on the sidewalk, "I didn't expect to see you here."

"I'm sorry I couldn't make it last night," she said. "I kept hoping maybe you'd come tonight."

He put one foot on the first step, casually, and, still standing, said, "I just happened to be walking by. I go past here quite often. As a matter of fact, I like to walk."

"I don't," she said.

He sat down on the step below her. "You don't?"

"No," she said, "I get tired."

Thomas put the palms of his hands on the step behind him and pulled himself up so that he was sitting beside the girl. "Well, then," he said, "I guess you don't mind sitting here a while?"

"No," she said, "I don't mind at all."

"Funny thing," he said. "I passed your place last night."

"Were you whistling?"

"Yeah, sure," he said. "Well, I mean, I generally do whistle, you know, when I walk . . . I suppose I was whistling."

"Petrouchka," she said.

"Gee, do you like Petrouchka? I've got a swell recording of it."

"Columbia?"

"Yeah. Say, this is wonderful. You didn't tell me you had a Victrola."

"I don't," she said.

"Oh. I was going to lend you some records. That's too bad."

"I sold it," she said.

"What kind was it?"

"Oh, it was just a portable; it was old, anyhow."

"But you've still got your records?"

"No, I sold them, too."

"Well," he said, "to think of your hearing me whistle Petrouchka. . . . Say, how could you have been there? There wasn't any light when I went by. Didn't you say you lived in the front room upstairs?"

"The light globe burned out," she said.

"Well, what'd you do? Just sit there in the dark all evening?"

"I went to bed."

Then he remembered that it was last night she'd been going to meet him and all that time he'd been standing there waiting she'd been lying in bed. Anybody ought to know better than to believe a story like that. All that talk about Petrouchka had made him forget last night for a little while.

"Well," he said, standing up and stretching, "well, I guess I'd better be going . . . I. . . ."

"Oh, Thomas," she said, "it was the last light bulb I had. I mean I wasn't even through dressing and it went out. I couldn't borrow one because nobody in that house ever buys but one at a time and there I was not even dressed yet and the thing went out on me and I felt around in the dark and finally got dressed and just as I was starting to go I caught my heel in the hole in the rug and fell down. I was trying to hurry because I didn't know what time it was for sure and, well. . . . Oh, Thomas, it was my last pair of stockings and I busted the whole knee right out of one and somebody was in the bathroom taking a bath so I couldn't go in there to mend it and. . . . Oh, I don't know, I just started to cry and I lay down on the bed. I was tired I guess because I went to sleep and when I woke up it was too late to come and I had a headache and I was so cold. . . ."

Thomas was back on the step again, sitting close to the girl.

"Here," he said, "here's my handkerchief. Well, Ursula, don't cry about it now. I mean, if you cried about it last night that was enough."

"Thanks," she said. "I'm not crying about the light globe; I'm not crying about anything, really. I been sitting here so long. I kept thinking you wouldn't come."

He looked away while she blew her nose and dried her eyes and tried to stop crying. It was certainly easy for people to surprise you, he thought. Now, the way she looked, that first night, with that quiet face, you never would have thought she'd be one to go to pieces over a light globe. Well, he guessed, the way he looked, you'd never think he'd be one to throw bottles all over a bar, either.

He thought again of the bar, the mirror and the reflection of Ursula's face. There was something incongruous in that reflection tugging at his brain, demanding to be recognized.

That's it, he thought, there wasn't any glass below the face: just space. She didn't have any drink. Sitting at a bar with no drink before her, going to pieces over the "last" light bulb, the "last" pair of stockings—no wonder she was crying.

She handed him back his handkerchief. "Thanks," she said.

"Sure."

"Have you got a cigarette?"

He fished one out for her and one for himself and held a match. They followed the two lines of smoke with their eyes, each to his own, and finally Thomas said without looking at her yet, "Did you ever notice a light bulb just before it goes out— how it'll sing for a while first?"

"Uh huh," she said, "but they don't always do it."

When they had finished their cigarettes Thomas stood and stretched.

"Come on," he said, "let's go."

"Where?"

"Well," he said, "*I* haven't had any dinner yet."

She took his hand to help herself up. "Oh, wait a minute," she said.

"Oh, come on, Ursula. I'm starved."

"Well, so am I," she said, "but my feet are asleep."

At five o'clock Thomas put his desk in order, went to the men's room and washed not only his hands but his face as well, walked down a flight of stairs, punched the time clock and went to meet Ursula.

"Well," he said, "you certainly look great. What happened to you?" "Say," she said, "you brought me luck. You know that restaurant we went to the first night? I went in there today and they gave me a job!"

"That's swell, Ursula. What doing?"

"Cashier."

"When do you start?"

"Tomorrow night."

"Tomorrow *night*?"

"Uh huh. They've got a day cashier, already, but the night one's leaving tomorrow."

"What hours?"

"Five to twelve."

"Five? But, Ursula, I don't get off till five."

"I know, but, Thomas, I couldn't let it go. I mean I've been out of work so long."

"Sure," he said. "You had to take it, of course."

"Just think," she said. "After the first week I can move out of that room. I've looked at the hole in that rug till I thought sometimes I never would have a job again."

"Yeah," he said. "You could get a better room. That'll be fine."

"You know, Thomas, I think I could even get an apartment, maybe, because I get my meals at the restaurant."

"That's swell," he said, "but gee, it's going to seem funny not being able to spend evenings with you any more."

"Twelve o'clock's not really so awful late, Thomas. I mean we could see each other after I get off work for a little while, couldn't we?"

"Sure," he said, "that's not so late."

"And, Thomas," she said, "there's Sunday."

"Sure," he said, "that's right. There's Sunday."

And now it was Ursula who slapped pennies and nickels and dimes down smartly on the counter and smiled up at the customers while she asked, "And is that all?"

Thomas called for Ursula at midnight at the restaurant and they walked through the silent streets to the church. They climbed to the top step to be away from the street light and sank wearily onto the stone.

"Tired?" Thomas asked and yawned.

"Just a little," she said. "It doesn't seem like it's only been two months since we ran here the first night, does it?"

Thomas yawned again.

"You shouldn't come every night, Thomas. It's two or three o'clock before you get home, and you have to be up at seven. That's not enough sleep."

"I know it," he said. "I mean to stay home every night, but somehow I'm always in front of the restaurant at midnight." He yawned again and shook his head.

"Oh, Thomas," she said, "you're so tired."

"Oh, hell," he said, "this is no way to live: spending an hour or so together every night walking around the streets and sitting on church steps. We can't even go to a movie; they're all closed by this time."

"We could go on Sunday, Thomas."

"Who wants to go to a movie in the daytime?" he asked, rubbing his eyes. "There's something indecent about it."

"Come on, Thomas. We'd better go; you're just dead."

"Wait till I smoke a cigarette," he said. "Maybe it'll wake me up. I was so sleepy I didn't even kiss you."

"Yes, you did."

"I'm sleepier than I thought," he said. "Anyhow, I love you, Ursula, even if you do work the craziest hours of anybody in the world."

"And I love you," she said, "even if you do throw bottles in bars."

Suddenly they were no longer tired and they sat very still, conscious of being two people awake and together in the midst of a sleeping city, and finally, Thomas said, "Well, Ursula, are you coming to live with me or shall I come to live with you?"

"Which place is better?" she asked.

"I've got a Victrola," he said.

"You can move that," she said, "but I've got a kitchen now with two windows."

"You'd love my west window, Ursula. You can see the river."

"And I've got a nice bathtub," she said. "Private."

"Is the water hot?" he asked, for he began to think that perhaps it might be fun to move, to have everything changed and new.

"Well, sometimes it isn't," she said, "but of course you can always heat it." Thinking of hot water that was not always hot she began to think, too, that it might be nice to move.

"To tell you the truth, Ursula, the furnace at my place is never quite up to January. Other months it's pretty good, but. . . ."

"I know," she said. "My roof leaks."

"And I forgot to tell you. I've got neighbors."

"Tap dancers or drunks?"

"I don't know," he said, "but they fight."

"Oh, well," she said, "I've got mice."

Thomas jumped up. "I know what we'll do."

"Yes, of course," she said, standing up, too. "We'll get a new place."

"With thick walls," he said, as he stepped down the first step.

"And hot water," she said, stepping beside him.

"And big rooms," he said on the next step.

As they swung into the street they both said together, "And a lamp you can turn off in bed."

When they found the place it needed a great deal of fixing, but at least they were spared audible neighbors and mice. They were on the ground floor so the roof was no longer their problem and they moved the Victrola. Since, by their union, they had twice the usual number of blankets they could allow the furnace a certain amount of temperament. Thomas was pleased to discover that Ursula cooked rather well and she, that he not only would pick up his own clothes but sometimes hers too.

In a couple of months they had their own vocabulary and already a little history that was theirs together and, while they hadn't forgotten that *yes, this is all*, they began to think that it just might be enough.

Mostly at nights they fell asleep together upon the very good mattress which they had bought on installments and which was now seven-tenths paid for and hardly worn at all, but of course that couldn't always happen and sometimes one of them would leave the other lying awake and alone in the dark.

This night it was Ursula who went off to sleep and left Thomas looking at the thick unrelieved darkness and lying very still and being terribly aware that the two inches between them might just as well be two miles.

He told himself that they couldn't always go to sleep at the same time and that it might as easily have been Ursula who was left awake alone and probably it had been lots of times. He reminded himself that he felt perfectly well and that losing a little sleep was of no importance, but it did no good and after awhile he thought of Jesus. This had happened to Thomas many times—this lying alone in the dark—and, always, he thought of Jesus. He tried not to, but he couldn't help it, even though he knew it would make him very sad.

To Thomas, the tragedy of Jesus was not that he was crucified, but that Peter couldn't stay awake just those few hours and went to sleep leaving Jesus all alone on the mountain out of doors and maybe the wind was blowing.

Thomas began to resent Ursula's sleep and even though he knew the morning would surely come with breakfast and hot coffee and another day he could not help but feel deserted and sad that all this could be happening to him and she could be maybe dreaming of something all her own, miles and miles away.

He was tempted to squirm and pull the covers and maybe groan a little so that Ursula would come back and be with him. He knew, though, that if he did Ursula would say, "What's the matter, Thomas?" and he would answer, "Oh, nothing." Then Ursula would ask "Can't you sleep?" and he would say "No" and she would say "Have you got a headache?" and he would say "No."

But they had learned a few things in these months and, even though he was tempted, he did not squirm and waken her, but he just lay still for a while and pretty soon he began to think of Ursula instead of Jesus and he remembered the first night he had ever seen her and how she had helped him to break the bottles and he remembered how quiet her face had been and he knew that he didn't have to squirm and groan and fuss. He could just tell her.

"Ursula," he said.

"Huh?"

"Ursula."

"What is it, Thomas?"

"Ursula, I'm lonely."

She opened her eyes and held her breath. She allowed a second or two for the earth, the town, the room and the bed to swing an arc and come to a full stop, for the look on her face was there for a reason. She had come by it from saying most often the second thing that came into her mind.

Now she reached out her hand and touched him (oh, very lightly) on the chest the way that children put out their hands in April to understand the sudden softness in the air and then she moved her hand and just barely touched his chin, his cheekbone, his forehead and then she took her hand away.

"Close your eyes, Thomas," she said, "and I'll tell you a story."

"They're closed."

"Well, when we are rich, I will buy you a baby leopard so that when you are awake at night you can listen to the leopard stalk. We will give him whiskey so he will never get very big and we will feed him soothing foods like tapioca and then he will lie in front of the fireplace and smile at you and you can pat him on all the fat places."

"Is that all?"

"Yes," she said, "that's all."

Thomas took Ursula's hand and held it tight.

"Thanks, Ursula," he said, and yawned. "Thanks."

Comfort the Small and Tender Grass

There was no need now to put it off any longer. If there was no mail in the box by 4:30, there was not going to be any.

Melissa made her way through the clear and silent house from the kitchen to the mail box and back to the kitchen again. There had really been no point in putting her hand in the box, because she could see through the holes in the front of it, but she always made herself sure.

Time now to heat the water. Harry would be home from work at 5, and wanting his coffee. She sat by the kitchen window, looking out on the fine spring day (how many thousands had she seen in 60 years?) and thinking of the times when she had wished for just such leisure as this. Now she had it, it only seemed to her she did not have enough work to do any more.

Quiet in a house, thick quiet like this, did not make her feel like working. She'd worked like a horse in the old days, though, she could tell you, and not so long ago either. Three children, a husband, all of them clean, always clean (she'd seen to that), and food three times a day (and often four), and everybody always telling her she shouldn't slip in and out of the house without putting on a coat, and all of them having more colds in a winter than she'd had in her whole life.

She added the coffee, now the water was boiling, and turned down the flame.

"I'll just have a cup now, I guess," she said. "And then when Harry comes, I'll have another one with him."

Sitting again by the window in the big kitchen, she hoped the coffee would comfort her, as it always did, that at the first scalding sip, she would see the shining, polished floor, the white dishes in their blue cupboards, the fresh green of the garden with satisfaction and in this order.

Day after day at a quarter of 5 her eyes would travel this route: the floors, the white dishes against blue, and then out—out to the garden and the tamarack tree, and they seemed to her, these three, like a restful trinity that made everything all right.

I hope one of the girls, she thought, one of them anyway, will think to have a tamarack tree. I wonder if I ever told any of them about mamma's tamarack tree? I don't suppose I ever did. Next time I write to Evelyn, I'll tell her. Now that she's got a child of her own, I guess it wouldn't be hard to write it.

And she thought how tomorrow that would be a pleasant thing to do, to write to Evelyn and tell her about how her mother had had a tamarack tree in Butler County, in Kansas, to the west of the house, when there were no other trees for miles around, and of when she had got her own (it was the spring before Angela was born) and of how Evelyn could have one, too, and Evelyn's daughter.

She saw a line of them standing through generations, all of them blonde women and blue eyed, tall and a little on the sturdy side, keeping a tamarack tree in whatever corner of the earth they lived, and looking at it and thinking back.

She hoped that Evelyn would have a tree, all right, because the way they were now, she doubted if Gerald or Angela would have children. Evelyn might be the only one.

And after all, why should they have children? She'd had three and where were they now? Gone, all of them gone. If only one of them had stayed by her now she wouldn't be feeling like it was October on a spring day like this.

You ought to get smaller, she thought, when things go away from you. You ought not to be able to lose things and stay the same size.

She halted the coffee cup half way to her mouth while an

unrecognized feeling of familiarity rushed at her from the walls of the room.

Where had she heard that before, or read it or thought it? Because the feeling she had was as authentic as an unexpected odor out of childhood. It was as strong as the smell of simmering cucumber pickles and as certain as a coyote crying in the night.

The clock said 5 minutes of 5 now. But what was she thinking of? Why was she feeling sorry for herself? Had she not Harry? Every day and night and always?

Getting out the cup and saucer for Harry, she smiled. After all, Harry didn't get married; Harry didn't take jobs in New York. He didn't go away to college; he wasn't always flying off.

Flying off . . . flying off: so that was it. She sat down very slowly, still holding Harry's cup in her hand, and the sting of those old, old tears were even now behind her eyelids, just the same.

On such a day as this, standing by the tamarack tree in Butler County, had she looked up in the sky and seen her pigeon fly away, straight away, not even looking back.

"Why, that must have been fifty years ago," she said, "but I can see it just as clear. . . . And poor old Mr. Cartwright, he felt so bad. I wonder if I ever told Harry about Mr. Cartwright and my pigeon? I don't suppose I ever did."

"Fifty years. Why it's like nothing at all. For all it's changed me, you'd think I'd never moved to Wichita, or married Harry or had three children."

"As plain as if it was today I can see Abraham Cartwright walking through the bluestem carrying that pigeon in his hand."

Abraham Cartwright wore a long, black coat and a long white beard and the thing about his face that no one ever got used to, nor ever forgot, was that, in spite of the beard, his face was wider across than it was long.

He came upon Melissa sitting on the ground with the sun full upon her, holding in her arms an ear of corn wrapped in a square of cloth. She was patting its yellow silken hair with her small brown hand.

"Oh, Mr. Cartwright," she said, "how long can you stay?"

"Oh, a while, Lissie, a while."

"What you got in your hand?"

"A present," he said. "I brought you a pigeon." He bent down, then, and put the small warm thing in her two hands.

"A pigeon?" she asked. "It doesn't look like your pigeons."

It didn't look at all like Mr. Cartwright's fine, big, fat pigeons that sat on Mr. Cartwright's big, fat barn, which as big as it was, was still smaller than Mr. Cartwright's house because of the paint on its outside and the staircase on its inside.

"Your pigeons," Melissa said, "have got colored necks."

"You wait," he said. "You just wait till it grows up."

She had waited all right and Dove, as she called the pigeon, had grown up to have on its neck the most beautiful colors Melissa had ever seen. Dove had grown up in fine style and found out she wasn't the only pigeon in the world.

On such a day as this Dove had found it out, and without any faltering or question she'd taken off from the barn and sailed straight over the tamarack tree.

"Poor Mr. Cartwright," Melissa said, looking at the kitchen clock and not seeing the time. "He felt so bad."

It had not been sorrow to Melissa, though. It had been anger; big and dull and slow.

Her eyes wide, unblinking, straight ahead, her arms held stiff to her sides, not swaying as she walked, her fists clenched and locked, her whole body bent forward, as in sorrow, as in pain, Melissa moved with even, hard, determined steps: left, right, left, right, left, right, in a straight line toward Abraham Cartwright's farm.

Unseen, the tender adolescent spring about her; unrecognized, the weight of coming tears. Only the emptiness now she knew, the horrible gap and the white, slow fury. Nor did she change her steps, but kept on evenly and without greeting: left, right, left, right until she stood before Abraham.

Still were the little fists held small and white, still were the arms held stiff; only the head moved up and she looked into Abraham's face.

"Why didn't you tell me?" she asked.

"Lissie," he said. "What's wrong?"

"Why didn't you tell me?" she asked again and she thought she would be standing there forever, saying it: "Oh, Mr. Cartwright, why didn't you tell me?"

"Why didn't I tell you what, child? Lissie, what's wrong?"

"Why didn't you tell me they had mates?"

"Who, child? I don't understand."

She looked up to the sky then, alien and cruel and mocking sky. Her arms relaxed and the small fingers uncurled and hung separate and heavy and resigned.

"My pigeon," she said. "My Dove is gone."

Then the first tears broke in a loud, ugly sob and she stood there, a little girl alone and heavy in the tender springtime under the big, cruel sky.

Abraham bent down slowly and sat upon the ground and waited for the child to sit beside him. When she had stopped sobbing and, out of weariness, had sat down too, he said:

"When did it go?"

"Yesterday."

"What's so awful," Melissa said, "is that I saw it happen. I sat right there and watched it go away and I was happy, even. I could have stopped it. That's what's so awful. I could have stopped it if I'd known."

That was what Abraham was thinking: I could have stopped it if I'd known. It was bitter to think that he, who had sat such long still hours seeing the pigeons beyond identification of them, beyond knowledge, seeing almost as a pigeon sees, that HE should have forgotten to warn her of this thing.

"No, Lissie," he said. "It's something you cannot stop."

"Oh, but I could," she said. "I could have tied a string to it or shut it up. I had plenty of time. They've been coming for three days now."

"Who?"

"The other pigeons. There were three of them and they came all together and walked back and forth on the roof of the barn. My Dove flew up with them and I thought . . . I thought my Dove was having company. Mine was the prettiest of them all; the others were thin."

"And they all flew away together?" he asked.

"No," she said. "Not right away. That first day they all walked back and forth and talked to each other, my Dove with them, and then the three others flew away and mine came back and sat on my shoulder. I was glad, just thinking my Dove had company.

"Oh, I should have known, but I didn't, and when they did the same thing the next day, and my Dove came back to me again, I thought they were all going to stay with me. I thought how nice it would be to have four of them, only I would always love my Dove the best."

This she had said to her Dove, stroking its head and telling it how, when there were four of them, she would still love it the best and the memory of her innocence made her cry again.

"Lissie," Abraham said, "you couldn't stop it. It would have happened sometime."

"Oh, I could have," she said. "Why I even helped it to happen. When I got to thinking about having all four of them there, I was so afraid they wouldn't come back that I sprinkled grain all around the barn and Dove and I sat by the tamarack tree and waited and waited for them to come.

"When they came I even pushed Dove up in the air to go and see them, and sat right there and watched them. When they started to fly away, just like they had been doing, my Dove went with them. They all left the barn together and I stood up and watched them and I couldn't even call out until they were just little black spots."

Abraham got up from the ground slowly and stood thinking. He must get the child into the house some way. He must give her a doll or a cookie or a book; he knew he must do something.

"I waited and waited," Melissa said. "I kept thinking they'd all come back, but finally I asked Mamma and she told me."

The child stood up and looked at Abraham in defiance now.

"That pigeon should have stayed with me," she said.

"Why, Lissie? What makes you say that? The pigeon cannot help. . . ."

"It should have stayed with me," she said, *"because I loved it."*

Melissa turned abruptly and left him; somewhere, away at the back of her mind, she had had a faint hope that Abraham could get her pigeon back for her because he had given it to her in the first place.

Humble in his futility, Abraham did not try to follow her, but reached to the ground mechanically and pulled up a long piece of bluestem. He stood there pulling the blade of grass again and again through his fingers. He looked down at his hands and then his eyes followed Melissa, so desolate and small, walking slowly down the road.

"Oh, little blade of grass," he said, to the small back, the drooping head, "bound to the earth and bent before the wind, the sky is a long way off. But do not wail that it is so. Oh, husha, child. Don't cry. And never mind."

Abraham Cartwright is thirty years dead but that word of his lives on in every clock that keeps the time, symbol of man's only steadfast enemy.

No matter how disguised in oblongs or bird's houses or little snapdown cages, how haloed with diamonds and gold, clocks know the thing they do and you can hear them making recompense, apologizing, every second of the day and night.

Husha, husha, husha.

But, Melissa never heard the kitchen clock, thinking of Abraham Cartwright thirty years dead.

I'm glad I went back to see him that time, she thought, that time when Evelyn was little and I took her with me. I'm glad he got to see me when I was married and had a nice home and children. We were always so poor in Butler County.

Husha, husha, husha.

Melissa set the pot on the back of the stove over the small burner so that the coffee would keep warm but not boil, and still she did not see the clock.

Husha, husha, husha.

"I think I'll get out the cup that was Mamma's," she said, "and be using it. There's no need to keep it sitting on the shelf. The little cup: the one with the primrose on it."

Husha, husha, husha.

And suddenly she heard and saw the clock. "It's twenty minutes after five!" she said. "I wonder what's happened to Harry? He hasn't been late getting home since Harding ran for President."

The Little Woman

It was his fourth drink. You could tell it was his fourth because he was starting to talk philosophy. He was one of those people who could never get over the terrible wonder of the fact that he had actually got to and out of college. It was silly of him to go on talking like he did because it made it so obvious that he didn't have a girl. Everybody there knew if he had had a girl her intimate peculiar characteristics would be more important to him than anybody's philosophy. If he had had a girl, now, and been on his fourth drink he would have been thinking about how there were certain words she never could pronounce or how she always took off her clothes in the same order.

It was going to be the Bergson argument tonight. I'd heard it so many times already. But he was having it with Lucile this time. Lucile was new to the crowd and so it might be different.

"What do you think?" he asked her. "If no one is on the spot to hear a tree fall, did it fall or not?"

I laid my bets. Sometimes they said "sure" and sometimes they said "no" and sometimes "what d'ya mean?"

"Of course it fell," Lucile answered.

"You mean Bergson was wrong?"

"Sure," she said, "Bergson forgot the earth. The earth behaves and the earth records. That's about all a mind can do, even."

"Yeah," I said, "some of us can't even record." That was a stinger for the boy. Everybody knew he had a rotten memory.

I began to like Lucile. "She's the first one to get him," I thought. I started over to sit by her, but changed my mind. "Oh, Jesus," I thought, "I haven't got the energy to get interested in a new person. Not just now."

We started on another round. This would be the fifth. It was the signal for the griping to begin. Always on the fifth drink they started in about how they hated the lousy work they did. There were seven of us in the room and all of us worked at different jobs for pretty small amounts, and none of us, I'm afraid, loved our fellow workers. All of us fussed, too, about hours and wages and having uneducated superiors—all of us, that is, except Michael. Michael said it was none of it any consequence and that you got out of bed in the morning just the same whether you liked what you were doing or not. He said if you had six people with futures and six people without futures and you watched them get up in the morning you couldn't tell the difference. They all looked sleepy. So I thought I'd talk to Michael and stave off the whining for a minute or so. As always, he had sat smiling in a corner all evening without saying a word.

"What are you thinking about, Stupid?" I asked him.

"I was meditating," he said.

"On what?"

"I was thinking," he said, "on that terrible day of judgment when the goats are separated from the sheep—what, oh, what, will become of the fennecs?"

That was just like Michael, and if I hadn't been feeling rotten I'd have loved him for that remark. But tonight it was rather irritating that he was, as always, in perfect character. Always contented, always complacent, always dependable. Somehow it got on my nerves.

I hadn't, after all, been able to stave it off, because they were already talking shop—the illiteracy of their employers, the underhanded methods of their brothers in slavery, the monotonous and repetitious thwarting of enlightened progress—it wove itself into a familiar lullaby as I reached for my sixth.

I was one ahead. I was thinking about my grandfather. I always thought about my grandfather on the sixth. I was thinking about how the best way to sum up all my grandfather's wild and picturesque life was that arrogant and spirited fist-clenched threat: By God! you can't do that to me.

It was usually true; they couldn't. But sometimes it was so obviously true they could, that even my grandfather had to see it and change his threat. But when it was so obvious that even my grandfather saw it, he did not sit in a badly ventilated smoke filled attic drinking alcohol in pale beer and whine about it. For one thing, he drank whiskey, and he drank it straight, which is something that I can't do without getting sick, and when he had to alter his threat of By God! you can't do that to me, he merely added: "but if you can, I'll make you sorry!", and I am not sure but it is to his credit that it is I and not he who saw the humor in it.

Each generation we seemed weaker. It wasn't only my grandfather—it was their grandfathers, too. In two generations we had come down all the way from whiskey to beer which is quite a way to come. Our grandparents would never have sat as we sat in righteous discontent. They would have got mad enough to fight and smash something, or they would have done, each man for himself, a little clever swindling without discussing it with their friends, or they would have gone right on living in luxury on credit, never mentioning such sordid details as money at a social function.

And suddenly I knew I was sick of all of us in that room . . . sick to death. Why in hell did we all get to know each other so well? Lucile was new to the crowd and I already knew more about her than my mother knew about friends she had had for forty years. My mother had a friend named Mrs. Benton whom she'd know for thirty years and she still called her "Mrs. Benton." They didn't even know each other's first names. If Mrs. Benton happened to call on one of those rare occasions when my mother had been crying, my mother always told Mrs. Benton that she had "such a cold." She knew, I'm sure, that Mrs. Benton could tell that this was no cold, but she also knew that Mrs. Benton would give no sign either then or later that she had had any other thought than that my mother had had "such a cold."

While I was thinking of this I could see in the far corner that if Helen stayed a half hour longer that she would have a crying jag, that we'd all listen to everything she said, and, though it wouldn't make any difference one way or the other, we'd remember.

Yes, by God, I was sick of them all, and it was time for me to leave again. Just about every six months I got this way and then I'd move someplace, quit work and be alone until my money ran out. It never lasted, of course, I always got hungry for people again and I'd call Michael up and pretty soon the others would be back. I'd find another job and talk a lot and drink beer and then in about another six months I'd get sick again—sick of knowing them all too well and do it all over again. That was the nice thing about living in a city; there was no limit to the number of times you could move.

I got up and left right then and Michael came home with me. I told him I was going away again and he didn't ask me where. He even packed my things for me. I was disgusted that when I was tired of Michael and the rest of them and running away without telling him where I was going, I'd still let him do my packing for me, but I let him all the same. For one thing, he's good at it.

The next day I went out to find a cheap place to live. Now the place I did live in I did not consider a cheap place. It was five dollars a week, which is not twenty dollars a month, as you might think, but twenty-two. And the jobs I usually got paid ten dollars a week, which is not forty-four dollars a month, but forty. So I was looking for what I considered a cheap place to live and I found it. It was the attic over a garage and it was two dollars a week.

Well, after I'd got my Victrola and records, my books and bed and trunk, the white rat and her cage and my store of milk bottles moved in I went down to the office where I worked and got my check and quit.

Now the thing about milk bottles is this: milk bottles are worth three cents apiece. If you take a bottle with you each time you buy a bottle of milk, the milk costs you eleven cents a quart, and if you don't take a bottle it costs fourteen. But on the other hand, if you get your milk for eleven cents, when your money is all gone, it's all gone, while if you keep storing your milk bottles away there comes a day when you *think* your money is all gone. Then after you have been through all your pockets and desk drawers and all the other places where you sometimes put small change and forget about it, and after you have eaten the last of the crackers and other kinds of food that aren't exhausted at one meal, you suddenly remember with great joy and a feeling of salvation that negotiable store of milk bottles.

Theoretically, if you pay fourteen cents instead of eleven each time for your milk, you should run out of cash just that much sooner, but it doesn't work out that way for some reason, and besides, if it did, you would still miss, on the eleven cent plan, that joy of finding buried treasure, that extra amount of clear gain. It is wonderful that a human being can fool himself like that month after month and find pleasure in it each time.

Walking back to the garage after leaving the office I was quite happy. For as long as the check lasted I was going to live the way I wanted to live. I was going to make that attic into a little stronghold for me and the white rat. I was going to read novels and play the Victrola and sleep. I was going to clean house and putter. When I worked I never had time to putter and make curtains and rearrange things. I had almost a whole month's check and that would last me long enough. This wanting to be alone and safe and sweet and clean and domestic—it never lasted very long. Ultimately, one always gets lonely; one always comes to respect people once again.

Well, I went back to that garage and I started to work. There was a gas plate, a table, a chair, one electric light and a toilet. It was not a bathroom because there was no bath tub in it. If Helen had seen it she would have said it was definitely and simply a terlit, an unassuming terlit, a little timid and surprised to find itself in a garage. I thought there ought to be some word to express all that and finally I hit on the word garlit and we've called it that ever since. The garlit was downstairs in the garage proper and so was the faucet. There was no sink. The faucet was outside and gave out cold water which was originally intended for the lawn.

I scrubbed the floor with soap and I set up my bed and unpacked my trunk which I used for a table. Then I took out my curtains and washed them. I borrowed an iron and pressed them on the trunk and hung them up.

I went to the lumber yard and bought me some yellow pine for five cents a foot and I got out my old hammer and built me some book shelves and set up my books. They looked fine.

I made the bed, spending lots of time over it, pulling the sheets tight and making squares at the corners.

There was some lumber left from the book shelves and I made a shelf against one wall and fastened it up with brackets. I got out all my bottles and jars of cosmetics and dusted them off and lined them up in a straight row on the shelf. I always liked bottles.

After I'd been to the store I came back, got a pan of cold water, carried it upstairs and heated it on the gas plate. The last place had had a bath tub and I was a little out of practice washing out of a pan. I spilled quite a lot on the floor, but I had got the water good and hot and it felt fine. I washed my hair, too. When I had finished I put on a clean robe and brushed my hair and made up my face.

I let The Little Woman out of her cage and fed her. Then I washed my hands and cooked my own dinner. After I'd washed the dishes I put a record on the Victrola and lit a cigarette and sat down in the chair. I felt clean and pleasantly tired and I looked around at the room so changed now. I was very drowsily proud of all I'd accomplished.

The Little Woman crawled over to me and sat on my shoe. I reached down and lifted her up on my knee. She was a white rat that I had had for a long time. It was no longer necessary to keep her in a cage. She was as tame as a dog. Usually the steps of a person entering a room will cause a rat to scurry to a corner. The Little Woman was so used to me that she'd come to meet me and lick my shoes.

She sat now on her hind legs and washed her face and whiskers with her tiny pink hands. She was the daintiest thing I had ever seen and while I sat very still and watched her as I had many times before I remembered what it was that made her so delicate. She was full grown—old for a white rat, but she was not larger than a small mouse. She had been used in a protein deficient dietary experiment and it had stunted her growth. She never would be any larger and I was glad. I shouldn't have liked her so much if she hadn't been like a tiny fur clad pink handed ballet dancer. Well, it was funny. For the first time it had occurred to me that it had taken sixty days and six rats like The Little Woman to prove that if you don't have enough to eat you don't grow. Well. I started to laugh, and I laughed so loud you could have heard it for a mile. The Little Woman scurried away from me in terror. A rat can understand almost anything else. A rat reacts to Beethoven differently than to Stravinsky, even. But a rat cannot understand laughter. Titters, now, a rat will tolerate, or a polite noise that denotes faint but vague amusement, but laughter—laughter scares a rat to death.

I quit laughing and reached for The Little Woman. I put her on my hand, not holding her so she'd feel caught, but just letting her sit on my hand and with the other hand I smoothed her fur.

"I'm sorry," I said to her, "but would you take my laughter from me? Surely, just when I've found a stronghold against sordidness, a nice clean place with our own curtains newly laundered, just when I'm easy and at peace—don't for God's sake deny me my laughter."

She shrugged her shoulders and beat her long slender tail against the palm of my hand, and I knew of course that she *would* deny me laughter. She would demand all and more that the little women of all time have been demanding of each other.

"Well, Jesus!" I thought, "that is funny. I wouldn't let a human being get away with that. There isn't a soul I'd let inhibit me. I even got sore at Michael once because he didn't like the blue mascara I'd just bought. And here, for the delicacy of a rat's ears, I forsake laughter."

The irony of it struck me as being so funny that I started to laugh again, but I clapped my free hand over my mouth in time. After all, one has to maintain a certain consideration . . . a certain delicacy.

Loopus

Old Loopus, he just hung down. The old biddies that came in the kitchen to have tea with his Mamma, they'd look at Loopus and yap: "That dog, he just hang down," and the other little whelps at school, they'd snivel: "That dog Loopus, he's sad."

Poor Old Loopus, his legs sank into his feet and his back sank into his legs. His ears hung down and his eyelids hung down and when he yawned his jaw kept falling and falling.

Oh, he was a sad dog, Loopus was, and he was embarrassed. It was all because of his tremendous tail. Loopus' Mamma, she used to whine to the old dams sitting in the kitchen drinking their tea: "That Loopus when he was born, I thought they'd be no end to it. The Dogtor he say to me, 'I never see such a tail. Is there no end to it, Dam?'"

"Poor soul," the old terriers would mewl, "poor soul."

Then Loopus' Mamma would cry in her tea and think she never would get over the disgrace of it.

Poor Loopus, he'd go over in a corner and walk around and around till he'd get that tail all wound up like a garden hose and then he'd lie down and try to look like it wasn't there. When he'd walk along the street he'd look ahead of himself real eager like he saw something interesting and a long time ago it used to fool the other dogs and they'd all start running ahead of him. Sometimes Loopus himself even believed there might be something interesting up ahead, but there never was.

It was the worst when he went to school. He could stand to have his Mamma talking about it all the time and he could even stand having all the old greyhounds drinking their tea and looking at him like he had too little of something, but when he went to school it was terrible.

The first morning Loopus sat down in his seat at school and his tail was still out in the school yard under the teeter-totters.

"Loopus," the teacher yelped, "bring that tail of yours in here so I can get this door closed."

"Yes'm," he said and he started to walk around in circles in the school room to take up the slack in his tail, but by the time he got it all in so the teacher could get the door closed it was already time for recess. All the puppies were sniggering at Loopus and the teacher got so mad she tripped over his tail.

"Loopus," she said, "you tell your Mamma she's gonna have to do something about that tail or teach you at home her own self. I can't have this room in an uproar every morning until recess time."

"Yes'm," Loopus said, and he hung down further and further until his eyelashes were lying out flat on the desk top.

Loopus didn't go out for recess because he knew he wouldn't have any fun; he never did. And when school was out for the day all the rest of the pups were through fighting and home and ready for supper by the time Loopus had got his tail untangled from around the desks.

"Mamma," he whimpered when he finally got home, "teacher says you got to do something with my tail else I can't go back to school no more."

"It's a curse on me, that's what it is," his Mamma whined. "I never to my dying day will live it down." And she began to sniffle again and the old worn out tears stood like catkins all along her whiskers until finally she licked them off and swallowed them, being, as she was, very thrifty.

"It seems like," Loopus whimpered very softly, with his eyelids hanging way down, "it seems like you could do SOMETHING."

"It might could be," his Mamma said, "that we could tie it up." So they wound up Loopus' tail around and around the way one puts away a garden hose for the winter and then Loopus'

Mamma tied the tail with a blue ribbon to keep it from coming unlooped. Poor Loopus, he looked like he was carrying around an automobile tire.

"It's heavier this way," he said.

"You'll soon get used to it," his Mamma yapped. "You'll get so you don't hardly notice it."

"Huh uh," Loopus said and he lay down in front of his tail and tried to look as though it weren't there.

When the teacher saw the new arrangement she said Loopus could keep on coming to school. Loopus would sit down at his desk and leave his tail out in the aisle, but all day the school pups kept calling: "Keep the aisle clear! Keep the aisle clear!" and each time one of them went up to the front of the class to recite he would trip over Loopus' tail elaborately and Loopus would whimper, real low, to himself, "It's a man's life," and he would act as though he had something in his eye. But finally the teacher went to the school board and they had a special meeting, voting to have a trap door made by Loopus' desk with a hole in the top of it for the tail to go through.

Loopus almost felt good over this. He raised his chin up a sixteenth of an inch and in a couple of weeks he could have managed a grin, but the decision of the school board got around in the town and the townsdogs began to yelp about taxes and of how even this wouldn't be the end of it unless Loopus failed every year, because each year that Loopus should go on to a new grade, they'd have it all to do over again. An influential poodle was heard to remark that the town was going to the mongrels.

This was the way it was for Loopus year after year and each year the mumbling got worse in the town about the high taxes and some dogs being too smart for their own good. Even some of the old dams, when they came to sit in the kitchen and drink tea with Loopus' Mamma, weren't so sympathetic any more. They got so they'd look at Loopus and then they'd say: "Tsk, tsk, it must take a lot to feed that tail," and Loopus' Mamma, she wouldn't stand up for him at all. She'd just scratch her old calloused elbows and yap, "Keeps me skin and bones, skin and bones," and poor old Loopus he'd get further down and further down on the floor and he wished there could be a trap door big enough for him and his tail, too.

But the year that Loopus graduated from high school something happened. That spring it began to rain and it rained so constantly that even the old biddies wouldn't come out in it and Loopus' Mamma's kitchen was almost always empty. Loopus' Mamma said the rain made her feel right dauncy and druppy and no count and she got crosser than ever with Loopus about tracking in the whole town on his tail and getting it all over her carpets.

Poor Loopus, he just hung down further and further and played like he had millions of things in his eyes.

But then one day on top of the rain noise there was a new noise. First it was a low mumble like the old dams slupping their tea in the kitchen. Then it got louder and louder and finally the church bell began to ring and everybody ran out of their houses toward the bridge because they'd been afraid of a flood for several hours now and on the other side of the bridge was high ground.

Loopus was there, too, with the crowd, but not so tall or so far forward, of course, as any of the other dogs. Still, though, he heard the terrible moan that came out of them all at the same time when they saw the bridge swept right away and crumbled into little pieces.

Loopus didn't moan because he'd been for a long time so that he just didn't care. He nosed up to the edge of the river and saw the bridge being crumbled and then he bit the blue ribbon on his tail loose and he stood there in front of the crowd for a while and then he looked at the wicked river and he smiled a very wicked, conquering, bitter smile. He shook his rump back and forth several times and then he gave his tail a swing. He swung that tail of his clear across the river and back again and across and back again and made a bridge for all the dogs to cross to high ground.

When they were all across they took hold of Loopus' tail all together and they pulled Loopus across and then he was a hero.

Loopus' Mamma she made him some hot tea and she washed his tail and brushed it and patted it and Loopus' teacher from the high school came to see him and she brought him her well pawed and man-eared copy of Keats which she had rescued from the flood. Then Loopus lay right down in the midst of that admiring crowd and went to sleep with a smile on his face and all the dogs tiptoed out very softly so as not to disturb him.

They had a pretty hard time of it there in the flood, those survivors, but Loopus had the driest place to sleep and Loopus had the hottest coffee and the freshest food.

After about a week the water went down and the sun came out and all the old dogs and puppies got to work and built a new bridge, but the water was still too high on the other side for them to go back there yet to live. One day Loopus brushed his tail up fine and went off across the bridge. He had a new picked dogtooth violet hanging from the corner of his mouth.

He looked for his old house, but it was gone, and he looked for the butcher shop, but it was gone and then he waded through a lot of muck and twisted weeds and old papers until he got to the school house. The school house had fallen, though the bricks were still there all lying in heaps and the Maypole was still upright.

Loopus walked alone among the damp and desolation slowly and then he stood up straight and took in a deep breath and looked about him. Something of the nobility and the grandeur and the potentialities of the canine race began to well up in Loopus and he swung his tail around and lassoed the Maypole, giving it a good, strong, friendly jerk. Then he let out a moan that was the spirit, the soul of Loopus . . . Loopus, an individual, a canine being, a power. Then he went back across the bridge.

Most of the survivors wanted to go back to the old side of the bridge and start over again, back where they had lived before and had their homes and been happy, but there was a small group who said it was wiser to stay on the high side of the bridge and this group had already started building houses and stores and beauty shops and even a gymnasium.

It was into this gymnasium that Loopus wandered, home from his little journey. His head was high, his ears were erect, his eyelashes even curled up and his tail stretched for blocks behind him. There stood the young bloods of the town all of them with their tails shut in a door, straining at the neck in an effort to stretch their tails like Loopus'.

Loopus strolled in and looked them over. He had a big black bone in his mouth. It had a fine, mellow, ten cent odor.

"Hi, ya Dawgs," he barked.

"Hi, Loopus." It was a regular chorus. One of the pointers opened the door, releasing the tails of the group. These tails were quickly dropped between legs and ignored. Some of the swains even pretended to have something in their eyes.

"Where you been, Loopus?" one of them yipped.

"Oh, across the bridge," Loopus said and nonchalantly dropped his bone, only half gnawed. "Been looking the old place over."

"How's it look, Loopus?"

"Pretty bad," he said, shifting his weight onto his back feet, "pretty bad."

"Anything left at all?"

"There's a few bricks left of the school house," he said, "and the Maypole's still standing."

"That was a great old school house," one of them said, eyeing Loopus' cast off bone.

"Yeah," Loopus said, "yeah, we used to have some great old times there."

Night's Comin', Miss Alice

"Work, for the night is coming, work for the night. . . ." The old woman hummed in a high, off-tune whine, as she inched along toward the barn, carrying the milk bucket. Always loved that hymn, she had, though she never could carry a tune. Old Tootle used to make fun of her tryin to sing. Poor old Tootle. Been a week now since they carried him off to State. Well, could she hepp it? He couldn't work no more, lyin there heppless in the bed. "You'll have to send him off to State," her daughter had said. "You caint take care of him." Well, God's truth, she couldn't. Still, it had been fast, everybody hurryin her, her daughter come to get it over with and get back home. And as for not workin, he never had been much good.

"What you want to marry that ole man for?" her daughter had said. Come from trash, he did. Ever body knew it. His mother a plain whore and a witch to boot. Cast spells she did. And Tootle a bastard. He could stanch blood, too, like his ma, and take off warts. Well, yes, she knew all that. She knew what people said. She was ashamed. "The idea, Miss Alice marryin at her age and marryin *that*." But they hadn't known how scared she'd been after Mike died. Just plumb *scared* to be there alone. Many nights she'd sat up by the stove all night just holdin her breath for the daylight to come. So *scared*. Lord, that night Claudie Joe come after dark to get some butter and her so scared to open that door she'd grabbed the shotgun and shot right through the door seven times.

"Hee, hee," the old woman stopped and wiped the sweat from her forehead on her arm. She could hear Claudie Joe yellin yet. "Miss Alice, Miss Alice, it's Claudie Joe, your own cousin. Put down that gun and git away from that door." Well, she hadn't hit him. Fool that he was. Ought to know better than come after dark like that and her only widowed a month.

Bad clump of weeds there by the path. Ought to be cut down. Likely be a snake in there. She'd ought to get the lively lad and cut it down herself, she supposed, but Lord, her old arms wouldn't hardly do what she wanted. Like as not she'd swing at them weeds and cut her foot clean off. Place needed a man. Well, that's what she'd told them about marryin old Tootle. He could hoe, at least. He did keep the garden long as he was able. She didn't suppose she'd have a garden ever again now.

She shuffled on to the barn, putting each foot down flat, as though it were made of iron. Herself she appeared to be made of knots, tied tightly. Knots on her hands, knots on her face, one big one grown out on her forehead. She would be able to go on as long as the knots all held, but there in the evening light the knots seemed to threaten that if one of them came loose, all would dissolve.

White saucers of blossom bobbed at her from the wild elderberry bush across the road. Shorter and smaller, the blooms of Queen Anne's lace surrounded it. Must be June, the old woman thought. June in Tennessee was mostly white. For brides, people said. They looked so cool, the white blossoms, and it was hot today, sticky hot, like before a storm. Miss Alice rubbed the sweat off her forehead with her arm again, and then her old face came apart, rather like a landscape being inundated by a lava flow. It was what was left of Miss Alice's famous smile, and it was for the cow who stood waiting by the shed.

"Hello, Sweetheart," she said. "Am I late?" The cow was a jersey, glossy and golden, sleek and fat. Miss Alice had a real way with dairy cows, had made a right smart living off them, too, over the years, and never sent one off to auction. People bought them right out of her barn and they paid her price. Now she had only Sweetheart left, and this one she wouldn't sell. Hadn't been a week since there'd been a buyer here, though. "Sell my last cow?" Miss Alice had said. "What'd I do with no cow now? You tell me that."

Miss Alice was very slow opening the door to the shed. She slapped the cow with affection as she went through the door. "You fat thing, you," she said. She like to find the little nubbins for Sweetheart and while she rummaged around in the corn bin, the cow became impatient. It made the old woman laugh to see how far Sweetheart could put out her tongue reaching for the ear of corn. Lord, what would they do when the corn was gone? First year in her life she hadn't planted corn. Old Tootle hadn't been able to make a crop and what would she do now when the corn was gone? Have to buy corn, she guessed. The idea. Buyin corn.

She leaned on Sweetheart as she walked around her through the manure and sat down on the milking stool. Old Tootle had made her that stool. "I don't need no milkin stool, she had said. "I squatted down and held a bucket between my knees for fifty years and more."

"You're gonna need one," Tootle had said. Well, he was right. Her legs wouldn't hold her now for sure.

But how had the titty rag got in her hand? There for a moment she'd been afraid she'd forgotten it. Yet when she started to wash off the udder it was in her hand. Well, sixty years, morning and night, ever day of her life since she'd been a girl she'd left the house with a titty rag in her hand. She guessed she didn't have to remember it.

"You got a scratch on your titty, Sweetheart," she said. "I told you not go down by them blackberry briars." Sweetheart munched noisily and switched her tail hard against the old woman's head. "Heah, heah, you stop that now. I'll tie your tail to your leg, you don't stop that."

The old woman leaned her head against the cow and began to milk, giving herself over to the sound of the milk hitting the bucket in its familiar rhythm and to the sensuous pleasure of the softness of the udder caressing her hands. "Skin like a baby," she said. And why not? Hadn't she let her nurse up to the time she'd sold off her ma? "Fresh yourself and still suckin," she said. "Some sight." The big thing had had to kneel to get under. It was comical. But Miss Alice liked a fat cow. Sweetheart would most likely be her last cow, she'd known that. That's why she let her nurse so long. That's why she liked to see her in the pasture, grass up to her belly, and it all hers.

Miss Alice tried not to see the manure on the floor. Not the way she'd always kept her barns. But she couldn't shovel it out any more, and old Tootle never would. She'd nagged him and nagged him to clean out the shed. "Don't hurt nothin," he'd say. "Leave it there."

Oh, she'd kept a pretty barn once. Fresh straw on the floor every day. Mike used to make fun of her, fussin so to keep the barn clean. When he'd be away from home and people ask him what Miss Alice was a doin, he'd say, "Oh, she's standin behind the cow with a pitchfork, waitin for a pat so she can carry it out of the barn soon as it falls." Pretty barn then. Mike kept it painted. Hadn't been painted since he died. And it was about to fall over, too. But at least the roof didn't leak, even if it had cost her a broken leg. She'd got so mad at old Tootle not fixin that roof, she'd got up there and fixed it herself and then she'd fallen. Just fell right down all the way, hard, and broke her leg. And that old fool kneelin down beside her, cryin, sayin, "Miss Alice, I caint lift you. I don't know what to do." Couldn't even lift her in the house, him so weak. "Well, leave me then, and go get some hepp," she'd said. And she'd lain out there half a day before the ambulance finally came. Healed all right, though. "Miss Alice you goin to live forever," the doctor had said, "if you got what it takes to mend bones like that."

How long ago was that? Well, she couldn't rightly remember. Six years? Seven? Lord have mercy, how the time went by.

Bucket so full of milk she could hardly lift it back out of the way. And rich! She could have kissed it. Such fine milk. Half cream, too. She slapped Sweetheart and watched her move out of the shed, her great glossy bulk bouncing like a rowboat over her thin Jersey legs. "Git on out now, Sweetheart," she said. She carried the bucket outside and set it down so she could fasten the shed door. It took both hands now and she could hardly do it. When she got the door shut and the bar across it, she leaned against it, breathing hard, her body covered with sweat. Hottest job in summer; coldest in winter, that was milkin.

But she'd done it. She'd done it once again. She'd done her work. She straightened up and let the air cool her. A little stir of a breeze blew on her and it felt mighty good. She started slowly back to the house. Yes sir, she could still do it. She could still work.

"Caint work no more. Caint do nothin. And fergits ever thing soon as you tell him. Don't know even where he's at hardly." That's what they'd said about Tootle. That's what her daughter had said to the doctor. And he'd signed the papers. "Yes," he said. "I understand." He'd signed the papers right then, fast. No argument. Well, she'd signed too. And then they'd carried him off to State.

But if it had been Mike. That was the thing. The wrong thing that worried her all the time. Because if it had been Mike, she would never have let them take him off that way. She knew it. She'd have kept him at home. She'd have managed somehow. She'd have done for him. She'd have put out cash money for a nurse. "Oh, Mike, Mike," she said. "Oh, *no.*"

There in the pale green evening light, she stood on the path in agony, her gnarled hands crossed over her abdomen, trying to deny what was coming. For weeks at a time, even months, she didn't think of it and then something, somewhere, would set off the awful memory and she knew she was in for it. For once started, she couldn't stop it. She had to live the whole thing clear through to the end. She couldn't help it. She was powerless. Right from the moment when Mike stood in front of the fireplace, saying impatiently, "Miss Alice, I'm too *tard* to eat, I told you. I'm goin to bed." And he had reached for the poker a little angrily and begun to fix the fire for the night.

And then he'd fallen. Right down hard, right into the fire. Big, he was. And in her fright, she was all helpless. His hair had caught fire before she could drag him free. Oh, she could smell it, that hair burning, and her beating at the flames and trying to pull him free of the fire and knowing, knowing he was dead.

And snow on the ground two feet deep. Where? Where would she go? To the north, to Skid's cabin, or further, to the south, to the Mathis place, with three times to cross the branch? Only two places to wade between her and Skid's place. Fool she was, she'd gone north. Waded the branch and her dress and petticoats froze stiff on her and weighin a ton to lug on and on, breath killin her chest and cryin, and thinkin of Mike back there alone and maybe comin to a little and rollin back in the fire. "God," she had sobbed, "God, hepp me. Hepp me."

And then to reach Skid's cabin door and pound on it with her frozen fists and finally to kick the door open and there find Skid, dead drunk, silly drunk, sittin propped back in a chair, a jug of moonshine over half gone on the floor beside him.

"Skid," she said, "come quick. Mike's dyin. He's had a heart attack."

That grin, that silly, happy grin on his face. "Aw Miss Alice, Mike's all right. Why, I seen him this mornin. Why, Mike's alive. You all *wet*, Miss Alice. Whass the matter?"

"Skid, he's dead, I tell you. Please come hepp me. I caint lift him. He's in the fire."

"Now, Miss Alice, you just stop talkin that way. Why Mike's all right, I tell you. He's *all right*. Aint nothin gone happen to ole Mike. I *seen* him."

Oh, it was hopeless. She took him by the shoulders and shook him and shook him but he was like rubber and when she knocked his head against the wall, he just grinned that silly grin. "Oh, Mike, he's all right," he said. "You wanna drink, Miss Alice?"

She could have killed him. Just killed him. If she'd had anything to do it with, and if there'd been time. But there wasn't time. She'd have to go. Go on. Go on to the next farm. Wade the branch in the heavy frozen clothes again. Half crazy she'd been, stumbling through the snow, her feet frozen, crying and praying, "Oh, God, just hepp me. Just hold me up till I do what I have to do."

And He had. He had held her up. She had done what she'd had to do. She got help at last. She had got back home.

The snow blurred now before her eyes and the landscape became green all about her. She saw the white elderberry blossom. She saw her house. She walked on slowly to the house. God, it was over. It was all over again. He had helped her, yes He had. She'd done what she had to do. She stepped up one step slowly with the good leg and brought the other up even to it. Her shoes were caked with manure and she leaned on the door and kicked them off and walked in the house in her stocking feet. She went in and sat down heavily before the stove. She'd had the fireplace boarded up after Mike's death and a big wood stove set in front of it. She couldn't stand the sight of that fireplace.

She was tired. Terribly tired. And she sat there, resting, knowing the dark was coming, knowing there was something she must do before she fell asleep. The milk. She hadn't strained the milk nor set it in the springhouse. She hadn't. . . .

She could feel her old heart beating hard and fast with the fear of her knowledge that she hadn't even brought the milk in the house. "You ole fool, she said, "you *forgot* it. You set the bucket on the ground to close the shed door and walked off and left it there." Bad as old Tootle she was.

She tried to pull herself up by the arms of the chair because there was no time to lose now. She had to get that bucket before someone came by and saw it there. What if they said *she* couldn't do her work no more? *She* forgot? The tears, confronted by such a multitude of channels in the old face, hung for a moment on the old eyelids and then, unable to decide a path, split into a thin film over her cheeks while she tugged and pulled at the arms of the chair, trying to get up.

No Special Hurry

If people bring so much courage to this world the world has
to kill them to break them, so of course it kills them. The
world breaks everyone and afterwards many are strong at the
broken places. But those that will not break it kills. It kills
the very good and the very gentle and the very brave impar-
tially. If you are none of these you can be sure it will kill
you too but there will be no special hurry.

—Ernest Hemingway, *A Farewell to Arms*

As soon as she woke up in the morning she knew she couldn't
put it off any longer.

"This is the day I got to think," she said. "I could sleep
through yesterday and I read all the day before, but sooner or
later I've got to come to it. It's either Thursday or Friday, I don't
know which, but this is the day the little boys are out to get
me."

There was a bench outside the house perched on the edge of
the mountain. There was nothing in front of it but a valley and
half a dozen hills on the other side. If you got to the point where
there was really nothing better for you to do, why this was as fine
a place as any in the country for sitting and thinking.

So that was where she came to sit and think after she had
thrown some water at her face, run the tooth brush from left to
right inside her mouth and spit thoughtfully onto the white
porcelain of the lavatory.

She sat down and gave the distant hills a nod of acknowledge-
ment to make it up to them for not being able to impress her and

then she leaned her elbows on her knees and looked out over the valley and waited.

Sure enough she didn't wait in vain because way on top of the most distant hill, like a piece of tired old gray mist, she could see it.

"I'll wait for you," she said to the thing. "You've got to go clear down that hill and across the valley and climb all the way up here to me, but I'll be here, don't you worry. I won't go away. Not me."

That thing she saw clear on the top of the distant hill coming so laboriously but so surely to her—it was not a stranger.

It was an old broken down second hand Trouble. It was a weary and bored old Trouble on familiar ground just putting in another day's work with vague and futile dreams of a vacation.

She sat right still there watching the Old Trouble advance and making no move to get away. Old Trouble was out of breath when he got to the top of the mountain.

"Sit down here by me," she said to him, "and rest yourself. I've been waitin' for you."

"That's the best way," Old Trouble said, "might as well get it today as tomorrow." He sighed heavily for he was glad of the rest. The girl looked at him closely.

"Oh," she said, "I remember you."

"Sure," he said, "of course you remember me—from three years ago."

"You bet. I remember you well. You were the professor, the doctor and the young boy."

"Ah, that was a marvelously complex interlude," said the old man, reminiscing, "and, before that. . . ."

"Before that you were the drunk, the melancholy girl and the mad poet."

"Those were the days," he said. "They called me Real Trouble then. I felt like a million in those days: plenty of exercise, good food, on the go every minute."

"But, even before that," she said, "you were a good deal different, but I remember you all right."

"Back in the experimental days, huh? When I was the playmate, the bully, and a vague ambition."

"I remember the first day you came."

"You were squatting on the sidewalk—a fat little girl watching the ants in the dirt."

"You scared me some the first time." She laughed at the memory of her childish fright.

"I watched you for a long time," he said, "and then I came up behind you."

"That was a sneakin' trick."

"I know it was, but in those days you didn't sit and wait for me the way you do now."

"Yeah," she said, "those days. . . ." She stared out over the valley for a while lifting her toes off the ground and putting them back again. The old man shook himself free of his nostalgia.

"Well," he said, "shall we get back to the folio?"

"The folio?" she asked. "That's a new one on me."

"Didn't I ever tell you about the folio?" he asked.

"No," she said, "you never told me."

"That," said the old man, "was a grave oversight. Always, with our steady customers, we explain about the folio."

"You missed me there, my friend. I never heard of it."

"I can't understand such an oversight," he said.

"Come on," she said, "come on. What is it?"

"Well," he said, "the minute you're born, the very minute, your folio is ready and waiting for you."

"Everybody gets one?"

"That's the fascinating thing of the whole business," said Old Trouble. There were moments when he really loved his work and explaining the folio was one of them. "It's even a greater achievement than finger prints."

"Yeah?"

"We feel it is. You see, each person's folio contains his own individual peculiar combination of trouble. Think of it. For each person a worry folio of his own and there are no two identical combinations. You've heard of geometrical progression?"

"Oh, sure."

"Well, it's bigger than that."

"So your own little set of troubles belongs just to you? It's all yours to keep?"

"Till the day you die."

"What about the people that die almost as soon as they're born? They kind of cheat you, don't they?"

"It is impossible to live so short a time that you don't have *some* use for your folio. It's never been done."

"Well, how does it happen, if this thing has been worked out so thoroughly, that you keep getting the same old stuff over and over? This is the third time, now, that I've swung into you."

"There you have the one drawback to the system. In order to keep the individual note (and that's what people like!) each folio is of necessity limited in the variety of raw material. But this is compensated for by the. . . ."

"You mean the variations."

"Yes. The variations on one kind of trouble are infinite, My Dear."

"To the point of disguise."

"You must agree with me, it's a fascinating business."

"My friend, it's stupefying."

"You're quite right," he said. "That's the very secret of its success."

"Well," she said, "are we going to sit here philosophizing, or are we going to get down to business?"

"To be sure," he said. "Back to the folio. Well, I suppose we can skip the introduction this time?"

"That's the part about 'once the client admits the limitations of his own power, everything is easier'?"

"Yes, we've been over all that before. Now, how about Article I?"

"That would be the one that goes: 'If the client has successfully hurdled his first compromise. . . .'"

"I see we don't have to waste any time on that."

"No, that's old stuff. Nor do we need to tarry over 'having a drink with the boys' and 'what I need is some violent exercise.'"

"Now," he said, "to get to the current issue. Have you a preference in how we start this thing?"

"Well, I'm sick of the 'What am I doing here?' approach, because I know perfectly well what I'm doing here. I'm getting myself mixed in so deep and so fast into other people's lives that I'll never be able to crawl back to what I had."

"And if you ARE able to?" he asked, although he knew the answer.

"It won't be what it was, that's all. It won't be a future any more. It will be something I came back to."

"I suppose," he said, "that you've already been over the ground on How-Did-I-Ever-Get-Here?"

"Oh, yes," she said, "that's what I started on. And I know perfectly well how I got here. I came here. On purpose."

"Not without warning, I suppose."

"I should say not. Why, I had some of the very best warning you can get."

"That would be Kenneth," said the old man.

"Yes, it was."

"We've had a great deal of trouble troubling Kenneth."

"You see, it doesn't really begin where it looks like it began. It starts way back. . . ."

"It always does," said the old man. He began to gather up his papers quietly.

"I remember I said to Kenneth, oh, a long time ago, 'If I could just swing this one thing, it would solve so many problems. It would make everything so simple for me' and Kenneth said the minute I stuck my head out of obscurity, then I'd be in a real maze and the only difference would be that it would be bigger than the one I had and of other people's making."

"But you didn't listen to him."

"Oh, no. Not me. Since Kenneth had never stuck his head out yet, I couldn't see how he'd know."

"That guy's getting advance dope. There's a leak somewhere."

"And it wasn't only Kenneth."

"No?"

"No, it was Joseph, too."

"Oh, Joseph and Kenneth. I remember that mess."

"That was all settled a long time ago. It isn't Kenneth and Joseph any more; it's Joseph and . . . and the new one, now."

"Yes, of course. That's why I came today. You know, that's a really magnificent touch, that. I hope you're not missing it."

"What?"

"The way you always get a link with the past. That's real artistry the way you never get a new variation, but that there's a throwback to an old one. A marvelous thread of continuity, there, My Dear. You mustn't miss it."

"Not me," she said. "I couldn't miss it; I fell right into it."

"And what was it Joseph told you?"

"Joseph said I'd have to come here, you know. I was afraid of this right from the start, but Joseph said every time you made any move at all, committed any act, you immediately and auto-matically got a new set of responsibilities to go with it."

"That's a very simple fundamental."

"I hadn't thought of it like that, before."

"Not you."

"But Joseph said if you wanted to live a full life you had to take care of those things that you got automatically because they were your. . . ."

"Well," said Old Trouble, "I see everything is going nicely. I'll leave you now, as we say in the trade, to your own troubles."

Off he went down the mountain just as quietly as he had come. The girl watched him till he disappeared in the valley.

"The truth is," she said out loud, "the truth is I don't want to live a full life."

She felt much better after she had got that far and, just then, to remind her, the little old man showed himself making the ascent up the distant hill.

"It's more than that," she said. "It's that I don't want to live at all."

So off she went to hunt for a rope to hang herself by, but after she found it and held the strong coils of it in her hand, she let it slip to the ground.

"I wouldn't be surprised," she said, "if all those stories are true. It would be just like me to go to all this bother and then get myself messed with a lot of goddamned angels. No thanks; I'll keep the mess I've got."

She went into the house and once inside she leaned against the closed door and yelled as loud as she could: "By God, the trouble with me is, I'm hungry!" although she knew there was no one there to hear her and if she wanted anything to eat she'd have to fix it herself.

Change

In the office where they worked they always called the big one, Thorson, by her last name, but they called the little one Amy. These two were riding together now on the bus from the city out to the little town near where Thorson's family lived.

"Maybe we should have taken the train," Thorson said.

"Don't be silly."

"I never thought about maybe all this bouncing around wouldn't be good for you. I was just thinking about getting home quick. The train doesn't leave until two hours after the bus."

"I'm all right," Amy said. "Don't worry about me."

"How much longer you going to work?"

"My God, Thorson, I don't know. I'll work as long as I can. I've got to."

"Well, we'll be there pretty soon. Probably nobody'll be in the house but Grandmother and she stays in her own room most of the time. Everybody'll be out doing the chores and you can go up and lie down a while."

"I wish I had some clean clothes to put on. Coming straight from the office like this, I feel dirty."

"I'll give you something. You can take a hot bath and I'll find you something to put on."

"Something of yours would look fine on me all right."

"What do you care?"

"Well, after all, I never met your family," Amy said. She looked out the window. Maybe not being there to look in the mailbox would make the letter come. She wanted the weekend to be over now so that she could get back to the mailbox. She felt sure that this time the letter must be there. Probably just sitting there in the box all over Saturday and Sunday while she was out here on Thorson's farm.

"No," Thorson said, "you got them all wrong. It's just like I told you this morning. You can do what you please. You don't have to stick your head out of that room if you don't want to. Buddy'll even bring your meals up to you. I just want you to rest. I just want you to be where it's quiet and eat some real food."

"Who's Buddy?"

"The kid brother. God, he's an ornery devil. He won't study. Dad gets so mad he could kill him, but Buddy just laughs. He's been in the first grade two years now. He just don't care."

"Oh," Amy said. After all, they were only an hour from the city. A long distance call wouldn't cost much. Maybe she could call up someone in the building and ask them to look in her mailbox. It might even come special on Sunday.

"Well, this is it," Thorson said when the bus stopped. "It's only about half a mile from here. Do you feel like walking or should I call Dad up and ask him to come in after us?"

"I'm all right. Let's walk."

"You got on low heels? It's a dirt road."

"They're all right."

"It's nice further on to walk," Thorson said. "Maybe tomorrow if you feel good we could go down back of the house. There's a creek down there."

"Yeah." Maybe, though, if she called long distance, that would make it not be there. And, besides, if she knew for sure she couldn't be hoping for it. She wouldn't want to go back if she knew it wasn't there.

"You see?" Thorson said, opening the door. "No one's here, just like I said. You'll have plenty of time to bathe and take a nap before the news."

"The *news*?"

"Well, they all come in at six o'clock and listen to the news," she said. "I only meant you could meet them then, that's all."

"Oh," Amy said.

She had not thought the living room would be so large, so much like a "city" living room. It was a very long room with a fire place at one end of it. It was very cool and dark to them because they had been walking facing the sun.

"Come on," Thorson said. "I'll show you your room right away so you can get a nap in before Buddy finds out you're here. Buddy'll talk an arm off you if he gets a chance."

Thorson began to climb the stairs out of the living room and Amy followed her. She would tell him about this next time she wrote, because she went right on writing whether he was getting the letters or not. He would be glad that she had been out of the city, been on a real farm, for the weekend. And she would tell him about Buddy, too.

Thorson left her in the room and went into the bathroom and turned on the water. She came back carrying a faded pair of pajamas. "Here," she said, "you can wear these." She crossed the room and opened the windows. "This is the best room in the house to sleep in," she said. "The bed's not much, but it's got more windows than any other room in the house and it's quiet. You can't even hear the radio up here."

Amy began to undress. "Won't your folks think it's funny, me coming in here and going straight to bed?"

"Hell, no," Thorson said. "They know what goes on."

"Oh," Amy said.

She woke up hearing strange voices and for a moment she could not remember where she was. Then she heard Thorson say, "I brought Amy home with me."

"That girl from the office?" a woman said. "The one that's going to have the baby?" That must be Thorson's mother.

"Yeah," Thorson said.

"Where is she?" a man's voice said. It was a very low voice, slow and rich.

"She's asleep now. She's all worn out. And listen, whatever

you do, don't talk about the war and tell Buddy not to while she's here."

"That'll make him do it for sure." It was the man's voice now, again. Probably she was at the rear of the house and they were all on the back porch because she could hear everything they said. She could hear every word distinctly coming through the windows.

"Does Buddy know her husband's in the Navy?" Thorson said.

"No, I don't think so," the woman said. "Hasn't she heard from him yet."

"No. Not for three months. They won't let them send letters now."

"I think that's terrible," the woman said.

"Now, Mamma," the slow, rich voice said. "You know they have to be careful. You know they can't afford to let anything slip out."

"But he doesn't even know she's. . . ."

"Don't talk so loud," Thorson said. "She'll hear you."

Amy closed her eyes self-consciously, holding them shut tight in case Thorson should come upstairs and look in on her.

When she woke up again she felt very rested and better than she had in a long time and the smell of the food cooking was very pleasant to her, as it hardly ever was any more. She dressed in her own clothes and combed her hair carefully and went downstairs. She went down very slowly and softly because the news was just ending and she did not want them to be embarrassed for her. She could hear the radio being clicked off as Thorson came to meet her.

Thorson's father was very big like Thorson and his eyes, brilliantly blue, were like his voice. Thorson's mother was a little woman, not much bigger than Amy. The grandmother, in the corner, was very obviously the man's mother, by her eyes, though she, too, was small.

"And that's Buddy," Thorson said.

"You missed the news," he said, looking up at her, smiling, looking straight into her eyes. They all looked at him.

"I was asleep," Amy said. She would certainly write to him about Buddy. Maybe even she could sketch his face. He did not look in the least like any of them except maybe a little like the grandmother. He seemed much *lighter* than any of the rest of them, as though he had more air in him. It was almost impossible to believe that he was a devil, as Thorson had said.

"Well now, Amy, you just sit down and talk to Papa," the mother said, "while we finish getting supper." Amy went over and sat down by the grandmother.

"You should have called up from town," Mr. Thorson said. "I coulda come in after you."

"I like the walk," Amy said. "It's nice out here."

"I been here all my life," he said, "almost."

Buddy took the newspaper and spread it out on the floor. He lay on his stomach reading the funnies. Suddenly he looked up at Amy.

"Say," he said, "you know Ben?"

"Ben?"

"Ben's my oldest boy," Mr. Thorson said. "He's away at college."

"I'll be glad when Ben comes home," the grandmother said. "He's going to graduate this year. Ben's a very smart boy."

"All my kids is smart," Mr. Thorson said, laughing, "all of 'em but Buddy here." He reached out and pushed Buddy's foot. "Buddy here can't seem to get through first grade."

Buddy looked over his shoulder at his father. He began to laugh. Mr. Thorson began to laugh, too. "I got to make a farmer out of Buddy," he said. He reached out suddenly and picked the boy up by his feet and stood him on his head. "There," he said, "that's good for your brain."

"Let go," Buddy said, twisting his head around. "I want to read the funnies."

Mr. Thorson held the boy's feet together. He looked at Amy and smiled. "Wouldn't you think there was something queer with a boy that could read the funnies easy as pie and couldn't get through *The Little Red Hen* in two years' trying?"

Buddy gave a sudden kick and freed himself. He turned over and sat up. "Aw," he said, "I just look at the pictures."

Long before the rest of them were through eating, Buddy slipped away from the table. They were all very much interested in Amy and it was good for her to be the center of so much attention, to cause them so much amusement by her comments on the thickness of the cream, the flavor of the butter, the smell of the hot bread. Just by having been brought up in the city she was somehow made to feel interesting and curious and important. Mr. Thorson got up from the table and went out onto the back porch and stood looking out over the farm.

"Now you go in the living room and sit down a while," Mrs. Thorson said, "while we clear up the dishes. You play the radio or do anything you want."

But at the door to the living room Amy stopped, entranced, holding her breath. Buddy stood before the fireplace, his whole body concentrated in shooting an imaginary ball into an imaginary basket. He held the ball by his finger tips, easily, lightly. His mouth was open and, while he aimed the ball carefully, he jumped into the air and shot the basket. Amy could tell, easily, by the way he caught it, that he had made it and she stifled a cheer just in time, because she wanted him to go on being unaware of her. She leaned back very close to the door, so as to be in a shadow.

When she looked back into the room he was stamping his feet on the floor, holding his arms like a windmill, making violent faces at the staircase. Now he was dribbling the ball down the length of the room and he was being desperately pursued. So real was the pantomime that long afterwards when Amy remembered the scene, she remembered the sound of the ball hitting the floor.

Now he was trying for another basket. He was having a hard time keeping the ball and he had to make a difficult shot. He had to make it with almost straight arms, across the basket. But he made it, and another and another and another, though the last one was a rimmer, riding around and around the rim of the basket. Amy's head followed the boy's exactly around and around as his followed the path of the ball. But this one, too, finally narrowly, fell through.

Amy was not aware that she was standing at all, or of how long she stood there. She saw the boy dribble the ball the length of the room many times, saw him triumphantly score one basket after the other. There was another rimmer and Amy could see in the boy's back how he was trying to make himself miss this one, just to make it real, but at the last second the ball slipped through. At the last second, he couldn't NOT score.

And this struggle, this almost physical compulsion to triumph, was so understandable to Amy that she left him, lest he catch her spying, and went back into the kitchen.

The women were not in the kitchen and Amy went out and stood by Mr. Thorson. "Where is everybody?" she said.

"They went up in your room," he said. "They're arguing about which bedspread you should have, or something. Mamma wants to get out all her finery and show it off."

"They shouldn't do that," Amy said.

"Aw, you let them show off, now. Don't you go and spoil it."

"All right," she said, "I don't know what to make of all this attention. . . ." Her voice broke and she looked out over the farm, looked hard, holding her eyes wide open.

Mr. Thorson pointed over to her right. "See that house there?" he said. Amy nodded her head. "That's where I was born." He swung his arm far to the left. "And that one over there. My wife was born in that one."

Amy was safely past the tears now and she could look at the

man's face. "All that in between," he said, "that's all mine." There was something very wonderful in the man's eyes, looking straight out over the farm, holding in his eyes all that was his.

"I've been watching Buddy play basketball," she said. "It's the most beautiful thing I ever saw."

"He must nota seen you."

"No," she said.

"I seen him do it once, too," he said. "Him and his basketball. He won't study; he won't learn. He just thinks about basketball, basketball, all the time, and even then he don't ask for a real ball to play with. He'd just as soon stay in the first grade all his life and play basketball in the parlor."

Thorson and her mother came out on the porch behind them. "He lets on like Buddy was dumb," Mrs. Thorson said, "but he's not."

"Well, he acts like it," Mr. Thorson said.

"You ought to quit talking about it in front of him," his wife said. "You must make him worse. I think he just does it to devil you."

"I know it," he said.

That night in her room Amy wrote her husband a long letter. She felt very confident that he was going to receive this one. She was excited about trying to show him exactly what Buddy had looked like and finally she quit writing and began to fill the pages with sketches of the boy leaping into the air to shoot a basket and dribbling the ball furiously down the room only a step ahead of his pursuers, but the best one she did was the way Buddy had watched the ball that kept ringing the edge of the basket before it fell through. She was very pleased with that one and she fell asleep imagining how her husband would look reading the letter, seeing her husband study the sketches carefully. She fell asleep feeling quite confident that if she didn't call up long distance the letter would be there waiting for her when she got back.

Sunday, after breakfast, Thorson said to her, "I'm going into town. You want to come in with me?"

"No," she said, "I think I'll go for a walk."

"You want me to bring you anything?"

"No," she said, "no, thanks."

She was glad that Thorson was not with her because she wanted to be alone for a while out of doors. She was feeling as though her husband were very near her now, as though if she spoke to him he could hear her and she wanted to hold onto the feeling because she did not have it often any more.

It seemed to her that she had walked a long way, but when she turned back to be sure of her direction, she could still see the house and she could see Buddy running toward her.

"Say, Amy," he said, when he came up to her, "you want to see where the cows go in the winter time?"

"Sure," she said.

"Well, it's in the straw stack. They build whole houses in there with rooms and tunnels and everything. Come on," he said, "I'll show you."

He crawled into an opening in the side of the straw stack, and Amy crawled in after him. She would have to wear these clothes back to town, but she did not care and she crawled on her hands and knees after the boy down the tunnel and, at a right angle to it, they entered a hollowed out place, larger than the tunnel.

"Sit down," he said. Amy looked around her. As far as she could see there was a network of tunnels and places like this one.

"Don't worry," he said. "There aren't any cows here now. Here's where they come in the winter when they get cold. They let you come in and sit right down by them and it's warm."

"I didn't know they did this," she said. She would write him about his, too, about this labyrinth of rooms and tunnels hidden inside the straw stacks. Probably in the car, in the old days, they had passed by a lot of straw stacks like this and never known.

"Say," the boy said, "you going back to the city today?"

"Yes," she said, "this evening."

"If I told you a secret would you not tell it to anybody?"

"I won't tell," she said. "Honest."

"Well," he said, "I'm not really dumb like they told you."

"I know it," she said.

"How did you know it?"

"Oh, you don't act dumb," she said, "and then I saw you reading the funnies and you were reading, I could tell."

"Yeah," he said. "I forget sometimes."

"Why do you do it?"

"Because," he said. "The teacher. I love the first grade teacher. I don't never want to leave her." He looked at Amy very carefully, but there was no need to because it did not seem amusing to her. It seemed very serious, but even though she felt like a traitor to the child, she was remembering that she was a guest here, that she owed it to Mrs. Thorson to try, that perhaps even for the child, she ought to try.

"But maybe you would like the second grade teacher, too," she said.

"No," he said, "I seen her already."

"Oh," she said. "Well, sometimes they change them just at the last minute."

"They might not," he said. "This one's been there a long time."

"Well, maybe you could go to a different school," she said. "Maybe in another school there would be a fine second grade teacher."

"She might not be a pretty as this one, though," he said.

"She might, though."

He thought abut this a while. He picked up a straw from the floor and examined it, as though it were another school with a beautiful second grade teacher in it. He clasped his knees in his arms and looked up at Amy, with that wonderful, clear, *light* look the way he had watched the basket that almost missed.

"No," he said. "Even if I knew for sure it would be as good as this one, even if it would be better, I wouldn't want to go. I like everything to stay just the way it is. I don't never want anything to change."

The boy blurred before Amy's eyes. Only his fine clear eyes stood out against the yellow straw, stood out large and blue against the walls of the cow shelter, the safe warm place that the cows had made against the snow and the winter wind. She reached out and grabbed the boy and held him tight to her. She put his head back over her shoulder and held it there that he might not see her face, that only the yellow straw should witness the tears streaming down her face. Oh, he was too little to know this already, to want this. He was too young to be so human.